TRUCK BLACK II

The Hunt

S. M. ANDERSON

iUniverse®

TRUCK BLACK II
THE HUNT

iUniverse books may be ordered through booksellers or by contacting:

iUniverse
1663 Liberty Drive
Bloomington, IN 47403
www.iuniverse.com
844-349-9409

ISBN: 978-1-6632-2843-7 (sc)
ISBN: 978-1-6632-2842-0 (e)

Library of Congress Control Number: 2022913765

Print information available on the last page.

iUniverse rev. date: 07/20/2022

DEDICATION

All the truckers past, present and future.
Without you America would stand still.

To our Veterans, especially those from WWII and Vietnam. Your service is appreciated and we are honored to know you.

PROLOGUE

A small town in Illinois, a body found behind the mom-and-pop truck stop. Twenty-four hours later, the body disappears from the coroner's office. It is as if the body just got up and walked away. Then the woman is seen back at the truck stop and at the coroner's home. The woman's brother disappears.

Thus, it starts. Every night the number of disappearances doubles. Sheriff Warren is stymied. Until two truckers arrive at his office door with a totally plausible explanation; at least it seems plausible to them. Krys explains that Ty drove for three years with his partner, Blake, who only drove after dark and never after sunrise. When Blake left him in Kalamazoo, Ty drove back to Illinois to Krys. They cleaned out the truck and found that the bottom bunk was actually a coffin, filled with dirt.

When Warren later proposed this theory to his deputy, Earl, he was amazed to find out that Earl had been thinking the exact same thing. Together they began their search of the town with stakes and holy water in hand. To the Sheriff's amazement, he soon had three more teams of military Veterans helping to eliminate the problem.

Warren received a call from Kalamazoo. Kee had been Warren's boss when he worked as a detective in Detroit and then helped with a case in Kalamazoo. He had fallen in love with his new partner, Lisa, but left for home without a word to her. When Warren called Ty, the dates and times coincided with earlier deliveries in Kalamazoo and Blake's disappearance there.

Warren, along with two volunteers from Hebert, drive to Kalamazoo to join Ty and Krys and the entire police force in hopes of eliminating Blake and his followers, including Lisa's sister Pat.

The day after Warren arrives back home, he receives a call from Kee. Lisa is missing. Someone had broken into her house, the front picture window was shattered inward, glass all over the floor. They found a body in her hallway, shot. There were footprints in the blood on the floor, more than one set.

It was obvious to Warren that Blake had Lisa. And it was obvious to Earl that the other set of footprints probably belonged to Pat. He explained how she could have been brought back.

So, what did Blake intend to do with Lisa? Why take her? Revenge or need of another driver? Where were they going and how were they going to get there?

It became a sit and wait game and sitting and waiting were not things Warren was used to doing, or very good at.

CHAPTER 1

Warren sat at the kitchen table watching the clock. The call from Kee had come in at 2 a.m. It was now 7 a.m. He had gotten up immediately after the call and dressed in his uniform, then made a pot of coffee. After throwing most of the coffee down the drain when it got cold, he made another pot. He sat staring at his second cup from that pot, now cold.

Warren knew it had to be Blake who took Lisa. He knew why he was being so vengeful. What he didn't know was what Blake intended to do with her. He imagined all sorts of evil things that Blake might conjure up. The worst of which would be to make her just like him and her sister Pat, evil and unable to show emotion, especially love.

The sun was now shining directly through the living room window. This was Saturday, Warren's day off from work. But he had his uniform on and still sat wondering what to do. The next few days would be his time for decision making.

Warren was too fidgety to sit any longer. He walked out the side door to his patrol car. The drive over the country road and then the highway towards town was quiet. He turned on his police radio but, like the countryside around him, it too was silent.

As he passed County Road 1235, his thoughts went directly to Cliff Raynes. He had only known Cliff for a day or so but he had felt emotionally bonded to him. He was with Cliff when he had identified his sister Sandy at the coroner's office. It was then that he had learned that Cliff had been dating Joe's daughter, Mary.

Warren and Joe went way back, had been best friends since they were kids. Cliff was very young, very shook up over his sister's death and was invited by Mary to stay with her at Joe's house that night.

When Sandy appeared outside the front porch, Cliff left the house and was not seen again, not until he was later discovered in the basement with Mary, where they were lying in boxes next to each other.

Warren reached the police station and parked in behind Earl's vehicle. When he had left Hebert for Kalamazoo, the streets had been deserted, the town deathly quiet. Those still alive had gone into hiding.

He stepped out of the car and looked around. He was both surprised and elated to see the different businesses already opening up their doors, even though it was only 7:30 in the morning. People were milling around the courthouse square. In front of the drugstore, two old retirees were already sitting playing checkers, coffee cups sitting on the table by each player. The town looked to be actually back to normal. He wished his life was as normal as the town at this moment in time.

Warren took out his key ring, then realized with Earl in the station, the door would be open to the public. He walked in and immediately noted that there still was no receptionist. Before he left for Kalamazoo, both the day and night receptionists/dispatchers had been absent from work. He didn't know if it was from fear that they stayed away or if they had been infected by someone and were out stalking other victims, like most of the other people in town had been doing.

Warren walked past his office and headed to the break room. He found Earl sitting at one of the tables, eating a TV dinner. Earl jumped up, surprised. He walked around the table up to Warren and started shaking his hand.

"I'm glad you're back, Sheriff. So glad you're back." Earl said, smiling broadly, still shaking Warren's hand.

"I'm glad I'm back too, Earl. Go ahead and finish your meal. Then come on into my office. We need to talk."

When Warren entered his office and sat down behind his desk, he noted a stack of papers lying in the middle of the desk calendar. He started shuffling through the stack and realized it was Earl's hand-written roster of all the people in town according to addresses and businesses.

Earl had written down the name and address, then the business. He then made columns labeled alive, staked, buried, burned, missing. Under each name, he had listed other family members and marked off their status.

Evidently, Earl had painstakingly listed every resident of the town along with all those who resided out of town. The lists made it clear to Warren exactly how many of the people were still alive and functioning in Hebert.

Warren sat for almost twenty minutes, leafing through the pages, when Earl appeared at the office door.

"Welcome back, Sheriff." Earl beamed.

"You said that before. But it's still good to be back." Warren said. "Just not sure how long I'll be here."

"You're leaving again?" Earl asked.

"Eventually. Just don't know when or to where."

Warren explained the situation to Earl. Earl asked how it could have been Pat if she had been staked and beheaded but Warren explained that they had taken care of her but that Lisa would not allow them to cut her head off. He didn't know why Blake wanted Lisa if he had gotten Pat back and he didn't know where they would have taken her or how they would be travelling.

"I only know one thing for sure. If he does turn her to one of his, I'll be the one who frees her. Me. No one else." Warren stated emphatically.

"Do your trucker friends know what happened?" Earl asked.

"Oh, my God. I didn't think to call Ty and Krys. I better call them."

"Go ahead," Earl said as he stood up out of the chair. "I've got to get cleaned up and ready for work."

Warren dialed Ty's number. Krys answered on the third ring.

"Hi, Warren. How are you?" Krys asked immediately.

"Not so good. Lisa's gone. Blake has her."

"Do what? How?" Krys asked, the tremor evident in her voice.

Warren proceeded to tell her about Kee's phone call this morning. He explained that he believed the window was imploded in order to put someone in the house who could open the front door and invite Blake in. After all, a vampire can't enter a home unless invited.

After listening to Warren, Krys asked him to hold on a minute while she let Ty know what was going on.

"So, what's next?" Krys asked when she returned to the phone.

"I don't know right now. If I leave here and try to find her, where do I go? Where would he take her?"

"I know it seems hopeless right now, Warren, but I'm thinking like you are. Where would he take her?"

There was silence for a minute.

"Listen," Krys continued, "just stay put for now. Let me and Ty monitor the CB and put the word out to the truckers. You keep watch on that new data base that was set up to monitor homicides and disappearances. When we all know something substantial and have solid evidence regarding Blake's whereabouts, we'll all get together and take care of things. Once and for all this time. Okay?"

"Okay, but it's going to be hard. I can't just sit and wait and not do anything."

"I know, Warren, I know. But we all need to sit tight. And you know that when the time comes, we'll be there for you. Ty isn't going to stop hunting until Blake is disposed of. He has a score to settle for the years he drove with Blake not knowing who or what he was. He won't stop hunting until it is all over."

"I know and I appreciate you and Ty, more than you'll ever know. Call me if you hear anything, okay?" Warren asked.

"You know I will," Krys said. "Ty said to tell you to take it easy. Business as usual until the time comes. Hopefully, we'll see you soon."

After Warren hung up the phone, he sat staring intently at it. There had to be something he could do. He was frustrated that he couldn't figure out what that was. He had loved her for so long, had literally begged her to return to Hebert with him and get married. But she was strong-willed and stayed in Kalamazoo. He had no idea that she was actually considering moving to Hebert to be with him. Even then, how could he not be expected to look for her?

He prayed she would be alright and not be turned by Blake or her sister Pat. He knew in his heart that the other set of small footprints belonged to her sister.

The pain and frustration weighed heavily on him. He was a man of action and decision, so how could he be expected to Just sit and wait and not do anything to try and find Lisa?

As Warren sat at his desk, he slowly realized that Krys was right. It was going to be a waiting game and he knew that Blake would eventually appear again. He had the new police app that he could monitor every day and sooner or later the disappearances and re-appearances would begin again. Blake was too prideful not to continue what he had started in Hebert and then in Kalamazoo.

But which town would he decide to start new again? There were so many that he and Ty had visited over the three years they drove together. Which one would he go back to or would he pick a new town they had never been in to throw them off his trail?

Warren said a short prayer that the wait would not be too long and that Lisa would still be Lisa when he found her. And he knew he would find her; one way or another.

CHAPTER 2

Earl appeared in the doorway once again, hair combed, shirt neatly tucked in and boots shiny as the badge he so proudly wore.

"Take a seat for a minute." Warren said.

"So, you saw my lists?" Earl asked.

"Yeah. Great idea. Must have taken you a long time to compile them."

"Not too long," Earl said. "I worked on them at night. The guys were all great about keeping track of names and addresses when they knew the people."

"How are all the guys doing?"

"Dan is doing great. He's been helping with the cleanup. Everyone we staked is buried, stakes intact. The ones that burned up, we put their ashes in urns and buried them. At least as much of the ash that we could get off the ground. Those three at the truck stop, I went back out and got their ashes out of the trash bins. We buried them out of respect, though their markers don't have names on them. I got some wood from Mack down at the hardware store and we made some makeshift crosses for everyone, some with names and some without."

"And town businesses?" Warren urged.

"All but two have reopened; one that small thrift store on Main and the other a beauty parlor on First Street. Of course, we're looking for a new coroner too."

"How about Doc Marlow for coroner? Is he still in town?"

"Yup. He doubled as our coroner for a while. He also wrote out the death certificates when we had the names."

"What in hell could he put on the death certificates that would be legal?"

"Most of them were congestive heart failure. A lot of them had been his patients and he listed different diagnoses he had been treating them for."

"Maybe we can talk the Doc into continuing on as coroner. It doesn't pay much but he lives right here in town." Warren speculated.

"Don't know about that. He said he was getting too old for all this excitement. He said it nearly wore him out keeping up with the bodies and the paperwork."

"In the meantime," Warren changed the subject, "why don't we run out to the truck stop and get something to drink?"

"Sounds good to me." Earl said as he got up from his chair, ready to leave.

Warren drove them out to the truck stop in his patrol car. After all that had happened and the fact that the truckers knew this is where everything supposedly began, he was surprised but pleased to see a dozen or more semis parked on the lot and as many cars parked out front of the restaurant. He hoped it was not for the wrong reasons.

When he and Earl entered, the restaurant was full. There were two waitresses who Warren did not recognize serving the customers in the booths and at the tables. Then he saw Sharon working behind the truckers counter. Warren led the way to two empty stools at the counter.

Sharon brought Warren his coffee and a Pepsi for Earl.

"So, how's it going, or do I have to ask?" Warren said.

"It's great, we're busier than ever." Sharon told him.

"That's all your dad and mom ever wanted." Earl said.

"They'd be really proud of you." Warren added. "How are things going at home, if I'm not being too inquisitive?"

"Home is good too. We moved into mom and dad's house when we first got here. Now I'm there alone. But not really alone. Mom and dad are buried in the family cemetery up on the hill overlooking the place. They'll always be with me. And John's buried with mom and dad. He didn't have any family and he was like a son to them, cooked for as long as I can remember. It just seemed so right to keep him with the family."

"That's good. Beth loved that farm." Warren said.

"I know, I love it too, always have."

Sharon left menus and walked over to the other side of the counter to take a trucker's order. When she came back, Warren gave her his order. She took the ticket back to the kitchen.

"Aren't you eating? Or are you still full from your TV dinner?" Warren asked Earl.

"Sharon knows what I want." Earl answered, not looking at Warren.

"Does she know everything you want?" Warren asked.

"I think I made that apparent on our last date."

"Your last date?"

"Yeah. We've kinda been seeing each other since she got back. I helped her bury Gene and Beth. I really liked that old couple."

"Me too," Warren said pensively.

Warren sat silently pondering his situation. He was still the sheriff. If he left again for an indeterminate length of time and made Earl acting sheriff again, would he eventually lose his job. It came down to a choice, continue working as sheriff or leave to look for Lisa. He knew he had to find her, even if it meant losing his job. No job is worth losing the one you love.

Their meals came and Warren realized he was actually very hungry. Sharon, like her parents, took pride in what she served her customers. It was apparent that the rest of her family felt the same. He had been watching the other two waitresses and they were continually walking around with a coffee pot or tea jug and making sure every customer was taken care of.

When Warren and Earl were finished, they lingered over their drinks.

"Oh, yeah," Earl said unexpectedly, "I called the companies about those two trucks out back. One company sent a driver to pick up their equipment, the one we found the people in the back of the trailer. The other company sent a tow truck, said they couldn't find anyone who wanted to drive the rig. Wonder why?"

"Did you tell the companies about their drivers and how they died?"

"Just that they had died under mysterious circumstances. But it seems everyone knows about Hebert and understands exactly what went on down here."

"Guess I better get back to work." Warren said. "You can go ahead and take the day off, and tonight. I can handle Hebert on a Saturday night. Besides, I need to keep busy. I'll drive you back to the station to get your truck."

"That's okay, Sheriff," Sharon interrupted. "I'm off in 30 minutes. I'll take care of Earl."

"I bet you will." Warren said with a smile and a knowing wink. "You two have fun. I'll see you tomorrow, Earl."

Warren stood up from the stool, left thirty dollars on the counter and walked out of the restaurant to his patrol car. It was sunny outside, but still chilly with a crisp coolness. The air smelled clean for the first time in a long time. Warren pulled out of the parking lot and drove slowly back to town, his window down, enjoying the fresh air of autumn.

At the outskirts of town, he made a left turn instead of going through town to the station. He drove up in front of the hardware store. There were a few customers around the store and Warren observed three pickup trucks out in the lumber yard when he drove through the lot.

He parked in the first available spot in front of the store. He walked inside, then down the aisle to the counter. Mack was sitting at his desk, ledger in hand, smiling.

"Come to settle up?" Mack asked.

"Give me a tally and I'll bring a check by on Monday. I just came to say hi, how are you and thank you."

"Well, hi Sheriff." Mack said. "I'm doing fine. And you're welcome, but for what?"

"Your help. But mostly your understanding." Warren told him.

"At my age, understanding is a given." Mack laughed. "So, how was your trip, fruitful?"

"The trip was basically successful, we were able to clean up Kalamazoo. We didn't find Blake though." Warren answered.

"And?" Mack asked.

"And what?"

"The fact that you didn't find Blake isn't the only reason you're so out of it." Mack stated bluntly.

"It isn't." Warren then proceeded to once again tell the story of how Lisa was abducted and he believed it was Blake and his woman, Pat, who had done it.

"Maybe this Blake just needed a driver." Mack suggested. "And in that case, he won't dare harm her, she's much too valuable to him."

"I hope you're right, Mack."

"I'm always right. You can ask Earl." Mack laughed. "But seriously, I'm very sorry to hear about Lisa but, from what you've told me of her, she seems to be very resourceful. I'm sure she'll be okay."

"I better get back to work. Just wanted to come over and say thanks."

"You can thank me by paying your bill." Mack said, smiling broadly.

"Yes, sir." Warren said. He saluted Mack, then turned and left the store.

CHAPTER 3

Warren spent most of the afternoon and evening going over Earl's lists. He left the office and returned home around 9 p.m. As he drove up his driveway, slowly cruising toward the house, he kept looking at the front yard. Although it was empty right now, it still spooked him. He could still see his friends standing there staring at him while he stood inside his living room peering out through the curtains. Then the horrific spectacle of them taking down the deer and drinking its blood. He had seen one episode of the Living Dead and that program reminded him of events here in Hebert. Except they were zombies and he had to deal with vampires. One other difference, on TV when the credits rolled up the screen, it was over. Here, it would never be over. The credits were the tombstones with the names of close friends, there forever.

He watched the 10 o'clock news and then went straight to bed. Although he was still worried about Lisa, it only took him minutes to fall asleep.

He spent the entire day Sunday cleaning up around the house, inside and out. He walked down to the pond behind the house early in the evening and after fishing for only a few minutes, he caught a bass large enough for his dinner. He walked back up to the house and scaled and cleaned the fish on a makeshift wooden table on the back porch. He loved the smell of fresh fish searing in the pan. He ate, put his dishes in the dishwasher and then turned on the TV. He watched for a few hours before retiring for the night.

The next morning, Warren was up early. He made a pot of coffee and filled his to-go mug full before he left for the station. He got to work earlier than usual, even for a Monday.

He was sitting at his desk when he heard the front door open. Someone entered and he wondered why they had not come into the office. He got up and walked around his desk to the office door where he stopped dead in his tracks.

"Leslie." He called out, astounded.

"Who else did you expect?" she answered as she stood up from her desk and walked across the room toward Warren.

Warren stood still, staring at Leslie. She had been like a mother to him since he had taken on the job of sheriff. When she didn't show up for work during the vampire scare, he had thought the worst. He now realized he didn't even know where she lived. There was so much about the people of Hebert that he had never bothered to learn about.

Finally, Warren took a step forward, then enveloped Leslie in a huge bear hug.

She eventually squirmed out of his grasp, looking up at him puzzled.

"I'm so glad to see you, you just don't know." Warren blurted out.

"I'm glad to see you too. But what happened to professionalism in the work place?" she asked.

"After all that's happened, to hell with professionalism." Warren told her. He bent down slightly and hugged her again.

"If I had known a few vampires would have brought this out in you, I would have ordered them up years ago." Leslie laughed, not attempting to squirm out of his grasp.

When he finally released her, he smiled down at her. "I thought you were gone."

"I was. I left a note on my desk for you. I went to my daughter's for a while. It was much safer at her house than it would have been at mine."

"I never saw the note. When you didn't come in and neither did Judy, I just assumed you were both infected, that we'd find you in a basement somewhere."

"Judy's gone. Earl found her in her crawl space. We buried her bones in the town cemetery."

"I'm sorry." Warren said.

"So am I," Leslie repeated. "Now, back to work. Enough lollygagging around." Leslie turned and walked back to her desk. Warren watched her until she was seated before he finally turned back to his office.

Once he was seated behind his desk again, he picked up Earl's list and started rifling through it once more. When the phone rang, he reached for it, then realized that Leslie had already picked it up.

"There's a Lt. Morgan on the line." Leslie called out.

"Hello, Pete." Warren said when he picked up his phone.

"Hello, Warren."

"How are thing up there in Chicago?"

"Pretty good," Lt. Morgan answered. "We followed your lead and have our city back under control, at least where the vampires are concerned. They never did get a good foothold here. How is Hebert doing?"

"Hebert is clean and businesses are opening back up." Warren answered.

"I talked to Kee this morning," Pete continued, "I just wanted you to know that we'll keep our eyes and ears open for Lisa and Blake."

"I appreciate that. We've got some truckers listening out for any news too. And I'll be monitoring the new police data line. We'll get Blake eventually. I just hope we find Lisa in time."

"We'll all be doing our best to help you out. I'll call if I hear anything."

"Thanks." Warren said. "I hope to hear from someone somewhere soon." With that, they ended their conversation.

Warren went back to the list. He soon realized he didn't know a lot of the names on the list. He could relate to the addresses but couldn't put faces to names. He was relieved to see only a few children's names on the lists.

He looked up from the desk when he heard the front door open. A male voice was asking Leslie if the Sheriff was back in town yet.

"I'm in here," Warren called out, "come on back."

Dan walked through the door, a big smile on his face, his hand held out ready to shake Warren's. Dan was a huge man, not fat but tall and well built. His mother would have called Dan a brick shithouse. He reminded Warren of Mean Joe Green from the Pittsburgh Steelers. A giant of a man but all heart.

After Warren motioned to the chair in front of his desk and they were both seated, he commented, "Nice to see you. What's up?"

"I talked to Earl this morning. Hope it's okay he told me about what's going on with your Lisa."

"It's fine," Warren said. "It's not a secret."

"I talked to my guys and if you have to leave again, we all want you to know we'll be here to cover your ass."

"I appreciate that." Warren said with a chuckle.

"So, is Kalamazoo clean now?" Dan asked.

"Pretty much. The Chief got together with the other police departments across the U.S. and now we have a data base set up to follow crimes across the states. Even our station will be able to get online and check things out."

"That'll help keep track of the vampires. Should make it a lot easier," Dan noted.

"Hope so," Warren said. "The longer it takes to figure out where Blake has gone, the more likely Lisa will be one of them."

"You know, he may have taken her just for spite or to make her drive for him. Earl said you thought he had brought her sister back from the dead."

"Looks that way. They found two sets of footprints at Lisa's. We didn't know the part about chopping their heads off."

"Yeah. We didn't either. But I doubt we'll have that problem here in Hebert again anytime soon."

"Hope you're right." Warren agreed.

"Anyhow, the main reason I came by is that me and all the guys got together and came up with an idea to get the town back on track. We want to have a dinner, the Sunday before Thanksgiving. Invite everyone in town. We can have it at the school gym. And being on Sunday, all the businesses in town are closed so no one has an excuse not to come."

"How are we going to feed so many people?" Warren asked.

"That's the easy part. Neal said he'd supply the turkeys and hams. Being the owner of the town's only grocery store has its perks. Me and the guys are ready to start cooking. Then everyone else can bring a side dish to fill up the tables." Dan paused for only a few seconds to let the idea sink in.

"It's a chance to get to know everyone and honor those who are gone." Dan went on. "So, what do you think about our idea?"

"I think it's a great idea. Gives me a chance to meet the people I don't know. And I have a dish that you'll love and I bet you've never had before."

"Okay. That means we'll do this in two weeks. We'll put up flyers all over town and advertise in the newspaper and on the radio."

"Okay. No time like the present to get started."

They talked a while longer about the dinner, then Dan left, whistling as he walked out the front door.

Warren went back to work on the list. He found himself stopping often to think about the dinner and the prospects of meeting the people he was hired to serve in Hebert.

He had basically stepped into the position when Sheriff Peters had retired unexpectedly and moved away to Florida. He had eventually run for reelection and was then voted into the job. He always felt the people had re-elected him because he had been doing a decent job and wasn't what he would call an absentee sheriff. He was in the office six days a week, sometimes seven. He kept the finances available for anyone who wanted to see the books and didn't hide anything that would have been considered public information.

Warren hadn't made but a few arrests since taking the job, those mostly for drunken and disorderly and a couple for breaking and entering. The B&Es were both at the liquor store which was equipped with a very good security system.

Both times Warren was surprised to find the thieves still in the store, since the alarm could be heard halfway across town and they had to know someone would show up to see what the commotion was. Of course, both times the perpetrators had been drunk already. The second incident, when he walked into the store, the perp was sitting on the floor with a bottle of whiskey in his lap and asked the sheriff if he wanted a drink.

Warren sat for a while longer, then walked out of his office and let Leslie know he was headed home and he would see her in the morning.

CHAPTER 4

Ty and Krys had kept busy driving since leaving Kalamazoo. They would deliver a load and then Ty would call his broker and immediately be on the road again. Krys drove mainly during the day and Ty enjoyed the night traffic or what there was of it. He had driven with Blake for three years and had never driven after dark during that time. He was enjoying it now, though, especially when he would top a hill and be able to look down on the lights of the next town or city up ahead.

So far, they had driven to the east coast, delivering in New York. Their delivery was after dark, so Ty had called ahead and had a police car escort them to the warehouse.

"Why the police?" Krys had asked.

"Security. Going through town, if we get caught at a red light, we could lose half the load by the time the light turned green again."

"How?"

"They roll up in a pickup or flatbed. One guy jumps out on the hood and cuts the lock. He then throws boxes to his accomplices until they fill up their truck. The light turns green, we drive on unaware of what has happened until we get to the warehouse."

"Oh, wow. I've heard truckers' stories about that sort of thing but thought it was just stories. You know truckers, you can tell their lying when their lips are moving." Krys said, laughing.

"Thanks a lot. But, may I remind you of what you are doing for a living now too?" Ty asked.

"Okay, point taken."

After their delivery, Ty drove out of New York City, then continued driving until dawn. Krys had slept most of the night but came out of the sleeper right after sunrise, dressed and ready to take over.

"Hungry?" Ty asked.

"Famished." Krys replied.

"Good. There's a truck stop just up the road with a great breakfast buffet."

"Sounds good to me."

"We can get breakfast, then I'll call in for another load." Ty said.

"I think I'd like to call Jimmy, back in Hebert. I want to know that Warren's okay with everything that's been happening. You know Warren will put up a strong front, but Jimmy will tell me the truth."

Ty drove another twenty minutes, then pulled off the highway and into the lot of a TA Truck Center. The lot was full but he managed to find an empty spot on the second row. He backed the rig in and they were soon walking hand in hand across the lot toward the store.

The restaurant was packed but they only had to wait five minutes before a booth became available. The waitress cleared the table quickly. They sat down and immediately ordered coffee and the buffet.

Krys got up first and was delighted to find one whole section of the buffet with fresh fruit, including sectioned Ruby Red grapefruit. As soon as she returned, Ty got up and then came back with two plates fully loaded.

"Great minds think alike," Krys laughed when Ty returned and one of his plates was full of nothing but the grapefruit.

Breakfast was exceptionally good and Krys was pleasantly surprised to find the coffee not overly strong. She liked her coffee but only if she could see the bottom of the cup when it was poured. She hated it when it was too strong and she had to add cream and sweetener.

After breakfast, Krys ordered another cup of coffee and sat enjoying it while Ty went to call in for a load.

"Well, I'll be damned." A very low male voice called out. "Hello, Krys. You working up here now?"

Krys was startled to hear her name but recognized the voice immediately.

"Hey, Billy," Krys said as she scooted out of the booth to face a very tall, very slim and very black trucker. They hugged each other almost passionately. Billy lifted her off her feet and swung her around, laughing boisterously.

When he put her down, he smiled at her and said, "I'll have to stop in here more often. The buffet is great, but the waitress is even more delicious."

She slid back into the booth, Billy sitting down next to her, his long legs stretched out into the aisle.

"You still blush like a schoolgirl. Guess that means I haven't lost my touch. So, how long have you been up here?"

"About an hour now. I don't work here, Billy. I'm driving again. Me and my partner are here to get breakfast. He's calling in for another load."

"Really? He must be something else, if he talked you into going back on the road when I couldn't. So, who is he?"

"That would be me," Ty said, sliding up beside the booth, his hand held out to shake Billy's.

Billy stood up out of the booth and shook hands, towering over Ty. He moved to sit on the opposite side of the booth, but Ty cut him off and motioned for him to sit back down next to Krys.

Krys introduced Ty to Billy, or "Weeping Willow" as he was known on the CB.

"So, now I'll ask you. How in hell did you talk my girl into partnering up with you when I couldn't, even as irresistibly charming as I am?" Billy asked, laughing.

Before Ty could answer, Krys piped in, "It was me who talked Ty into partnering up. I had to convince him, not the other way around."

"Okay, I see how it is. Well, congratulations old man." Billy said, smiling broadly.

They talked on for quite a while before Krys told Billy about Hebert and Kalamazoo.

"I heard a lot of different stories on the CB, never thought you'd be involved. But knowing you like I do, I'm not surprised." Billy stated.

"By the way, you never mentioned Denver." Billy added.

"What about Denver?" Ty asked, no longer relaxed but sitting up straight and leaning over the table, alert to Billy's every word.

"I live in Denver, don't listen to the TV news because it's too depressing. When I'm off the road, it's party time."

"How well I remember," Krys said. "Just means you haven't changed in your old age."

"Old age? Who you calling old, little girl?" Billy asked. "I'll be old when I'm dead."

"Back to Denver?" Ty pleaded.

"Oh, yeah. Anyhow, when I was out at one of the clubs last weekend, Magic, a biker friend of mine, was talking about a friend of his who got killed, then disappeared from the morgue."

"Is that the only one he mentioned?" Ty asked anxiously.

"Yeah, for Magic. But the guy he was talking to said a friend of his who was usually at the bar every weekend hadn't been seen in a week or two either."

"That makes two," Krys said, looking over at Ty.

"Think we should call Warren and let him know?" Ty asked.

"Not yet," Krys answered. "He's probably still settling in at home. And we want to be completely sure before we make that call and take him away from Hebert again."

"Well, I got to get going." Billy announced. "Catch you on the flip side. Still Wyldfyr?"

"Always." Krys answered. "And Ty is Krafty Fox with a K."

"Krafty Fox?" Billy asked.

"Yeah, Kraft is my last name."

"Makes sense to me." Billy said as he stood up out of the booth. He shook hands with Ty and looked questioningly from Ty to Krys, then back to Ty.

"Go for it." Ty said, smiling.

Billy turned and embraced Krys once again. He hugged her tightly, whispered something in her ear, then released her and kissed her on the cheek.

Krys said, "I know." She sat back down in the booth and watched Billy as he walked across the restaurant and out the front door.

"He's a good friend, isn't he?" Ty asked when he sat back down across from Krys.

"A great friend, has been for over ten years. When we both lived in Denver and I'd have trouble with my middle son, he was always there to help. He was and always will be my best friend."

"Okay. But you know I have to ask what he whispered in your ear."

"You got a good one is what he said. That's why I said I know. Because I know I do and I trust Billy's instincts explicitly."

"Well, we better get out of here too. We got a load to Florida, to Jacksonville."

"Really? We've got to make a short stop at the beach. It's flat, white and absolutely gorgeous."

"Bet it's not as gorgeous as you though. I'll have to check it out and see."

Ty held Krys's hand as they walked out of the restaurant, then across the lot to the truck.

CHAPTER 5

Warren called to Leslie that he'd be on long distance, so hold his calls for a while. He dialed and asked for Lt. Morgan.

"Lt. Morgan here." The voice on the other end of the line answered.

"This is Warren. How are you?"

"I'm fine now that it's nice and quiet here in the Windy City. How are things in Hebert?"

"Hebert is okay. And before you ask, I hear Kalamazoo is okay too. When I left, there were still some vamps around that we hadn't found but the police department is staying vigilant."

Pete asked if Warren had heard anything about Lisa, to which he was said no, nothing.

"Well, like I said before, I'll keep an ear out and keep watching the data base. Anything shows up, you'll be the first to know."

"I appreciate that. I've just about got everyone and their brother looking out for her. We have truckers on the lookout too, two on the east coast and one on the west coast and north of Colorado. We also have Kee up in Michigan and you in Chicago. We should have our bases covered."

"Any idea yet how Blake is traveling?" Pete asked.

"None yet, but doubt he'd go by semi again, too conspicuous. But then, who knows how Blake thinks. Even Ty, who was with him for three years, can't figure the man out and, truthfully, who would want to?"

"Okay." Pete said. "Keep in touch and I'll do the same."

"Thanks again," Warren told him. They said their goodbyes and hung up.

"I'm off the phone, Leslie," Warren called out.

Leslie appeared in the door. "You have a visitor."

"Who is it?" Warren asked.

"A Bud Peterson?"

"Peterson? Let him in."

A young, well-dressed man walked through the door. He shook hands with Warren, then sat in the chair Warren had pointed to in front of his desk.

"Sheriff Warren, I'm Bud Peterson. Bud is short for Buford, so you can understand why it's been shortened." The man said in all seriousness.

"Peterson. You're Joe's son." Warren stated.

"Yes, I am. And I'm here to find out what happened to my dad and my baby sister."

"I don't know if you've heard anything about what happened here in Hebert, or up North or a number of other cities across the U.S."

"I've heard the rumors but being a doctor it's kind of hard to believe any of it."

"If what you've heard is that vampires are here and elsewhere, it's true. They are. I've seen them, I've got up close and personal with more than one of them.

"And my dad and sister?" Bud asked.

"Our first known vampire was a woman named Sandy. Her brother Cliff was next. Cliff chose to be with his sister when she showed up at your dad's place the night after her body disappeared from the morgue. Cliff was at your dad's house because he and Mary had been dating for quite a while. Your sister left the house when she was summoned by Cliff the next night. Twenty-four hours later, your dad went missing. We thought he was with Mary, but we were wrong."

"Where did you find them? What did you do to them? I really need to know."

"We found Cliff and Mary at Joe's place. They were in boxes in the basement. Your dad was next door with his lady friend and her family, a son, a daughter-in-law and two kids. They were all in coffins."

"And..."

"And we took care of them. I released your father. He had been one of my best friends for years and I felt I owed that much to him."

"Okay. I guess that will have to do, for now. But my main reason for being here is twofold. Number one, can Hebert use a second doctor, a general physician and surgeon?"

"I'm sure there's room for another doctor here. We only have Doc Murdock right now and he's ready to retire. All the death certificates and bodies he had to deal with wore him out. Your dad wasn't just the coroner, he had his own private practice that was flourishing. Everyone in town loved Joe. So, what's your second reason?" Warren asked, curious.

"I'd like to apply for the job of coroner. I've got the credentials, thanks to my dad's upbringing and encouragement. I'm also executor of his will and I'm now the proud owner of the family home as well as the coroner's office. So see, it's the perfect fit."

"I really don't see any problem with either of your requests. City Council meets tomorrow night. You be present to plead your case and I'll be your first yes vote."

"I appreciate that, Sheriff." Bud said. "I've been to dad's house already and checked it all out. It's clean inside and out."

Warren breathed a sigh of relief. He knew from Earl that Dan and the rest of the crew had been cleaning up the houses, removing any and all evidence of what had occurred in so many of them. He told Bud about Earl's list and would let him know tomorrow night where Joe and Mary were buried.

"I appreciate that too," Bud said. "I'm sure we'll want to put proper markers on the graves. And if this Cliff was that close to Mary, I'll want to take care of his grave site too."

Warren rose from his chair and walked around the desk to shake hands with Bud. Uncharacteristically, Warren gave Bud a hug. It seemed like the natural thing to do with Joe's son.

"Will it be just you moving in?" Warren asked.

"Sorry, no. I'm married. My wife's name is Julie, she's a middle school teacher. We have three kids, a 12-year-old girl named Kelsea and twin 10-year-old boys named Jason and Jordan. So we will definitely help you re-populate the town."

"Great idea as far as I'm concerned. And I know the City Council will agree. So, see you tomorrow night. Do you know where the city hall is?"

"Yes, I do. I was raised here, remember. I didn't leave until I was 18 and off to college. And I've been back numerous times. So, I'm okay."

"Oh, by the way," Warren began. "The town is planning a Thanksgiving dinner the Sunday before the holiday. A bunch of the guys are fixing turkeys and hams and the rest of us are bringing side dishes. You and your family are officially invited to come. I can promise a good time and lots of good food. And that will give you a chance to meet the rest of the townspeople."

"Sounds good. We'll be sure to come. My wife makes a mean sweet potato pie."

"Think she could maybe make two?" Warren asked with a smile. "I'm a sucker for sweet potato pie."

Warren walked Bud out of his office as far as Leslie's desk. They shook hands once again and said their goodbyes.

Warren went back to his office. He was anxious to tell Earl the good news, since good news had been so scarce in Hebert for such a long time. He dialed Earl's home phone but got no answer. He tried his cell phone and Earl answered on the first ring.

"Hi, Sheriff," Earl said. "I'm on my way in. Anything you need?"

"Nothing that can't wait until you get here. See you soon."

CHAPTER 6

Krys and Ty drove to Jacksonville without incident. They left the trailer at the warehouse to be unloaded and bobtailed to the ocean. Ty marveled at the white sands and crystal clear blue waters. They sat in the truck for a few minutes before Krys coaxed Ty into taking off his shoes and going for a walk on the beach.

"The sand is so hard, like cement." Ty commented.

"I know. Years ago we could drive our car down here and spend the night on the beach. It was so peaceful with the waves and all."

Ty admitted to delivering in Florida quite a few times in the past, but never taking the time to stop and smell the ocean. He admitted to never taking time off to enjoy any of the things around him.

"Stick with me," Krys said, "and I'll show you a lot of things you've never taken the time to see."

"You can count on me sticking close." Ty told her. "You've already shown me a life I never expected to experience."

They walked up and down the beach, Krys collecting seashells along the way. Ty found a sand dollar that was completely intact and handed it to Krys to add to her collection.

Krys told Ty to stay on the beach and she would be right back. He stood staring out over the water. The waves were so small but the sound of them on the beach had a soothing effect on him.

When she returned from the truck, she was carrying a blanket and two bottles of Gatorade. Ty helped her spread out the blanket and they sat down, relaxing totally. Ty kept his feet off the blanket on the sand, enjoying the warmth.

"Once before," Krys began, "I asked you where you were from. You didn't answer me."

"Yes, I did." Ty said.

"No, you didn't. Everywhere is really nowhere. So, now is as good a time as any to start talking."

"Okay," Ty finally spoke, "I'm originally from North Carolina. My parents, both gone now, were teachers. I'm Cherokee Indian, descended down from my Grandma, who was full-blooded Cherokee, a medicine woman which was rare in her day. She knew all the herbs needed for just about any ailment. She had a soft, quiet voice and a way about her that put everyone at ease."

"She sounds wonderful." Krys commented.

"She was." Ty said. He sat for a second or two before speaking again.

"The Cherokee were a highly spiritual nation with ceremonies and customs. They called themselves Ani-Yvwiya or 'Real People'. Grandma grew beans, corn, squash. These were called the 'three sisters' and were the staples in her diet. She also farmed potatoes and had peach trees. She taught me crafts like basket weaving, pottery, beadwork and carving gourds."

"She sounds like a very knowledgeable woman."

"She was that. In the Cherokee Nation, the woman owns the land and has the authority to pass it on to any member of her family. I am the proud owner of 20 acres and a log cabin."

"No teepee?" Krys asked.

"Only one, it stands alongside the cabin. Years past, it was used as a medicine sweat tent. The old chiefs would have something serious to discuss, they would start a fire, use just enough water to make steam and sweat through their decision. Claimed the steam cleared their heads and they would make the right decision with nothing else clouding their thoughts."

"Sounds reasonable. Isn't that what a shower does for us some times?"

"True. Anyhow, Grandma is gone now and I will always miss her and hold her in my heart."

"I'm sorry," Krys said.

"Don't be. You are my family now. You are all I need to keep me on the straight and narrow and keep me sane."

They sat for another hour, comfortably silent, each deep in their own thoughts. Eventually, Ty stood up, held out his hand to help Krys up, then helped shake out the blanket and fold it.

When they returned to the truck, Ty asked Krys if she was hungry yet.

"Famished." Krys replied.

"I know a truck stop out on Highway 10 that has a seafood buffet. Sound good to you?"

"Seafood? Sounds perfect to me."

Ty drove away from the ocean and travelled a good 40 miles before he turned into the truck stop.

After they were seated and had their drinks, Krys walked over to the buffet. She was loading up a plate with crab legs and mussels when a lady trucker stepped up beside her with an empty plate. They both reached for the tongs at the same time and bumped plates in the process. They laughed and excused themselves and then Krys proceeded on down the buffet line.

Krys walked back to the booth and sat down. Ty immediately got up and headed for the buffet. While she was still cracking the crab legs and only had a small pile of meat on her plate, Ty returned with his plate loaded high with numerous shrimp, from boiled to breaded and fried to coconut covered.

"Excuse me." A female voice spoke up from behind Krys.

Krys turned around and looked up to see the lady from the buffet.

"Oh, hi." Krys said.

"If I'm not being too presumptuous, could I please join you?" the lady asked.

"Sure." Krys said, giving Ty a quizzical look as she slid over in the booth to make room on her side.

"You're Krafty Fox and Wyldyr, aren't you?" the girl asked.

"Yes." Ty answered. "But how did you know that?"

"I've been monitoring the CB for a while now." She answered. "My bad. I'm Cassy. Cassy Adams."

"Hello, Cassy. I'm Krys and this is Ty."

"It's nice to put faces to the handles once in a while."

"So, what's your CB handle?" Krys asked.

"Blond Bombshell." Cassy answered.

"The name fits." Krys laughed.

"My grandpa was a trucker and he gave me that handle when I was around eight years old. It just stuck."

"Bet you get a lot of grief with that handle." Ty said.

"Sometimes, yeah, I do. But I can handle that just fine."

For a while, the only sound at the table was the cracking of crab legs.

"Are you still looking for Blake?" Cassy asked suddenly.

Krys and Ty stopped eating abruptly and simultaneously looked up from their plates at Cassy.

"And you know about Blake how?" Ty asked.

"Jimmy Anderson is my cousin. We're real close, talk all the time. And I talk to my brother Jacob too. He volunteered in Hebert when they were disposing of their problems."

"That explains that." Ty said.

"I've been monitoring the CB, Jimmy asked me to. There've been a few deaths that were somewhat suspicious but no disappearances yet."

"Where was this?" Krys asked, anxious all of a sudden.

"Couple in Denver, one in Aurora and one in Arvada, both are suburbs of Denver." Cassy told them.

Krys and Ty looked at each other expectantly.

"Have you been to Denver recently?" Krys asked.

"I live in Aurora, have for the past five years. I'm out past County Line Road, though, kind of country living. Lots of open spaces."

Remembering what Warren had experienced in his front yard with the vampires taking down a deer, Ty asked Cassy if there was much wildlife where she lived.

"We used to get deer in the yard every evening. Also, raccoons, skunks and bobcats."

"Used to?" Ty questioned her.

"The last time I was home, which was only a week ago, I had a three day layover waiting on a load. We had about four inches of snow in the yard but no tracks, other than those made by my animals. Usually, there are at least deer tracks because I leave food out for them in a trough all year round."

"The food wasn't touched?" Ty asked.

"No. It was still there when I left out."

"What about your animals?" Krys asked. "Do you have a dog or cat that go outside?"

"I have both. Sam, he's a bobcat. He goes out when he wants to, which is usually every night. And I have a Husky/Wolf mix, Bright Eyes. He comes and goes whenever he wants to. But, thinking back, Sam only left the house during daylight hours on our last trip home. He never did go out at night. Neither did Bright Eyes, for that matter."

"How do you know this?" Krys asked her.

"I have a huge doggy door, one they use as they please. But Sam slept on my bed all night, every night. I would have felt him get up off the bed. And, come to think of it, Bright Eyes slept on the floor by my bedroom door every night, which is unusual for him."

"You have a bobcat?" Krys asked. "That's awesome. What do you do with him when you go on the road?"

"Sam comes with me, he always has. He's out in my rig right now, waiting for me to bring him some goodies. You'll have to meet him."

"I'd love to." Krys responded. "I love cats, always have. But a bobcat, that has to be way out there."

"Is he declawed?" TY asked.

"Hell, no. When he goes out, he has to be able to protect himself. In the truck and at home, I've never seen his claws. He's adorable. You'd love him."

Ty and Cassy both decided they needed dessert. Ty came back to the table with some banana pudding and a large piece of carrot cake for Krys. Although she protested, she dug in quickly. Cassy came back with some cotton candy.

"Can't resist. Whenever my dad and grandparents took me and my brother to Golden Coral, I got cotton candy. It just reminds me of the good times."

"Krys is the same way when it comes to carrot cake." Ty said.

"You know me so well," Krys responded, smiling over at Ty.

When dinner was finished, Ty picked up both checks, among protestations from Cassy that she could pay her own way.

They walked out of the restaurant and across the lot to Cassy's truck to see Sam. She was driving a company truck for Swift but instead of the normal white truck, she had a red one.

When they reached the rig, Cassy climbed up and opened the driver's door and said okay. Immediately, Ty and Krys could hear the animal jump off the bed onto the floor. He came out of the sleeper and walked around the driver's seat, then leaped out of the truck without touching the steps to stand by Cassy's side, wary of the two strangers standing so close. Cassy knelt down beside the cat, reaching over to scratch his ears.

"Ty and Krys, I'd like you to meet Sam Elliott Minsky. Sam, they're okay."

Krys walked slowly up to Sam, knelt down in front of him and slowly raised her hands to his eye level, so he could sense she wasn't a danger. She reached over and began scratching his head and back. Sam responded by taking a step forward, laying down on the pavement beside her and laying his head on her leg.

"He's adorable. He's really precious." Krys exclaimed.

Ty walked up behind Krys. Sam's ears perked up and he moved his head slightly in order to watch Ty. Ty knelt down next to Krys and reached over hesitantly to pet Sam, who then laid his head back down on Krys's leg and accepted all the attention.

"You passed," Cassy stated. "He likes you both."

"When he's out of the truck like this, don't you worry he'll take off, being wild and all?" Ty asked.

"I did at first. But we've been together now for three years and he's never made an attempt to leave my side."

"You two have a special bond. I love it." Krys said, still petting Sam.

"They've actually got a dog run here and, luckily, there aren't any dogs in it right now. Think I'll take Sam over and let him run a while. Want to come?" Cassy asked.

"You bet." Krys answered before Ty could say a word for or against.

Krys stood inside the dog run with Cassy while Sam ran back and forth from one end to the other, always running back to Cassy and Krys, looking up for their attention. He'd get his ears scratched and be off running again.

Ty stood outside the fence watching them play. It was a good distraction from his every day routine.

When it was time to leave, they all exchanged names and cell numbers and promised to keep in touch.

CHAPTER 7

As soon as TY and Krys were seated once more in the truck, Ty got out his phone and called Warren.

"Hi, Ty," Warren answered. "What's up?"

"I think we got a lead on where Blake might have gone. But it's not a given yet." Ty answered.

"Where?" Warren asked, anxiousness heard in his voice.

"We met a lady trucker today at a truck stop here in Florida. She mentioned four suspicious deaths, two in Denver and two out in the suburbs. She hadn't heard of any disappearances yet. She's a cousin to Jimmy and she mentioned being a sister to Jacob. She's been monitoring the CB and keeping in touch with both of them there in Hebert."

"And this morning," Ty continued, "a friend of Krys's said he had heard from a friend of his about one guy who definitely got killed, but then the body disappeared. There was also another guy talking about a friend of his who was at the bar every weekend religiously but hadn't been seen or heard from in a couple of weeks now."

"So, where are you now and where are you headed?" Warren asked.

"We have to go back to Jacksonville to pick up my trailer. Then I'll call in for a load, see if I can't get one into Denver or at least close by."

"Okay. I'll call the chief of police there, maybe get a heads up on the situation. Keep in touch." Warren said and immediately hung up.

"Ten-four." Ty said seconds after he heard the dial tone. "Warren's going to call Denver and talk to the chief of police up there. See what's going on."

"Hope we all don't get our hopes up for nothing." Krys mused.

"Yeah, me too." Ty added.

CHAPTER 8

Warren immediately got on his computer and into the nationwide police web site. He typed in Denver chief of police. The name that came up was Larry Moore. He wrote down the name and number and stuck the paper in his shirt pocket.

He stayed busy most of the day, going through papers on his desk. His mind kept wandering to the Sunday dinner coming up, now less than a week away. As much as he hated the idea of making a speech, he was determined to personally thank the men who had volunteered to eradicate the problem in town. And he wanted to say a special thank you to Earl because Warren felt that Earl had served the town above and beyond the call of duty. He was bound and determined to let the entire town know how much Earl had done for them, then and now.

Earl had completely surprised Warren when the situation involving the vampires had evolved. His knowledge and bravery were exceptional. Earl had always been in the background but Warren intended to put him up in the foreground on Sunday. He wanted everyone to know what kind of a man they had protecting them on a daily basis.

Around 2 p.m. that afternoon, Warren finally took a break from his paperwork and fished the paper out of his pocket, then dialed the number to Denver. A receptionist answered and directed his call to the proper office.

"Hello, Chief Larry Moore speaking. How can I help you today?" a very brisk voice answered the phone.

"My name is Josiah Warren and I'm the sheriff of Hebert, Illinois. I need to talk to you about some suspicious homicides in Denver and the surrounding suburbs."

"I know exactly who you are, I've been in the loop from the beginning. I've already talked to Pete Morgan in Chicago and Keenan Jones in Kalamazoo."

"Then you what I'm calling about?" Warren asked.

"I'd say the word vampire comes to mind."

"You do know then. Is this something you think you can accept as fact?" Warren asked.

"Fact or fiction. Right now, I'd say fact outweighs fiction by 99.9%." the Chief responded.

"Have your homicides disappeared shortly after being found?" Warren asked anxiously.

"Two disappeared from the coroner's office here in Denver. I haven't heard from Arvada or Aurora yet. I can make a formal inquiry though. I can also call you back when I find something out. Is this a good number to reach you at?"

"No. This is my office number. I'll give you my cell phone number. We're only an hour apart, but you can call me at any time, day or night. It's imperative that I know as soon as possible if there's any chance Blake is in Denver."

"I understand completely. I've been in the know because of Kee and I'm aware of the urgency to find your Lisa."

They exchanged their cell phone numbers and then said their goodbyes.

Warren sat at his desk. The phone call had proved interesting and somewhat productive. He wasn't about to rush to Denver until he was sure Blake was really there and it wasn't just a town he had passed through and left infected. And, unfortunately, it would take more than a few victims to prove one way or another.

As many cities and towns as Blake had traveled through, Warren knew he had to be one hundred percent sure that Blake was indeed in Denver. He checked the data base once again but nothing new had popped up.

Warren vowed to himself that if it turned out that Blake was in Denver, he'd be on his way immediately. This time he would find Blake and destroy him. He could only hope that he wouldn't be forced to do the same thing to Lisa. It was a constant worry to him as to what he could or couldn't do to Lisa. He had loved her for so long but did he love her enough to kill her? He prayed daily that Blake had not yet turned her into a beast of the night like her sister Pat.

CHAPTER 9

Ty and Krys picked up the trailer and drove a little over two hours before they stopped back at the truck stop. Krys went into the restaurant and got a booth while Ty went to call his broker. When he joined her, she had already ordered him a glass of iced tea. She was doctoring a cup of hot tea with lemon and some honey.

"I got a load to Aurora. We'll have to drive empty to Texarkana to pick it up though."

"So, what is it we're picking up?"

"Tires." Ty said. "But I know exactly where we're going. My LTL was called the three river run, never knew why. I ran from California up north to Washington State, across through Wyoming and down into Colorado. Then into Texas and back to California. In Texarkana I picked up tires and delivered them to numerous towns in California from El Centro to Modesto. In Washington State, I'd pick up apples. I liked the route cause it took me up Highway 1 which runs along the ocean. I could look out my driver's window at the water. Out the passenger window were cliffs topped with orange groves. It was really a spectacular run."

"But this time we go to Colorado." Krys remarked.

"Yup. And for Warren's sake, I hope it is Blake and that Lisa is with him and she's still herself."

"If she isn't, do you really think Warren can take care of her? You know he's loved her for a long time now."

"I know. But just like Lisa insisted she take care of her sister, I think Warren will take care of her if necessary. I just hope and pray it won't be necessary."

"I realize Blake took Lisa for revenge. But if he has her sister back with him, which is what the police in Kalamazoo and Warren believe, then why keep Lisa?" Krys wondered out loud.

"I don't know. I can't figure Blake out. And, truthfully, it would scare me to death if I could."

They left the restaurant, fueled up and then hit the road.

"You know," Krys suddenly said, "if Lisa is still okay, Blake may be using her like he used you, to drive during the day."

"Lisa can't drive a semi, or at least I don't think she can." Ty said.

"But it bet she could drive a motorhome. Just think about it. A motorhome would be perfect. Dark tint on the windows, dark curtains. All the RV parks that are available to hide out in."

"It would be completely inconspicuous. It's definitely a good way to get wherever you want to go. But there are too many RV parks to even begin to know where he would stop to park."

"A needle in a haystack." Krys said.

"Totally," Ty commented. "But I think we need to let Warren in on your idea. He may have one or two of his own, but I believe you might have hit the nail on the head, so to speak."

"Just full of old sayings, aren't we?" Krys asked, jokingly.

"Just like two old married people." Ty said, winking at her, then turning his attention back to his driving.

CHAPTER 10

The Sunday of the big dinner came around faster than Warren expected. Saturday evening he put together two large cake pans of what he called "Pizza Dip". It was restaurant style chips crushed and then doused in butter. Next layer was cream cheese blended with picante sauce. Top layer was chopped red, green and yellow bell peppers along with green onions, tomatoes and black olives. When it was all put together, it looked like a pizza.

When Warren arrived at the gym Sunday afternoon, it was already packed full of townspeople. As soon as he stepped through the door, Sharon appeared and took one of the cake pans. Warren followed her across the gym floor to a row of tables set up in front of the stage. Sharon moved a couple bowls of salad over to make room for Warren's cake pans. When they set the pans down, she removed the aluminum foil he had used to cover them.

"Oh, wow," Sharon exclaimed. "I don't know what it is, but it looks scrumptious."

Warren explained to her what it was and how to cut it into squares.

Suddenly, unexpectedly, Sharon moved closer to Warren and then gave him a big hug.

"What was that for?" Warren asked, a little startled.

"For the hell of it." Sharon said, smiling. "I appreciate all you did for mom and dad. I still get a little emotional when I think of them and how long the three of you had been best of friends."

"I wasn't here when they were found. Earl was in charge and he was the one who took care of your mom, dad and John."

"Oh, I've already thanked Earl. But you were my dad's best friend and you always treated both dad and mom with the utmost respect and love. For that, I can't thank you enough."

Before Warren could answer Sharon, Earl appeared from out of the crowd. He was carrying a large roaster. He put it on the table and took the cover off. The aroma of homemade bread dressing made Warren's mouth water.

"You surprise me more every day, Earl," Warren said, noting how Earl was standing beside Sharon with his arm around her waist lovingly. Sharon leaned into Earl and gave him a kiss on the cheek.

Bud Peterson walked up to Warren and shook his hand.

Warren introduced him to Earl and Sharon and then asked Bud if he and his family were getting settled in.

"Yes, thank you. We kept a lot of Dad's stuff in the house, but we also moved a lot of our stuff in. I just wanted to thank you for your input and vote at the City Council meeting last week."

"No thanks necessary, it was the right thing to do. By the way, how's the family adjusting to our little town?"

"I'll let you ask them yourself," Bud said as he turned and motioned to a woman and three kids who were standing off to the side to come join them.

"This is my wife Julie, my two boys Jason and Jordan and…"

"And this must be your gorgeous daughter Katy," Warren cut in as he held out his hand to shake Julie's, then the boys and then Katy in turn.

"You have a beautiful family. How do you kids like Hebert so far?" he asked.

"It's cool." The twins yelled out simultaneously.

"And how about you, Ka?"

"It's great." She answered. "I got my Aunt Mary's room and it's so neat. I got my own grown up bed now and really girly curtains."

"That sounds really great." Warren told her. He still remembered Mary's room from his investigation shortly after she disappeared.

Before their conversation could continue, the Mayor interrupted on the PA system on the stage.

"Can I have your attention please." The Mayor began. "We want to welcome the town of Hebert to its first annual Thanksgiving dinner. The first of many. Before we begin lining up by these tables full of such wonderful aromas, I want to call out a special thank you to the men who made all of this possible. As I call your names, please raise your hand so everyone can see who you are."

"Sheriff Warren. Deputy Earl Baker. Dan Roberts. Tom Wilson. Jacob Meyers. Joshua Meyers. Andy Anderson. Jimmy Anderson. Kevin Irwin. Craig Ivory. David Kennedy. Joe Gray."

When their names were called, each man raised his hand in acknowledgement. After all the names were announced, the entire assembly stood clapping, whooping, whistling and cheering for those named. The crowd eventually settled down and the Mayor continued.

"Now, I would like a moment of silence for all the friends, neighbors and relatives we lost. The list of names is entirely too long to name everyone, but just a few include Gene and Beth from our local truck stop, Joe Peterson our coroner, his daughter Mary, Judy Summers from the Sheriff's department, Susie Petty and John Adamson from the truck stop along with so many more victims."

The entire assembly quieted down and heads were bowed for those who were no longer with them.

"Now, Father Keller, will you give a blessing and then it will be time to eat."

Father Keller walked up onto the stage and took the microphone. "Dear Lord, please bless this congregation assembled here. Watch over all of us and keep us safe from harm. Bless this food which we are about to partake and let it nourish our bodies. Keep our departed close to you as they will always be close to our hearts. In Jesus' name. Amen."

In one voice, the assembly repeated the amen.

The Mayor once again stepped up to the microphone and simply said, "Let's eat."

Without a word said, the crowd had parted and allowed Warren and the rest of the volunteers who weren't serving to get to the tables first. When Warren looked at that first table, he was amazed to see it covered from one end to the other with turkeys. There were the traditional roasted turkeys but then he noticed that there were also two fried ones. There was Earl's roaster of dressing along with three others pans of cornbread dressing, one of which had jalapenos in it.

Warren opted for a slice of white meat from one of the deep fried turkeys, something he had never had before. He took a big scoop of Earl's dressing which was still warm. Then he moved on to the next table.

There were bowls full of different salads. One in particular caught his eye. It was full of all types of leaves he didn't recognize, covered in fresh sliced mushrooms, yellow bell peppers, tomatoes and green onions.

"You really should try my homemade dressing on my salad," the man behind the table commented. Warren looked up but didn't recognize him. He did put the dressing on the salad and then moved on. He cut a square of his pizza dip and placed it on his plate, which was now pretty full.

He walked to the last table which was covered in pumpkin pies and sweet potato pies, apple pies, pecan pies, a huge carrot cake, various cookies, fudges and brownies along with a huge bowl of fresh whipped cream. He took a slice of one of the sweet potato pies, then covered it with a ladle full of whipped cream.

Warren walked to a table near the far wall of the gym. A couple minutes later, he was joined by Jimmy and David. He smiled when he noted that David had two plates, both piled high with food.

"Some things never change." Jimmy laughed as he sat down next to Warren.

They were soon joined by two more of the original volunteers, Jacob and Andy.

"We all got together when we learned about your Lisa." Jimmy started, "and we talked about who could leave out if necessary. Here they are." Jimmy pointed across the table to the two men sitting there.

Warren reached across the table and shook hands with Andy and then Jacob in turn. "Are you sure about this?" he asked.

"Positive." Andy said. "I'm retired and don't have anyone to keep me here. I've been driving truck during the summer for Bridgeport Tank down in Texas. But that's summer and we're definitely not having summer right now. I've already made arrangements with Jimmy and David to take care of my horses and dogs, although I'm really thinking about taking Mickey with me. She's a Collie and I took her with me the last couple of days we were working here. She sniffed out them vampires real good. She may be an asset to us."

"What about you, Jacob?" Warren asked. "Are you originally from here?"

"You want the short or long version of my story?" Jacob asked, smiling.

"Really, I think we can all get the long version, considering how much food we have here to eat." Warren answered.

"Okay, then. I grew up here in Hebert. I joined the Navy right out of high school and, although I wanted to work on planes, they found out I knew computers and that's where they put me. My dad was in the Navy and I followed in his footsteps. Like him, I was the youngest recruit in boot camp. And just like him, I was the only one who shot 100 out of 100 moving targets. We both got plaques to prove it."

Warren could tell how proud Jacob was of his accomplishments as well as his dad's.

"Go on." Warren urged between mouthfuls.

"When I got out of the Navy, I came back to Hebert and opened up a computer store, next to Margie's flower shop. Within a year, I paid for the building. Two years later, I purchased the building next door and opened it up to make more room and increase my inventory. Also, I finally had a real office, not a corner of the storeroom."

"I've always worked with high school kids, teaching them and then sometimes hiring them. As of now, I have both a boy and a girl from the high school working for me. I hired Jason because he was so energetic, was always willing to learn and be hands on. He was always coming up with new ideas and, between the two of us, we actually designed a game that is now being played across the entire U.S."

Jacob stopped to take a drink of his tea, then continued.

"I hired Sharky a year out of high school. She worked for me in her junior year but, during her senior year, she got involved in a Gothic phase and more or less blanked out everything else. When she graduated, she went to work for Neal over at the IGA. She worked stocking shelves, then as a cashier. When she started helping him do the ordering and other paperwork, she realized she actually missed the computer. She applied for a job and I hired her immediately. She knows the basics of the computer but loves the mathematical end of it. And, she's great with the customers."

"When I volunteered to help out with the vampires, Sharky actually went into the office every day, locked herself in and worked on my books. I'm not exactly the best accountant. She found receipts that were a year old and more. When I went back to work, she showed me what she had done with my horrible bookwork. I told her she indispensable. I told her she was now my accountant with a pay raise."

"She still wants to deal with the customers though, I think she enjoys standing up to those big guys. I told her we both knew I didn't deal well with them, especially the irate ones. She stands up to them while courteously putting them in their place yet placating them. I made the mistake of telling her she was irreplaceable. She said she'd remember that word every year when it was time for her annual raise. I think I created a monster."

"Anyhow, with Jason working on the computers and Sharky doing everything else, I don't have any qualms about volunteering to go with you, Sheriff, wherever we have to travel to save your Lisa."

"I appreciate that, more than you'll ever know. It's not like I'm inviting you to a party, that's for sure."

Warren looked at Andy but didn't have to ask any questions before Andy spoke up.

"I've lived here my whole life, on a small farm just south of town. It isn't much, but it's mine and I love every inch of it. I have quite a few horses, my oldest son rode in the rodeo and I still have one of his old nags, can't make myself put her down. But she's in good shape and enjoying all the leisurely time she has now. I've got a couple of dogs, my Collie Mickey and a Shepherd named Mouse. They're both good dogs. I never have to worry about prowlers, the four or the two-legged kind, around my place."

"I've known Jacob's dad since we were in first grade. We've been friends since then, lifelong friends, more like brothers. I joined the Marines when John joined the Navy. We both made it through Vietnam and returned here."

"I have one son. John had a daughter and two sons, Jacob here is one of them, of course. John's kids look at me like their uncle and I wouldn't change that for the world. I love every one of those kids, even Jacob the squid." Andy said as he leaned over and tousled Jacob's hair.

"That's a jarhead for you." Jacob shot back.

"Then, now and forever." Andy said with pride. "Anyhow, with Jimmy and David taking care of my livestock and my dog, I'm more than willing to go. Any idea which way we'll be heading, Sheriff?"

"I've heard rumors about Denver from a couple of different sources, but nothing is written in stone yet. That's the only place so far that has bodies disappearing. Do any of you know Denver? Ever been there?" Warren asked.

"Been there more than once," Jacob spoke up. "My sister, Cassy, lives up there. She's outside the city, as country as she can get and still be close enough to enjoy the city. She has a mobile on an acre. It's in a park but she's buying the house. She has two cement pads nearby where she sometimes parks her truck and, if necessary, a trailer. I was thinking maybe we could take Andy's motorhome up there, park it near her place and some of us could sleep in it."

"Not a bad idea," Warren agreed. "We'll see what happens."

"Did you do anything other than computers in the Navy, Jacob?" Warren asked.

"Unfortunately, yes. I trained to be a sniper and used my training when they sent me to Afghanistan. But that also made me think of something that might be useful when we leave here. What if we were to hunt the vampires at night, when they're out walking around?"

"Don't know about that. They're only vulnerable in the daytime." Jimmy interjected.

"Yes, but I have something that I really think might stop a lot of them in their tracks."

"Really?" David asked. "What is it?"

"Wooden arrows. Wouldn't a wooden arrow through the heart do the same damage as a wooden stake?"

"It probably would," Jimmy said, "if your aim is on target. The only problem I see is that arrow tips aren't made of wood."

"The ones I've made are. Fashioned them myself and they'll pierce through flesh just fine." Jacob stated.

"You sure?" David asked.

"Positive. I brought down a ten point buck with one last hunting season."

"I'm not that good with a bow," Warren stated, "so I'd be of no help."

"I've fished with a bow before." Andy said. "I'd be willing to try it but I'd need some practice first."

"I'm sure even a Jarhead can learn from a Squid if he puts his mind to it." Jimmy said in all seriousness.

Andy glared at Jimmy for only a few seconds, then said, "Yeah, right."

CHAPTER 11

Warren was enjoying the socialization when Earl and Sharon came up to the table. Sharon spent time introducing her crew to Warren. He realized she had been totally accurate in her description of two burly men. Their muscular arms were as large as Warren's thighs.

Afterward, they all continued to sit, relaxing for a change. Warren leaned over toward the next table and asked Earl about the guy at the salad bar.

"Oh, that's J.R. He moved to town right after we had it cleaned up. You should get to know him, he's really quite interesting."

"How so?" Warren asked.

"You know that old building down on Main and Ash, the one that's been vacant for so long?"

"Yeah."

"Well, it's not vacant any more. J.R. bought it. He turned it into a workout center and health store. He believes in everything natural, no preservatives."

"Sounds interesting, if I ever want to go to a gym, which is highly doubtful." Warren said.

"He made that salad and dressing from all natural ingredients, everything made from scratch. He loves to cook and shares his cooking with everyone."

"That sounds like someone David needs to get to know." Warren commented, smiling over at David slyly.

As everyone started laughing, including David, Warren's phone rang.

"Gotta take this." Warren said as he stood up from the table and headed for the door leading outside. He answered it on the third ring and told Ty to hold on until he was outside and could hear him.

When Warren was far enough away from the door and the noisy crowd, he said, "Hey, Ty. What's up?"

As Warren listened intently, his facial expression changed from a questioning look to a more serious one. He listened for a good ten minutes, took his notebook out of his pocket, wrote a name and number down, then said his goodbyes.

When Warren walked back into the gym, he was greeted by many different people; some he knew, some he didn't. He made a mental note to really get to know them all.

When he passed a table near his destination, J.R. stood up from the table and shook his hand, formally introducing himself to Warren.

"I hear you opened up a gym. I'll have to come by and say hello sometime. But I've got to warn you, I'm not the gym kind of guy."

"That's okay, Sheriff," J.R. said, "We have more than just a gym. We have a health food store, cooking classes, classes on how to get in shape with or without exercising, all sorts of interesting and educational things going on."

"I'll definitely get by to see you. But you really do need to write out that recipe for your salad dressing. I've never tasted anything like it. It was really great." Warren said.

"I'll have it ready whenever you come by," J.R. said. "And I hope you'll visit real soon."

"Me, too." Warren said. He turned and walked back toward his table.

Before Warren could get seated, Earl came to the table and asked if that was Ty on the phone and did he have any news.

"Yes and yes." Warren said. "After this is over, meet me at the station. Andy, Jacob, could you also come by?"

"Sure thing." Andy said after Jacob had nodded yes.

The mayor once again walked up on stage.

"Attention, please." He began after thumping the microphone to make sure it was still working.

"We all want to thank Dan Roberts, Tom Wilson and the rest of the crew for their delicious turkeys."

Everyone in the gym began clapping as Dan, Tom and the rest of the men stood up, including Andy and Jacob. There was a lot of whooping and hollering from the crowd.

"Thank you," Dan bellowed from his position on the floor, not needing a microphone. "But thank you should also go to all of you for the great side dishes that really made this dinner a success."

Again, everyone started clapping and whistling their approval.

Warren slowly made his way through the crowd and up onto the stage. He tapped the mayor on the shoulder. The mayor moved aside, allowing Warren to get closer to the microphone.

"Can I have your attention for just a second, please?" Warren began.

The crowd fell silent and looked at Warren expectantly.

"You all know me but, unfortunately, I've not taken the time to know all of you. For that I apologize and make a solemn vow to correct that mistake."

"I wanted to come up here and personally thank the volunteers who were here for our town. Without all of them, our problem would never have been taken care of."

Warren paused to allow the crowd to once again applaud for the volunteers. When the applause died down, he continued.

"My main reason for being up here is for Earl. Everyone here knows Earl, knows he's my deputy. But when our town needed him, Earl stepped up to the plate. He knew and understood what was going on, much more than I did. When I left to go to Kalamazoo, I left Earl in charge. He did his job, did more than anyone could have possibly expected him to do. He led the volunteers, supplied them with information in what they were facing and how to take care of the problem. He should be our man of the hour."

Earl had silently stood next to Sharon, listening to Warren's speech. A single tear ran down his cheek.

"I'm sure you all know about my Lisa's disappearance from her home. We now have some idea where she may have been taken. To Denver, Colorado. I'll be leaving again in the next day or two. Once again, I'll be leaving Earl in charge. I have all the faith in the world in Earl's ability to protect this town and all of you."

Warren paused for a couple of seconds, then continued once more.

"This will be my last trip hunting Blake. I'll hopefully be coming back to Hebert with Lisa by my side. I realize that is wishful thinking at this point in time. But we all live with wishes. No matter what the outcome is, I will return."

Warren paused once again, looking across the gym at the crowd who were raptly listening to him.

"I make you all a promise here and now. I'll be back and when I get back, I'll be a better sheriff for as long as you want me to continue in that position. Once I retire, in 20 or 30 years, I'll totally back Earl to take my place."

The audience broke out in laughter and Warren turned and left the stage. As he walked through the crowd, everyone continued to applaud for him. Some of the volunteers patted him on the back and Earl stood tall and shook his hand when he reached him.

The mayor stepped back up to the podium.

"Now, if everyone wants a to-go box, we have them at the head of the table by the turkeys. You all take as much food as you want. We plan to have dinner like this every year around this time. It's our way of celebrating our lives and all that each one of us means to our town."

"What about a town barbecue in the spring?" a voice in the crowd shouted out.

"Great idea," the mayor said. "Bet we could talk Dan and his crew into some hellacious BBQ."

"I bet you could too." Dan said, his voice easily heard over the chattering of the crowd.

"Okay, then. Leftovers be gone! Have a great day, a great thanksgiving and see all of you in the spring for BBQ."

At least half of the people in the crowd lined up to fill the boxes with leftovers. David was second in line with two boxes in hand.

Jimmy leaned over toward Warren and said, "You know he's going to say that they're for both of us, but don't let him get by with it."

After the line died out, Warren got up and walked over to the second table to collect his pans. The first one was completely empty, the second one had only one square of dip left in it. Sharon had neatly folded the aluminum foil and placed each piece under one of the cake pans. Warren wrapped both pans up tight and headed toward the door.

He stopped when Sharon thumped the microphone and asked for everyone's attention.

"I just wanted to say how much I enjoyed all the dishes served here. Being in the restaurant business, I can truly appreciate new ideas, especially ones that are so damned good."

"Now, I have another idea. Why don't we all get together and put a recipe book together. I'm sure someone here in town could bind and illustrate it and I can type up all the recipes and organize them. What about it?" she asked exuberantly.

Everyone in the gym started talking at once and Sharon heard words like great idea, super, oh yeah and sure thing.

"My office can print the books and bind them." Jacob piped up from the middle of the gym.

"And I can actually make some of the recipes and then take pictures of the finished products for the book." J.R. added from the other side of the room.

"Okay, then." Sharon continued. "Bring me a recipe out to the truck stop. I'll supply free coffee or tea when you come in. Be sure to put your name on each recipe you bring out. Bring as many as you want. I never run out of tea or coffee. Thank you." With that, Sharon left the stage.

CHAPTER 12

Warren walked out of the gym, put his pans in the back of his patrol car and headed back to the station.

Within minutes of his arrival, Earl came through the door, followed by Andy and Jacob. Warren led them into the break room. When they were all seated, he began.

"I talked to Ty this afternoon. He met another trucker who is from Colorado. She said that there were a couple of incidences in Denver as well as the suburbs of Arvada and Aurora, of homicides that were suspicious. She didn't know if any of the bodies had disappeared or not. She was heading back to Denver. Ty got a load to Aurora and he and Krys are headed that way too."

"Did Ty by any chance mention this other trucker's name?" Jacob asked. Both he and Andy were on the edges of their seats waiting.

"Yes, her name is, let me see," Warren pulled the paper out of his shirt pocket," Cassy".

"Oh, my God." Jacob said. "That's my sister."

"And my niece." Andy added.

"I thought you two weren't related." Warren said.

"Not really by blood," Jacob said. "We're related by heart and soul. Me and Cassy have always thought of Andy like an uncle. He's always been in our lives. And Jimmy, he's been like a brother to me."

"Does this mean you're leaving soon?" Earl asked.

"Soon," Warren said, "just not this minute. I'm basically just putting you two on alert. It sounds promising but nothing positive yet."

"Do they know how Blake would have gotten to Denver from Kalamazoo?" Jacob asked.

"No one knows for sure but Krys does have a theory. Right now, it's only a theory though. She's been thinking a motorhome. It makes sense but nothing is written in stone." Warren answered.

"Okay," Andy said as he stood up from the table, "me and Jacob will get our things put together and be ready whenever you call."

"Want me to get my bows and arrows loaded up too?" Jacob asked.

"If you have time before we leave, you'll have to set up some targets and we can all get some practice in." Warren suggested.

"Already got the targets set up out at Andy's. So, any time." Jacob told him.

"Okay, then. How about in two hours we meet at Andy's, Earl too."

"Works for me," Andy said. "We'll pick up the bows and arrows at Jacob's on the way back to my place."

Jacob and Andy left. Warren turned to Earl.

"Ready to be Sheriff again, Earl?" Warren asked.

"I guess." Earl answered. "But truthfully, not really. I enjoy being your deputy because you make me feel like we're actually in this together."

"We are partners," Warren said. "But I feel we're more like family now, after all of this."

"I'm glad you said that cause I have a question to ask you, brother." Earl said, putting the emphasis on the word brother. "Would you consider being my best man? That's once you get back home and all business is taken care of."

"I don't have to ask who the bride is, do I?"

"No, you don't. We've known each other since we were kids. It's about time we made it all legal."

"It would be an honor and a privilege to be your best man." Warren said. He walked around the table, shook Earl's hand, then gave Earl a hug and a pat on the back.

"Great. "I'll let Sharon know today. She's the one who suggested we wait until you get back."

"Does everyone know I'll be leaving again?"

"Pretty much," Earl chuckled. "Just not to where or exactly when."

"Well, in a couple of days, I'll be making a call to Cassy. She's supposed to be on her way home to Aurora and she knows the Chief of Police personally. They'll keep in touch and she can relay any news to Ty and Krys and then I'll get it from them."

"I know who Cassy is, I've known her for years. She was really pretty with light brown hair streaked blond and legs that go all the way up to her waist."

Warren gave Earl an astonished look, then said, "That's basically how Ty described her."

"Spot on. She and Jimmy have been real close although they consider each other cousins. She was like a sister to me, we were always pretty tight. And she calls me at least once every other week or so to let me know she's okay and doing well."

"Good Lord, Earl," Warren exclaimed, "is there anyone or anything you don't know?"

"As a matter of fact, there is something I don't know." Earl answered seriously.

"And that would be?"

"The recipe for J.R.'s salad dressing. Man, that stuff was the bomb."

"Well, guess you and me should head out to Andy's and get in some target practice with Jacob's bows. You up to a little competition?" Warren asked.

"Any day, any time, Sheriff. I'll show you my trophies some time." Earl laughed as he led the way out of the break room and across the office to the front door.

CHAPTER 13

Ty and Krys drove out of Texarkana with their load of tires, heading for a warehouse in Aurora. Ty asked Krys to call Cassy, see if she was back home yet or on her way in, find out if she had heard anything else of importance.

Krys made the phone call. Cassy was at a warehouse delivering her load, then would be headed out to her place. She gave Krys directions and let her know that there was a pad between her truck and her home where they could park their rig. Krys told her she'd call when they got their delivery to the warehouse.

"Okay. She's delivering now, then going home. We're invited to park at her place if we want to." Krys relayed to Ty.

"Depends on what's going on. When we get to the warehouse, we'll see if we can drop the trailer. Then I want to get into Denver and talk to the Chief of Police. See if Warren gave him the heads up for us. Then we'll see about going to Cassy's place."

"Sounds like a plan to me." Krys commented.

Ty could tell Krys was thinking about something else, her mind not on the delivery or their future plans in Denver.

"Okay, what's wrong?" Ty finally asked.

"I can't stop thinking about Lisa and Warren. You know it'll break his heart if Lisa is turned by Blake. I know Warren will do what needs to be done, but what will that do to him mentally?"

"I'm like you. I believe Warren will be able to do what's needed. But I also believe he'll never be the same after that, it'll scar him for the rest of his life."

"What about us?" Krys asked.

"What about us?" Ty repeated.

"If I were to be bitten, could you put a stake through my heart?"

"The only stake I've got for you is mine personally," Ty stated, smiling mischievously.

"No," Krys said angrily. "I'm not joking. Could you do it?"

"I made a promise to you when we first started this venture, but I'll tell you again. No harm will ever come to you, I won't let it. So, that's a question you don't have to ask me. Okay?"

"Okay." Krys said, smiling back at Ty. "But I do have one more question for you and it's really important."

"What is it?"

"How long are you going to put your life on hold chasing Blake?"

"Until I find him. Which means, until I stake him and cut his friggin head off. When I know he can't harm anyone anymore, I'll stop hunting."

"Okay. You do know I'll be right by your side all the way."

"I know." Ty said. "I also know how lucky I am to have you here with me."

"And know I'll never let you forget how lucky you are to have me." Krys told him.

"That's okay. But you know actions speak louder than words, or so my Grandma always told me."

Ty drove to the warehouse and was directed to Dock 12. The security guard let him know that he could heave his trailer, the hostlers would take care of it when it was unloaded.

When Ty asked the guard if there was a time limit as to how long he could leave the trailer, the guard informed him there wasn't. He also told Ty that they had excellent security and had never had a break in or graffiti painted on any of the trailers parked on their lot.

Ty thanked him for all his help and information, told him he hoped it wouldn't have to be parked more than a couple of weeks, maybe a little longer.

The guard asked Ty if they were taking a vacation in Denver to which Ty responded something like that.

Ty took the paperwork into the warehouse while Krys moved over to the driver's seat and sat waiting. In about ten minutes, Ty appeared through the door and went straight to the hook-ups. He cranked the dollies down and took care of all the glad hands.

He walked around the front of the truck and got in on the passenger side. Krys gently pulled out from under the trailer and then drove out of the lot. Ty called information and got the number to the police station in Denver, then got an address.

Seconds after he hung up, his phone rang.

"Hello." Ty answered. After a few seconds, he replied, "Yeah, I understand. Give me the address." He sat listening, typed the street address and city into his GPS. He said goodbye and looked over at Krys.

"Change of plans. We're going to Cassy's after all. Warren will be leaving Illinois later today, along with Cassy's brother Jacob and her uncle Andy . They'll be here early tomorrow evening. In the meantime, we can start planning our next move."

"Does that mean Blake's here? And Lisa?" Krys asked anxiously.

"Don't know, Cassy didn't say."

"Okay, turn on your beloved GPS and let's get this show on the road."

CHAPTER 14

Monday morning, Warren went into the office early. As soon as he sat down, he called Denver. He realized that Denver was an hour earlier than he was, but he hoped the person he was looking for would be in.

The phone was answered immediately by a man's brisk voice.

"Larry Moore, what can I do for you this early morning."

Warren was taken back and wasn't sure he had reached the right number.

"This is Sheriff Warren."

"Been waiting for your call back. What took so long?" the voice on the other end of the phone said.

Warren sat for a few seconds, staring at the receiver he was holding in his hand, totally confused now. He heard the voice still talking and put the phone back up to his ear.

"Excuse me?" Warren said.

"No problem. When do you expect to arrive here?"

"Enough," Warren shouted into the phone, totally disoriented by now. "How do you know I'm coming to Denver?"

"I know you're coming because Blake and Lisa are here."

"They are? Where?" Warren asked excitedly.

"Don't know where exactly. I can explain all of this when you and your crew get here. You can bunk at Cassy's place. For now, it's our safe house."

"Okay." Warren said, still confused. "We'll leave out later this afternoon."

"See you soon. Safe trip."

Warren sat at his desk, the phone still held up to his ear, the dial tone loud and clear. He sat for a minute more before finally putting the receiver back in its cradle.

As Warren looked up from his desk, Earl walked through the door into the office.

"You look confused. What's going on?" Earl asked.

Warren told him about his conversation with the Chief up in Denver.

"How's he know so much?" Earl asked.

"No idea. Ty and Krys were delivering up there this morning. Don't think they've had enough time to talk to him yet."

"How can he be so sure about Blake and Lisa?"

"I don't know." Warren said, a puzzled look still on his face.

"So, when do you leave?"

"As soon as we can, which will probably be later today." Warren said.

"Okay. Why don't you go home and pack. I'll call the guys. Jacob can go pick up Andy and I'll pick them up at Jacob's house and bring them back here to the station."

"Yeah." Warren said as he stood up from his desk. Without a word, he walked through the station and out the front door.

Earl sat down behind Warren's desk and called Jacob. The conversation was short and to the point. He then called Sharon at the truck stop and let her know that Warren was leaving out in a couple of hours for Colorado and that he'd be working longer hours again.

Sharon told Earl she understood. He'd just have to patrol the truck stop more often so she could feed him his three meals a day.

Earl hung up after some small talk. As he sat there, Leslie walked through the doorway.

"Feel natural?" she asked.

"Feels unnatural." Earl told her. "And I don't ever want it to feel natural."

"Why not?" she asked.

"Cause Warren is the Sheriff, I'm his Deputy. I don't want that to change. It's how it's supposed to be."

"What happens when Warren retires?"

"We'll talk about that in 30 years or so, when it happens." Earl laughed. He got up from the desk and headed out to Jacob's place.

Leslie walked back to her desk. She loved Warren like a son. She hated to see him leave again to put himself in harm's way. She hoped that the woman he was leaving for would finally realize what a good man he was and would return with him back to his home, where they could live together, where he could finally be happy again.

Half an hour later, Warren walked through the door of the station. Leslie stood up from her desk and gave him a hug.

"I'll miss you," she cried.

"I'll miss you too. But, hopefully, I won't be gone too long this time." He told her.

"And hopefully you won't be alone when you return." Leslie whispered in his ear as she hugged him again.

Warren walked into his office. He sat down at his desk, ruffling through a few of the papers left unattended. Twenty minutes later, he heard Earl come through the front door.

"Andy and Jacob are outside by your truck. You ready?"

"You in a hurry to get rid of me and get out to the truck stop?" Warren asked as he rose out of his chair.

"Hey, a man's gotta eat, you know." Earl told him as they walked out of the office and through the front door.

Warren pushed the button on his key chain and his truck lights came on and the doors unlocked with a click.

"No motorhome?" Warren asked.

"No," Andy replied. "Cassy has two extra bedrooms. I figured it would be easier to get around in your truck. We can always rent a motorhome in Denver if we need one."

Andy turned to face the street and shouted out "come". A large Collie came around the front of Earl's truck. When Andy said "up", the Collie jumped into the bed of Warren's truck. He immediately lay down next to Andy's duffel bag. Andy rubbed the dog's head and scratched his ears while he waited on Warren.

Warren turned back to Earl. Without a word, they shook hands, then hugged, patting each other on the back.

"You be careful up there." Earl said as Warren turned toward his pickup.

Warren gave Earl the thumbs up and got in behind the wheel. Andy was already seated in the front passenger seat. Jacob was in the back, a laptop sitting on his legs, already opened.

"Hope you don't mind Mickey coming along. He's a good vampire dog. Sniffed out a bunch of them for me here in Hebert."

"No problem." Warren said. "I can use all the help I can get."

As Warren pulled away from the curb and started driving slowly through town, he found himself missing Hebert already. He waved to quite a few of the townspeople as he drove.

"I got a quick route to my sister's if you want it." Jacob spoke up from the back seat.

"Great." Warren said. "You navigate. We're on our way."

Warren drove out of Hebert, his mind racing ahead to Colorado.

"Well, the one good thing to come out of this," Andy began, "is we'll see Cassy again."

"That's a good thing?" Jacob asked.

"What's bad about it?"

"She'll still be an inch taller than me." Jacob said, smiling.

"Some things never change." Andy sighed.

"So, remind me how you are all related." Warren said.

"Me and Jacob's dad have known each other all our lives. We've been like brothers over the years. My Jimmy, Jacob and Cassy all grew up together. Cassy has always called me Uncle Andy, even though we're not related."

"What's your sister like?" Warren asked, trying to keep the conversation going so time would go by faster.

"Where do I start?" Jacob began. "She's a year older than I am. She's tough, real tough. I've always been small, skinny my whole life. I was bullied in school a lot. More than once she's punched out the bully."

"Really?" Warren laughed.

"I remember once, this girl kept at Cassy, poking her and calling her names and all. Cassy kept telling her to quit, not to push it. Eventually, since the girl couldn't get a rise out of Cassy, she called our mom a bitch. Cassy decked her, knocked her out cold."

"Did she get into trouble for that?" Warren asked, actually interested in the story and its outcome.

"Not really. The girl's dad called mom griping and threatening Cassy with the law because of what she had done. He said he was coming over to our house. Mom just told him he knew where we lived. He asked mom if she condoned what Cassy had done, if she encouraged such behavior in her daughter. Mom told him if his daughter called her a bitch again, Cassy had permission to deck her again."

"Did the guy come to the house?"

"Nope. He hung up the phone but never showed up. A week later, his sweet little girl was arrested for stealing social security checks out of mailboxes."

Warren found himself laughing out loud, grateful for the diversion.

CHAPTER 15

Ty's GPS directed Krys down County Line Road to Colfax, then south. They found the park without any problem and drove through to Cassy's place. Krys backed onto the empty pad between Cassy's truck and her house. She shut the truck down. When she stepped out, Cassy was already walking across the lawn from the house.

"Hi," Cassy said as she drew close, "see you found me okay."

"It's really nice out here." Krys said as she and Cassy hugged each other.

Ty came around the front of the truck and immediately stuck his hand out to shake Cassy's.

"You're kidding, right?" Cassy asked as she raised both arms and gave Ty a big hug.

"Now, come on in." Cassy said as she led them back across the lawn toward the house.

Before they had walked ten feet, Sam came running from behind the house toward them, followed by a huge Husky/Wolf mix. Sam ran straight up to Cassy, then over to Krys, who was already kneeling on the ground, ready to start scratching and playing with him.

"And who is this?" Ty asked as the dog slowly approached.

"This is Bright Eyes." Cassy said.

Ty knelt down on the lawn. "Come here, Bright Eyes." He said in a hushed voice.

Bright Eyes walked up to Ty, who slowly raised both of his hands. When the dog started sniffing at his hands, Ty lowered them to the dogs' head and started petting her gently. Bright Eyes lowered her head and then lay down on the grass by Ty. She rolled over on her back and Ty began rubbing her belly.

"You started something now," Cassy told him. "Be prepared to stop in a week or two."

"Okay by me," Ty said. "I love the Husky face and eyes, but you can still see the Wolf in her, especially when she's running."

"She's got enough wolf to make her even more precious to me." Cassy told him. "She's part Timber Wolf through her mother."

After another five minutes, Krys and Ty both stood up and started walking with Cassy to her house, the animals following close behind.

Cassy led them up onto the patio and then over to a table and chairs at the far end.

"It's so nice here and it's the end of November," Ty commented. "Kind of hard to believe."

"It's unusual. We've had only one snow fall so far and it was short lived. You do know we could have a foot of snow on the ground tomorrow." Cassy said.

"That would suit Krys just fine." Ty laughed.

"So," Krys began, "have you talked to anyone about our dilemma?"

"Just Larry." Cassy said. "I'm sorry. That's Larry Moore, Chief of Police in Denver. He's a friend of my dad's and my Uncle Andy's. Larry talked to Sheriff Warren this morning, then called me. Said Sheriff Warren, my brother Jacob and Uncle Andy are leaving some time this afternoon, should be here in 24 hours or so."

"Think I'll call Warren and let him know we're here." Ty said, already wrestling his phone out of his shirt pocket.

"Hey, Warren," Ty said after only a few seconds. "Where are you guys?"

Ty listened for a while when Cassy yelled out," Say hi to Jacob and Uncle Andy for me."

Ty didn't relay the message but started laughing instead.

"Okay, see you tomorrow." Ty said and turned off his phone.

"What was that all about?" Krys asked.

"A voice in the background said something about a loud mouth and then another older voice said he guessed he was going to have to be referee again. Then just laughter." Ty answered.

"Just wait til Jacob gets here." Cassy said. She then invited them into the house, led them through the living room to a formal dining room. The table was already set. Cassy went into the kitchen. After a trip down the hall to the bathroom to wash her hands, Krys joined her. By the time Ty came back from the bathroom, the food was on the table.

"Sorry, it's only salad." Cassy said apologetically.

"And, unfortunately, the cornbread is only warm." Ty added.

"Excuse me?" Cassy said.

"I'm joking," Ty laughed. "It all looks and smells delicious."

"Nothing fancy, just something quick and easy."

"This is definitely the best quick and easy I've tasted in a while," Ty told her, smiling broadly.

CHAPTER 16

The next morning, Cassy and Krys put together potato salad and macaroni salad. There was chicken in the sink thawing out. Ty had showered and then washed two loads of clothes. He had the clothes folded and put away in the truck.

With chores done, Cassy got out a jug of tea and they all sat around the table, finally relaxing. Cassy proceeded to tell them her story.

She was only 15 months older than her brother Jacob but had always been taller and bigger than he was. She loved her brother more than life itself. They had fought and teased each other all through their childhood. Once out of school, they had then matured and become very close.

When Jacob went into the Navy, Cassy and her dad were there for his graduation from boot camp. During his tour in Afghanistan, Cassy wrote him at least three times a week, letters full of nonsensical things. She only wrote funny or light-hearted stories and kept him apprised of new jokes from his favorite comedians.

She moved to Colorado when she was offered a job driving truck for a local company. Her dad drove for over 20 years and her mom had driven for a short while. Her dream was to be a veterinarian. Driving truck provided her the means to accomplish that goal along with paying off her double wide mobile home.

The house was rent to own and the lease option was for ten years. She had doubled her payments and, at the rate she was going, it would be paid for in two more years.

She loved her house. It had three large bedrooms, two baths. She had her office and craft room set up in one bedroom which was large enough to still accommodate a sofa bed. The third bedroom was set up for guests.

She had a huge country kitchen complete with a walk-in pantry. There were cupboards on all three walls. The dining area was large enough to hold a table with six chairs, a bakers rack, a huge entertainment center that housed all her baking pans and small appliances, a long table full of plants and a water jug on a rolling stand.

Her uncle and brother, on a long visit, had built her the large deck out front. She had her outdoor furniture on the back of the deck along with a huge BBQ. The deck was her favorite spot to sit with coffee in the morning or a drink in the evening, enjoying the peace and quiet and watching Sam and Bright Eyes romp in the yard.

Cassy loved plants and had at least two or more in every room. She had two palm trees, a gift from a neighbor, that were now on stands with wheels in the guest room. During the warmer months, they were always wheeled out onto the patio. She said she inherited her green thumb from her mom, grandma and great-grandma, the only difference being that her great-grandma was the only one who could grow African violets.

"Give me an African violet or a fern, guaranteed I can kill it within a month or less." Cassy laughed.

She explained her relationship to her Uncle Andy, that they were not actually blood relatives but had been close her whole life. He had always been her favorite uncle. Cassy and Jacob had grown up with his son Jimmy.

"You know Jimmy from Kalamazoo. I almost forgot he went up there with Warren and David."

Suddenly, Cassy's phone rang, she talked for only a few minutes, answering with only a yes or a no. When she hung up the phone, she was smiling broadly.

"That was Jacob. They'll all be here in about half an hour. Guess we can get the chicken and veggies started."

"Let's go." Krys said as she got up out of her chair and headed toward the kitchen.

"I've got extra chairs in the guest room along with a leaf for the table." Cassy told Ty.

"No problem." Ty said as he turned and headed down the hallway.

Cassy started flouring the chicken and getting it ready for the oven. Krys took some broccoli out of the freezer, seasoned it and then covered it with cheese. She put it in an electric oven on the counter and turned the temperature to 350.

Krys and Ty had just finished setting the table when there was a knock on the door. Ty answered it and greeted Warren with a huge handshake while pulling him through the door into the house.

Cassy ran across the living room and literally threw herself into Jacob's arms, almost knocking him over. They stood together, neither one of them moving or attempting to let go.

"Okay," Andy spoke up from the doorway, "I'm beginning to feel invisible here."

Cassy finally let go of Jacob and turned to Andy, who picked her up off the floor in a huge bear hug, laughing loudly.

Meanwhile, Krys had hugged Warren and then Jacob and Andy in turn.

Warren introduced Jacob and Andy to Krys and Ty. Then Jacob introduced Warren to Cassy. After all the hellos were said, everyone headed toward the dining room table. Krys went into the kitchen and came back with a large pitcher of ice in one hand and a similar pitcher filled with tea in the other.

"Something smells pretty good, sis." Jacob commented.

"Your favorite, little brother." Cassy called back from the kitchen.

"In that case, knowing my sister like I do, you had all better be super hungry."

The three men took turns washing up, then sat with Ty at the table talking weather and other nonessential things.

Krys and Cassy brought the dinner to the dining room table and everyone sat enjoying the food. There were comments from all the men about how good the dinner was, how good it tasted after all the fast-food meals on the way in.

After dinner, the girls said that they would clear the table and get the dishes in the dishwasher. Jacob and Ty offered to help and get things put away. Cassy insisted that Uncle Andy and Warren retire to the patio where Andy could have his after-dinner smoke.

The dishes were cleared and put away in record time. The leftovers were stored in the refrigerator. The ladies, Ty and Jacob then joined Andy and Warren on the deck. It was an unseasonably warm evening and they were enjoying the peace and quiet, not realizing that it had actually gotten dark while they sat and got caught up on their news.

"Good evening." A soft spoken male voice said from close by the patio.

Everyone on the deck jumped up, startled. They stood looking out from the deck into the night, not yet seeing the person the voice belonged to.

"I didn't mean to startle you. I apologize." The voice spoke again.

As they stared into the darkness of the yard, a man appeared, walking slowly toward the house. He stopped approximately three feet from the steps. He was now close enough for everyone to see clearly.

He was a short man, no more than 5' 8" tall, in his early to middle fifties. He was slightly built, but not skinny. He had curly blond hair with some gray streaks through it. Although he looked slightly pale, he didn't have the sallow look of the undead.

"Who are you?" Warren asked briskly. "What do you want here?"

"My name is Richard Cartier, my friends call me Rick. As to what I want, I'm here to assist you in your quest."

Without a second thought, both Warren and Jacob pulled their crosses out into view from underneath their shirts.

"Your response to me is completely understandable. Please take all the precautions you feel necessary." Rick said, looking directly at Warren.

"You said you're here to help us," Jacob interjected, "help us to do what?"

"Eliminate Blake and his followers before they overrun Denver and all its suburbs." Rick said emphatically.

"And why wouldn't we include you in their numbers?" Andy asked.

"May I join you and explain exactly who I am and why I'm here." Rick asked.

"Come on up." Cassy said.

"Are you crazy?" Krys asked. She had been standing beside Cassy but now started backing up across the deck to where Ty stood.

Everyone had backed away from the steps. Everyone except Cassy. While Jacob and Andy kept their eyes on Rick, Krys, Ty and Warren stared at Cassy in disbelief.

Rick slowly walked up the steps and stood at the railing of the patio silently.

Cassy looked back at the others and said, "I can't believe you all didn't see what I did. Both Sam and Bright Eyes are in the yard. So was Mickey. None of them attacked him. If he was a danger to me, Sam would have scratched his eyes out and Bright Eyes would have ripped out his throat."

"You got a point," Andy said. "Mickey would have been barking her head off by now."

While they all stood silently, Sam jumped up from out of the yard and walked across the top of the railing. He sat down next to Rick, purring loudly as Rick scratched his ears and under his chin.

Bright Eyes walked up the steps, sniffed at Rick and then lay between him and Cassy, totally at ease.

Close behind Bright Eyes, Mickey came strolling up the stairs onto the deck. She walked right past Rick and came to sit down next to Andy.

Cassy invited Rick to join them inside as it was starting to get cooler now that the sun had gone down. Cassy led the way, followed by Rick, then the rest of them.

Cassy motioned Rick to the couch and then took a seat across the room in her armchair. Everyone followed suit and soon everyone, except Ty who continued to stand by the front door, was seated in the living room. Sam sat near Cassy while Bright Eyes lay down in front of the couch at Rick's feet.

"We're all ears," Ty said, his eyes glued to Rick, still wary of this stranger.

CHAPTER 17

Rick proceeded with his story. He began by reminding Ty that two years earlier, he had been laid over in Denver for three days. That was when Rick had met Blake; wrong place, wrong time. Blake characteristically bit him and he found himself waking up in the morgue. He was still fully dressed, so it was easy for him to walk out without being noticed. The next day, he slept all day, waking up to find that he had been sleeping under his bed the entire day instead of in it. It was a very confusing time, especially that night when he began to crave blood.

That first night was total agony because he refused to follow his instincts. He did go to the grocery store and bought some steak that he ate raw later at his house. But he knew immediately that something was wrong.

He called a doctor friend of his, a Dr. Boykolov, who was from Russia. He told the doctor it was an emergency and waited for him to arrive at his house. Fortunately, he came right over, checked him out and found the bite marks on his neck. The doctor was evidently much more educated on vampires than Rick was and took him immediately back to his own house up in the mountains. That same night, Dr. Boykolov made several phone calls about Rick and his condition.

The doctor made arrangements for Rick to remain at his home while he and another doctor and some of his scientist friends worked on a cure for him, still not telling Rick what the cure was for. They did start giving him blood through an intravenous line and that seemed to help Rick immensely. But he still found himself shying away from sunlight and sleeping all day in a dark room.

After a week, Dr. Boykolov presented Rick with what he called the "V-Serum". When Rick asked him what the "V" stood for, he said, "Why, vampires of course." Rick was flabbergasted and disbelieving. He took the serum that night and then the next. By the second night, his cravings were squelched.

"Dr. Boykolov gave me numerous books about Dracula and what it meant to be bitten by a vampire and what symptoms would follow. Unfortunately, all of these books were fiction and I didn't want to believe them, although I knew at that point that I didn't have a choice in the matter any longer."

"Dr. Boykolov also gave me a journal to read. It was a record of his time spent in Transylvania studying vampirism. It explained in detail the myth that Dr. Boykolov believed to be fact. He had been working on a serum for three years now, along with four of his colleagues."

"The only reason I immediately believed him when he told me the serum was for vampires is because I've known the good doctor for years. He's helped the F.B.I. solve a number of cases that involved paranormal activity. And if a doctor of his integrity believed in vampires, why wouldn't a normal person like me believe also?"

Rick continued to tell them how the serum had been improved gradually and now he took it only once every two weeks. They were working on once a month and then once a year. The doctors and scientists were all diligently still working hard to perfect it enough to allow Rick and many others like him to lead a full and productive life, hopefully eventually during daylight hours.

"Your Blake is here in Colorado, doing his usual evil deeds. We've tried to keep up with his victims and bring them into our fold. Unfortunately, we haven't been able to convince all of them. Some of them actually like being vampires. I can understand them liking their new power and the fact that they can live forever. But what they don't understand is that with our serum, that part of it doesn't change, just their cravings do."

"So, what exactly are you offering us here?" Warren asked.

"I'm offering my help in your quest to eliminate Blake. He's a virus that needs to be wiped out because, truthfully, he's much too arrogant for the cure we can provide him."

"You want to work with us to kill one of your own kind?" Andy asked.

"He's not my kind," Rick said defensively. "I have never infected a single living person. Neither have any of the people we've been able to help. None of us have harmed anyone. Blake is not our kind."

After a short pause, Rick continued. "Warren, and basically all of you, except Cassy here, know the damage Blake has done to your lives, your town. How many have you had to destroy, how many friends lost? How many killed because that was your only option?"

Everyone remained silent, each deep in his or her own thoughts about those who had had to be destroyed.

"Although our option is much more humane, we don't want larger numbers. Which basically means we don't want him to continue to infect people so we have to either help them with the serum or eliminate them. We want him stopped, probably more than you do. I still am living in darkness and, honestly, I hate it."

They sat in silence until they were startled by a sharp yip heard coming from the deck near the doggy door. Bright Eyes' ears perked up but she didn't attempt to move from her spot.

"I'm sorry," Rick said, turning to the door. "Kaylee, come in."

Through the doggy door, a small head appeared. She came completely through, sniffed at Ty, then walked around the room sniffing at everyone else.

She stopped in front of Bright Eyes, who raised her head ever so slightly. They sniffed each other, then Kaylee gave the Husky a sloppy kiss on the nose. She walked over to Rick who picked her up and held her lovingly in his lap.

Cassy boldly walked up to Rick, held out her hand to Kaylee, who sniffed and then licked her fingers.

"If it's okay with Kaylee. She's very protective and usually won't go to anyone else."'

To Rick's surprise, Cassy slowly picked Kaylee up off his lap, cuddled her gently, then walked back across the room and sat down in her chair. Kaylee curled up in Cassy's lap and quickly fell asleep.

"I know now why you want to be a vet. You definitely have the touch. She's never gone to anyone like that before, ever."

"I love animals, any kind. Except snakes. Still not comfortable with a snake, still get goosebumps. But how did you know I want to be a vet?"

"That is one of the perks inherited with this condition. It helps me know who I can approach without fear of being eliminated by a stake or a wooden arrow." Rick said, looking toward Jacob, giving him a knowing smile and then a thumbs up.

"I feel I know all of you personally already. I know Krys and Ty drive truck, that Ty drove with Blake and now he hunts him. They met in Effingham when Krys was waitressing. She figured out what Blake was and teamed up with Ty. Now they love each other although they try hard to pretend they are just together to hunt Blake. I know Warren is the sheriff of Hebert and has had his run-ins with Blake before and that he is here hoping that Lisa is okay and he'll get her back, this time forever. I know you are all basically here for Lisa."

Rick stopped talking for just a minute, looking at those whom he had already mentioned.

"I know Jacob is Cassy's brother, a computer nerd but also the one who put the wooden arrows together with the compound bow. This, by the way, will prove most helpful in the future. And, last but not least, I know Andy isn't really your uncle but should be and that he's here not just for Warren and Lisa, but most of all for Jacob and Cassy, to help keep them both safe."

Everyone sat in stunned silence, each staring at Rick, then at each other in turn.

"So," Rick continued," What do you think, Warren? Do we all work together and get your Lisa back and maybe help her sister, Pat?"

"Sounds like you know something about Lisa that we don't." Warren said, now more interested than he had been previously.

"I can sense that Lisa is okay, being used by Blake." Rick said. He then turned his attention to Ty and Krys.

"You were right, Krys, they are in a motorhome. They're staying in RV parks, truck stops and rest areas. But they never stay more than one night in any one place. We haven't been able to track them down yet, but we will."

"What do you think about my wooden arrows?" Jacob interrupted, curious since Rick had already mentioned them.

"If we can't reform a person by talking him or her down, can't convince that person that our way is better, that arrow may be our only way out. We go out at night because that is when they are easier to spot and talk to. However, that is also when they are most dangerous. A sniper, so to speak, lurking nearby with good aim and one of those wooden arrows, may be our salvation when that vampire decides he likes what he's become and doesn't want to change anything."

"We try to usually approach one of them when they are new to the game, before they've become accustomed to the taste of blood. If we can talk to them and explain how much better our way of life is than what Blake's offering them, they usually see it our way and join us."

"What happens if they don't see it your way?" Jacob asked, now sitting on the edge of his seat.

"That's where you could be most useful. We've never been attacked physically by any one of them, but there were times when their intent was perfectly clear. I don't usually go out alone, I have backup to help in just such cases. But the idea of you and your arrows covering my back adds another element to the safety of me and my crew."

"Sounds scary and dangerous to me," Cassy commented, looking from Jacob to Andy, then back to Jacob.

"It is, child. It truly is." Rick stated.

CHAPTER 18

Suddenly, there was a knock on Cassy's front door. As everyone watched, the door was slowly pulled open. Ty stepped back cautiously and both Andy and Warren had stood up, prepared for whoever came through the door.

A very tall man in a nice blue suit walked into the house. He bent down just slightly when he came through the doorway.

Andy walked across the living room and shook hands with the stranger, then they hugged each other like long lost friends. Andy turned back to the living room.

"I'd like you all to meet Larry Moore, Chief of Police here in Denver and a good friend of mine."

"You forgot to mention undeniably handsome, super intelligent and an all-around nice guy." Larry added.

"Did I also forget to mention how unobtrusive and unabrasive you can be?" Andy said. "Be prepared for the worst, people."

Andy took Larry around the room, introducing him to Warren, Ty and Krys. When they got to Cassy, Larry bent over and kissed her on the cheek. Kaylee growled and nipped at Larry, much to his surprise.

"That's great, just great." Larry commented. "Your big dogs and that bobcat of yours like me. But I have to put up with this little pipsqueak trying to maul me? Come on, Kaylee, you know me."

"It's just that she likes me better." Cassy laughed.

Lastly, Andy directed Larry over to Rick.

"No introductions necessary." Larry said when he was standing in front of Rick. They shook hands and Larry sat down next to Rick on the couch. "I see you were invited in and haven't been shot with a wooden arrow yet."

Warren had watched all of this curiously. He wondered how he had come to the point where he was sitting in the same room with an actual vampire, talking nonchalantly about challenging other vampires to take what he called the "V-Serum."

Suddenly, there was a scratch at the front door. Everyone turned anxiously toward the sound.

As they watched warily, the doggy door moved slightly. All of a sudden, Andy's collie, Mickey, stuck her head through the door.

"Come on, Mickey," Andy called out, "It's okay."

The dog crawled through the door, stood back up, shook herself and walked straight over to Andy. She sat down between Andy's legs, silently surveying the room.

"I didn't know you brought her," Larry commented. "Where's she been?"

"Getting the lay of the land." Andy said. "Search."

Mickey stood up and walked around the room, sniffing at everyone. When she came to Cassy's chair, Cassy reached down to pet her, then introduced her to Kaylee. When she approached Rick, Andy held his breath. She stood staring at Rick, as if confused as to how to react to him.

Rick slowly reached out, extending his hand to the Collie. Mickey sniffed his hand, backed up one step, then came forward again. She sniffed once more, then licked the end of Rick's fingers. Rick slowly bent forward and began petting her head and ears.

"That decides our position with you, Rick." Andy said. "In Hebert, Mickey was our best tool in hunting vampires. She could sniff them out right good."

Andy got up out of his chair, walked over to Rick and extended his hand. They shook hands vigorously, then Andy returned to his seat. Mickey followed close behind and lay down across Andy's feet.

"Well," Larry began. "I want to welcome all of you to Denver. I know your history, Warren, as well as Ty and Krys. I know Andy personally and have had contact with Cassy in the past, in a good way of course. But I don't believe I've met Jacob before."

"I'm Cassy's brother," Jacob began. "I volunteered in Hebert and helped eliminate vampires there. I came because Andy volunteered and my sister lives here. I'm here to help in any way I can."

"What do you normally do for a living, when you're not hunting vampires, that is?" Larry asked.

"He's a computer nerd." Cassy spoke up.

"That's the second time I've been called that tonight. But just remember, even computer nerds have a place in this world." Jacob countered.

"I know," Larry began, "and I'll be the first to appreciate your skills. As a matter of fact, I brought a list with me."

Larry pulled a rolled-up sheaf of papers from his back pocket, rolled them backwards onto themselves and then handed them to Jacob.

"This is a list Rick's people have put together. It's all the places Blake has stayed since his arrival here. I also have my own list of all the RV parks, truck stops and rest areas in and around Denver, including the immediate suburbs and as far as fifteen miles in any direction outside of town. Maybe you'll be able to find a pattern of some kind as to where he's been staying and where he may be going next. If we can get one step ahead of him instead of ten steps behind where we are now, we might get a jump on this before it gets any more serious than it is."

Jacob took the papers and, without a word, walked down the hallway out of sight. He soon returned with his laptop. He went straight to the dining room table and became oblivious to everyone and everything else in the house.

CHAPTER 19

Everyone except Jacob sat silently in the living room.

"So, Larry, what's your story?" Ty asked suddenly. "I'm sure, being the Chief of Police, you already know all about us."

"Not much of a story, really. I served in the Air Force although promotions eluded me due to my lack of verbal control. For short, my mouth too frequently overloaded my ass. I went to the police academy and got a job in Denver. Been here ever since, been Chief for the past five years. I'm a member of the American Legion, the District Commander for Central Colorado. I like working with the Veterans and helping them in any way I can. I love pro wrestling, am an avid fan. When I'm not watching wrestling, I'm usually watching reruns of Star Trek."

"Wrestling, huh?" You and Krys definitely have a lot to talk about." Ty said. "She's the know all and be all of pro wrestling."

"Sounds good to me." Larry laughed. "When we are all over this, we'll have a sit down and see who knows the most. We may even place a little bet on who's the most knowledgeable."

"My bet is on Krys." Ty announced, smiling over at her. "I've seen Krys at work when it comes to wrestling and its history. You'll definitely have a challenge on your hands with her."

"You left a lot of history out," Andy cut in. "Like the fact that you limp because of an injury you received while serving your country. And that your time is completely taken up with helping other Veterans, always working different functions and raising funds to get the Veterans and the hospitals the things they need. I've never known you to say no to a Veteran or to one of your rookies at the police station either."

"Don't make me out to be a saint, Andy. We both know better and I wouldn't want these young folks to get the wrong impression."

"Oh, believe me, Larry, once they get to know you, they'll all get the right impression. They'll just have to get used to your obnoxious humor and learn not to be offended every time you open your mouth."

"Well, not trying to offend anyone right now, I really need to get home. Six in the morning comes early for an old guy like me. When you all get up and about, come on down to the station and we'll strategize."

With that, Larry rose from the couch, shook Rick's hand, then shook hands all around the room. He walked into the dining room to shake Jacob's hand and wish him good luck in his endeavors on the computer, saying he was much more suited for the job than he himself would be. When he reached the front door, he turned and saluted everyone, then walked quietly out.

"Well, he certainly is interesting." Krys commented.

"You don't know the half of it, girl," Andy told her. "Although he can be obnoxious at times, he truly has a heart of gold. He has gone out on a ledge for more than one rookie in their career, but has never been let down by any one of them. All of his men and women respect him. He won't allow them to call him Chief or Mister, he's just Larry to everyone. His office is probably the smallest one in the police station and I guarantee it will be cluttered with papers and files lying everywhere. But if you ask him for a specific file, he'll have it in your hands in seconds. He knows where everything is in that mess, always on top of the game."

"Doesn't he do anything for fun?" Ty asked.

"Of course. Besides wrestling and Star Trek, he's an avid bowler. And he has lots of friends. I've stayed with him before and he has a rigid routine."

"A work routine or a fun routine?" Warren asked.

"Both. Every morning before work, he stops at a little diner close to his house. He admits to being cranky in the morning until he has consumed at least two cups of coffee. He'll sit around this large table with a bunch of old cronies exchanging insults and solving the world's problems with their bountiful knowledge. After an hour and a breakfast of toast and hashbrowns, he leaves for work and tries to solve all of Denver's problems."

"He sounds like quite a guy." Ty said.

"He's a great guy," Rick interjected. "Larry was the second person I called when me and Blake had our encounter. He arrived at my house before my doctor did. He's been fully supportive of me ever since. And, believe me, when he tells his officers and patrolmen and women that we have vampires and we need to extinguish them, they'll follow him without question. His men and women believe in him and would follow him into hell if it was necessary."

"Wow," Cassy exclaimed. "You are very passionate when it comes to Larry. You and Uncle Andy both know him better than we do. I've known him as a friend of Uncle Andy's and we see each other once in a while and talk even less. But he's always been a perfect gentleman and more like another Uncle to me."

"What about you, Rick?" Krys asked. "What did you do before Blake? You present yourself as a well-educated man."

"I did the same thing before Blake as I'm doing now, only now I do it in the dark instead of in the light. I'm an F.B.I. Agent. I track down criminals from cold cases and bring them to justice."

"That explains why you're so anxious to find Blake and bring him to justice. Not just for what he did to you, but for what he and his followers can eventually do to the entire United States." Ty added.

"But you are one of the lucky ones who has been able to continue to lead a fairly normal life after Blake." Cassy said in all sincerity.

"You could say that in one aspect I am lucky. At least luckier than most of the people Blake has encountered. Hopefully, we can stop his reign of terror and bring this Dracula to a quick end."

"You can't really call him Dracula," Jacob said from the dining room, "cause he's nothing like the real Dracula, nothing at all."

"Okay, little brother, why not give us a history of the real Dracula. I know you're dying to enlighten us all." Cassy said, having turned around in her chair to watch her brother.

Jacob got up from the table and came into the living room, sitting on the opposite end of the couch from Rick.

"I've been googling the real Dracula and there was a real interesting program on TV about him a few weeks ago. He was a real Romanian prince, a true warlord. He was born and raised in Sighsoara, a very poor upbringing. Although there were few real amenities, it was considered the safest town in the region. His father was a trader, trading with the Germans in the 12th century. This kept his family safe. But his father was eventually assassinated by a rival clan."

"So, how did he get his horrible reputation and what about drinking blood?" Cassy asked, becoming totally enthralled with her brother's story.

"I'm getting there," Jacob continued. "In the 1450's, he lived in Bran Castle, the most secure fortress on the Romanian border. It's here where he launched his reign of terror. Being the Son of Vlad Dracula, he was a Knight of the Order of the Dragon. He built an image of power in Wallachia."

"In 1458, he invited voyeurs to dinner and impaled 500 of them on tree spikes. They were spiked through the rectum because this took two days or more for them to die in agony."

"He built a fortress called Poenari, on an inaccessible mountain. He would invite rich merchants to his castle and then enslave them to continue to build more of the castle. He was forever adding more rooms and more dungeons."

"What about the blood?" Cassy insisted.

"He attacked Brasov, the richest and best defended town in Transylvania. He attacked at night and impaled over 1,000 villagers. It was called the Forest of the Impaled. He had a table set up in the middle of those impaled and had his dinner served to him there. That's the blood part. He never drank their blood. That part is a myth."

"So what happened to him? Did he ever really die?" Krys asked.

"In 1462, he demanded help from the Christians in the war against the Turks. He used savage gorilla tactics including passing on diseases, poisoning the water and burning the crops. When he left there, he was then known as The Impaler Lord, leaving behind 20,000 people impaled."

"From there, he went to Castle Dracula in Peonari. His wife committed suicide. He left to fight again. He was exiled for ten years, then returned to Bucharest. He was killed in battle, question of fair fight or murder."

"So he was dead and buried?" Ty asked, now getting more and more interested in Jacob's rendition of the true Dracula."

"He was supposedly buried at the Monastery of Snargov. But it was also said his head was cut off and taken to the Sultan. The tomb is empty, there's no proof of a body ever being in it. To this day, in Transylvania, Vlad remains a hero despite the brutality of his battles. And there are a lot of people who believe he is still alive and walks at night among the villages."

"That's a hell of a story." Andy commented.

"Blake has, in some ways, the brutal mentality that Vlad was historically noted to have." Rick added.

"So the real Vlad never drank blood?" Cassy asked, almost sounding disappointed.

"Nope." Jacob answered. "Where that myth started is the million dollar question. But for centuries, monsters like Blake have been drinking blood and stating they are true vampires, true Draculas. Only other true monsters would understand why he does it. I wouldn't know where to start looking on the internet for that kind of information. What would I look for?"

"Got me." Cassy replied.

"Well," Rick interjected as he rose from the couch and walked toward Cassy. "I better get home. I'll take Kaylee; that is, if she'll let me take her away from you."

Cassy handed Kaylee over to Rick, petting her continuously until she was safely settled in Rick's arms.

"Thank you for coming." Cassy told him.

"Thank you for inviting me in. It has been a most interesting evening. I hope to see all of you soon and pray that together we can rid Denver of Blake and that those infected will listen to us and choose the right way of life."

With that, Rick walked across the living room and out the front door. Andy had followed closely behind him, then stood staring out the screen door.

"He's gone. It's like he just vanished." Andy said, puzzled.

"Guess that's another perk he didn't mention." Krys said.

Andy walked back into the living room.

"The dogs and Sam are all outside. I'll lock up after they come back in." Cassy said.

"It still amazes me that the animals all accepted Rick so easily. I believe he's a good man but nonetheless he's still a vampire." Krys said to no one in particular.

"Animals have an instinct that we people don't." Cassy began. "They know when they are threatened or when their humans are threatened. And believe me, if Rick had been a threat both Sam and Bright Eyes would have taken care of him real quick."

"Don't forget Mickey," Andy added. "In Hebert she could sniff out a vampire so quick it would make your head spin. She's damned good. But she didn't even blink an eye at Rick. It's all too mysterious for me."

"Well, guess we getter all get a good night's sleep." Cassy said. "I have one spare bedroom and the couch in my office folds out to a queen-sized bed."

"Me and Krys will sleep in the truck." Ty said. "With the doggy door and all this four-legged protection, we'll sleep just fine tonight."

Everyone said goodnight. Ty and Krys walked back out to the truck. Jacob and Andy and Mickey all bedded down in Cassy's office. Cassy, Sam and Bright Eyes snuggled up on her bed. Warren said he'd take the couch because he wanted to be close to the front door, just in case.

After everyone retired, Warren sat on the couch. He had locked the doggy door, not wanting the animals out in the yard after dark. He figured if one of them got up and needed to go out, he would let them out and watch them from the doorway.

He was still astounded that he was in Denver and had actually been sitting with a vampire in the house talking about Lisa. Rick had said Lisa was still herself and Warren took comfort in that. He only hoped that Rick could be trusted and that he wasn't lying to them just to make them feel better.

He could picture Lisa, her smile and sense of humor. He still kicked himself for leaving Michigan without a word to her. Things had been better in Kalamazoo but she still had refused to move to Illinois and be with him. He had realized after being back home for a couple of days that it was because of her sister Pat. He had had every intention of calling her the next day, but that was before he got the news of her abduction.

This time, if he got her back, he wasn't going to accept no for an answer. She was coming back to Illinois with him, they would get married and find something for her to do to keep her busy. Whether it was with him in the sheriff's office or somewhere else, it didn't matter. All that mattered was that they would finally be together and he was determined to never leave her, not even to help hunt Blake if they didn't manage to eliminate him here in Denver.

The property around Cassy's home was deathly quiet. Unknown to any of them, there was a shadow in the darkness just inside the tree line diligently watching the house and the semi. It was the shadow of a man with a very small dog standing quietly next to him.

He stood perfectly still, as if the cold never touched him. After a few minutes, he picked the small dog up and cradled it in his arms, covering it with part of his jacket.

He stood watching until just before sunrise, then disappeared into the wavering darkness.

CHAPTER 20

Just before 6 a.m., Cassy's phone rang. She answered sleepily but then quickly came awake. She got dressed, woke Andy and Jacob. Then she headed to the living room where she found Warren laying across the sofa bed, fully clothed, his boots beside the bed.

She gently shook Warren's arm. He sat up in bed, completely awake.

"What's up?" Warren asked.

"Lisa was spotted last night. Larry just called. He's got a witness at the station. Uncle Andy and Jacob are already up and dressed."

"I'll call Ty and Krys." Warren said, reaching for his cell phone.

Ten minutes later, Cassy, Andy and Jacob piled into her Jeep. Warren, Ty and Krys were in Warren's pickup, ready to follow Cassy to the station.

It took only thirty minutes to drive to the District 4 Station. Cassy got on the highway and with little to no traffic, they cruised to 6th Avenue. They were lucky to hit the lights green and soon came to Colorado Boulevard. The station was only blocks from that point.

They pulled into the visitor lot and parked close to the front door. The station was very modern, a one story brick building set on a gorgeous green lawn with lots of trees surrounding it.

When they entered the front doorway, Larry was waiting for them. He waved them around the metal detector, past the reception area and down a short hallway. Although there were a few police personnel in the building, it was ghostly quiet. Everyone looked busy, no one was standing around talking or drinking coffee. They all had jobs to do and were determinedly going about their business.

Larry stopped midway down the hall and turned back to face Warren.

"She was seen at a local truck stop. One trucker is our only witness. No one else present remembered anything. I'm going to question him, then let him get back on the road. You all can wait out here and listen in."

Larry turned and disappeared through a door nearby, only to reappear behind the one-way glass of the interrogation room where a man was already seated at the table.

"I'm back." Larry joked with the man. "Sorry to keep you so long. Promise this will be our last time going through this and then I'll have one of my officers drive you back to the truck stop."

"No problem. Glad to help." The trucker said.

"Okay. You are aware that this is being recorded?"

"Yeah. That's okay by me."

"Alright then. Please state your full name."

"It's Berl Winters."

"Your reason for being at the truck stop, Berl."

"I was laid over after delivering yesterday. Got a load to pick up this morning, heading back east."

"We'll get you out of here shortly. Don't want our commerce to shut down." Larry commented.

"Exactly."

Warren stepped up close to the glass, next to Andy. He was anxious to see this trucker and hear what he had to say about Lisa.

Warren stood watching the man closely from behind the glass. The trucker was a huge man, had to be over 6' 4" and about 350 pounds. He was stocky but not what Warren would describe as fat. He had scraggly hair that curled around his ears. He had a full beard that was very bushy, no thin spots anywhere with a very ruddy complexion. But the most prominent thing about this man was his eyes. They were the deepest blue Warren had ever seen, they were so dark as to be almost purple.

Warren listened as Berl answered Larry's questions. By the tone of his voice and Warren's experience with interrogating people back in Michigan, he felt that the trucker was an honest man and was telling the truth, as he knew it.

"Okay, Berl. Start to finish, let's hear what happened last night."

"Well, I had a late supper and had gone to the men's room, it's by the cashier near the hallway to the front door. I started to walk back out the door into the short hallway that led back into the dining area when I heard this lady screaming."

"What was she screaming? Could you make out the words?" Larry asked.

"She was screaming 'help me, call the cops'."

Earl paused for a second, a sad look on his face.

"I started to come out of the hallway when this really tall dude showed up. It was as if he appeared out of nowhere. He was just suddenly there. He put his hand on her shoulder and she seemed to shrink away from him. Then this other lady appeared from behind him. She looked a lot like the first lady, only taller, more queen like."

"Okay. What happened next?"

"Well, the taller lady grabbed the shorter lady and held her. The shorter lady kept struggling but the taller one just held onto her, like she didn't even feel her fighting to get away."

"Did you leave the hallway area?"

"Not then. The guy was staring at the customers seated in the restaurant, looking from one to the other. Then he looked all around the room and it got real quiet. No one said a word or moved to help the lady. Me included. And for that I feel so ashamed."

"No need to feel that way. Believe me, you wouldn't have been a match for that man. If you had acted, you probably wouldn't be here telling me your story."

"When he turned in my direction, I stepped back, deeper into the hallway and away from the door."

"Okay. What next?"

"The man picked up the shorter lady as if she didn't weigh a pound. He carried her out the door and the other lady just followed close behind him. Neither one of them ever said a word, not to anyone in the restaurant and not to each other. It was all really weird."

"What did you do then?"

"I ran into the restaurant. I just stood there, horrified. The customers and waitresses, they were all just sitting or standing there. The customers continued to eat their meals like nothing had just happened. I yelled "what's the matter with you guys? We need to help her". They asked me who they were supposed to help. No one remembered the ladies or the man. They were looking at me like I was drunk or crazy, or both.

"Did you, by any chance, see what kind of vehicle they were in?"

"No. I just kept standing there, not believing all these folks. How could they not remember what we had all just seen. It was like one of those horror movies where you're the only sane person left on earth."

"And then?" Larry prompted.

"And then I called the cops. They came out in minutes. They questioned all those people still there but no one said they saw anything. They asked me to come down to the station and talk to you. So, here I am."

"One last thing," Larry said. "Can you describe the three people in any more detail?"

"Sure. He was really tall, way over six foot, thin, pale with black hair that was combed flat to his head but looked kind of long. The lady with him was almost as tall as he was. She carried herself like a queen, like someone of royalty. She had on a long dress, to the floor, but she was barefoot. I thought that was kind of weird since it was pretty cold outside. She had long hair, but it wasn't pretty hair. It was really dull looking. And she was pale like him."

"And the other lady, the one screaming."

"She was shorter, pretty and feisty as hell. She fought like a wildcat, not that it did her any good. She looked a lot like the taller lady though.

Her hair was lighter colored but was messed up, like she had just got out of bed or something. And she had a huge voice, she sure could scream. That's another reason I can't believe those people didn't at least hear her scream. I know I'll never forget that sound. I wanted to help her so bad, I just couldn't make my feet move."

"I understand completely, Berl. You've been a great help to us. I'll have one of my officers drive you back to your truck. Be sure to leave a contact number in case we have any more questions. And here's my card. It has my cell number on the back if you remember anything else you think might help us."

"No problem. You all been real nice to me, believing me and everything. I just hope you can figure all of this out, cause I'm sure confused enough for all of us. And I'll say a prayer that that lady can get away from those two again and get some help."

Larry rose from his chair, shook hands with Berl, thanked him again for his cooperation and walked out of the room. When he had closed the door behind him, he motioned for everyone to follow him down the hall. He led them into his office.

The room was small, not what Warren expected for a Chief of Police. Larry's desk was covered in loose papers and files. There was only one chair in the office, but there was a long couch against the far wall. Warren sat anxiously in the chair in front of Larry's desk.

"Did your men find anything out there?" Warren asked.

"Nothing. They questioned all the customers still there, no one remembered anything. They also questioned some of the truckers on the lot but no one saw a motorhome coming in or going out of the truck stop."

"How can a vehicle as big as a motorhome continue to go unnoticed?" Cassy asked.

"It won't be invisible forever." Larry said.

"So, now what?" Warren asked.

"Now, we keep looking and Jacob keeps working on his computer. Hopefully, we'll figure out a pattern and get lucky or have a witness call us. It's a waiting game." Larry answered.

"I can't wait." Warren said. "I'm going to rent one of those RVs and visit a few of your parks."

"Day or night?" Larry asked.

"Both. Daytime, there won't be any activity around their RV. Night time, I'll have the guys with me. If we find them, we'll know what to do."

"Sounds okay except for a couple of things. I'd like to keep Jacob working on the parks and truck stops. But I also want him to work with some of our officers training them with the compound bows and arrows."

"I can work with your officers," Andy spoke up. "Been practicing and I'm almost as good as Jacob now."

"Almost being the key word." Jacob laughed.

"If someone can go with Warren during the day, then someone else at night, you can probably cover a lot of parks."

"I do want to take Mickey with me in the RV though, if that's okay?" Warren asked, looking over at Andy.

"It's okay by me." Andy told Warren. "She'll sniff out them vampires before you can shake a stick at her. She's real good at what she does, believe me. And she loves to ride. Just call her over to the RV and say 'up' and she'll jump right in and be ready to go to work."

"What about Rick?" Cassy asked.

"Rick will be out there." Larry told all of them. "He has his own way of doing things. I'll give him Warren's number to call if he finds Blake and needs help getting Lisa."

"I'm headed back to Cassy's. Jacob can get his list printed out of the parks, then I'll go rent the RV and we can get started." Warren said as he got up out of the chair and headed for the door. Ty, Krys and Cassy followed close behind.

Andy and Jacob stayed in Larry's office, Andy ready to get acquainted with the officers they'd be working with.

"You can set up your targets back of my house, if you want to." Cassy volunteered, peaking around the corner of the door. "There's more than enough room and no one will bother you."

"It's a good idea, but we have a rifle range out back of the station with targets already set up. And I don't want to draw any more attention to your place right now, not with Blake here in town. If Rick can sense Blake, we know Blake can sense Ty and the rest of you. Besides, we're in the process of duplicating Jacob's arrows and bows and we want our officers to start practicing immediately so they can get good with the crossbows."

"You won't have much problem with the bows." Jacob told Larry. "There are just one or two tweaks to accommodate the wooden arrows and Uncle Andy knows exactly what to do to get everything in sync."

"Okay, Uncle Andy," Cassy called out from down the hall. "don't worry about Mickey. I'll feed her before she goes with Warren."

"I'm not worried." Andy called back, then turned to follow Larry down the hallway in the opposite direction.

Warren, Ty, Krys, Jacob and Cassy all exited out the front door, heading back to the parking lot and their respective vehicles.

They all remained quiet in each vehicle on the ride back to Cassy's, each one lost in his or her own thoughts.

Warren spoke up first. "I'm relived to know Lisa's still alive. But, what will Blake do next? He has to know that Lisa will never cooperate with him or Pat. Our time is running out."

Ty answered Warren. "I made a pledge to eliminate him once and for all but I'm worried about the rest of you. Blake has no conscience when it comes to eliminating people, whether he knows them or not. It's like he enjoys watching them suffer and squirm."

Jacob sat silent, anxious to get back to his computer and determined to figure out some sort of pattern to try to trap Blake.

Cassy was worried about everyone. She didn't have a clear understanding of what was going to happen, she just knew she was afraid for her brother and her Uncle Andy, as well as everyone else. She was ready to help in any way she could. She had never backed down from anything in her life and she wasn't about to start now.

She was ready to grab a bow and join the hunt. She had been hunting with a bow for years, fishing too in a creek that ran by her property. She was adept at hunting, knowing when to be quiet and when not to move. She had shot her share of elk and deer up in the mountains, knowing it meant food on the table.

But, she just wasn't sure if any of her experiences with the bow would help her if and when she encountered a real live vampire. She had never shot at a real person, vampire or otherwise. She wasn't sure if she could actually pull the trigger when faced with another human being. Buts she was determined to help and anxious to get started. She decided to continue to think about the safety of the others and, literally, all the people in Denver and the suburbs. If it meant the difference between them staying alive or becoming like Blake, she felt sure she would have no trouble letting an arrow fly.

CHAPTER 21

When Cassy and Jacob pulled into her driveway, all three animals met them, tails wagging in welcome. Warren pulled his truck up on the street by the driveway. He, Ty and Krys exited the vehicle, walked up the steps to the patio and into the house.

Warren commented on the dark clouds coming in over the mountains and how cold the weather had turned since morning. It was only 11 and the temperature had dropped 15 degrees already.

"Looks like we may get some snow today." Cassy told them.

"That would be great." Krys exclaimed.

"For more reasons than one." Ty added.

"Besides the fact that Krys and I and all the animals love snow, what other reason could there be?" Cassy asked.

"Tracks." Ty said. "No tracks around a motorhome during the daylight hours. Fresh tracks after sunset.

"And," Warren added, "there won't be many campers in the parks with the snow, which will make our job a whole lot easier."

"I wonder why Blake came to Denver in the winter?" Krys asked to no one in particular. "Seems he would have gone to Florida or somewhere warm where there would be more tourists."

"Don't know why Blake does anything." Ty commented. "Doesn't seem like a real smart move. You'd think if he was determined to come here that he'd come in the fall or spring, when there are more people out and about."

"But in winter we get all the skiers and snow-boarders." Cassy reminded Ty.

"But don't they mostly stay up in the mountains, not down here in Denver proper?" Krys asked.

"True." Cassy agreed.

"Who knows how Blake thinks or why he does what he does." Ty added. "It just seems like a bad move to me, that's all."

Warren got a Denver phone book from Cassy and leafed through the yellow pages. He found an RV rental and made a phone call, giving them his credit card information over the phone. He was able to get it for a discounted price since it was off season for the company and they had a lot full of RVs. He wrote down the directions to the RV Center. He asked Ty and Krys to go with him so they could drive his pickup back to Cassy's. They left immediately.

Cassy sat down next to Jacob at the table while he worked on printing out the names of all the parks and truck stops in the Denver area, as well as the outlying suburbs as far west as Golden and as far south as Colorado Springs, including the directions and quickest routes to each one.

"That should do it." Jacob said as he put all the papers together for Warren.

"So, little brother." Cassy began, "Did you ever in your wildest fantasies believe we'd be together again to fight vampires, much less have Uncle Andy here with us?"

"Does the word never seem a plausible answer to your question?"

"Yeah. Me too."

"If Warren takes any of the animals with him in the RV, I don't want him to take Sam. I want Sam here with us." Cassy said.

"Okay."

"I feel safer with Sam here. He's truly fearless, you know. When we went hiking in the mountains, Sam killed a rattler that was in our path. I hadn't even seen the snake and would have walked right up to it."

"You don't have to convince me of Sam's bravery, sis."

"I know. I think I just need to remind myself of it."

Jacob leaned across the corner of the table and uncharacteristically hugged Cassy.

"While you're being so nice to me, tell me what it's like to hunt these vampires and kill them."

"You really don't want to experience it if you don't have to. Hunting isn't the problem. You do it during the day when they're sleeping. You either pull them out into the sun so they burn up, like spontaneous combustion, or you put a stake through their heart. In the end, we decapitated them. Earl, Warren's deputy, said if the body is left intact, they can actually come back."

"Like Lisa's sister Pat did?" Cassy asked.

"Yeah. It isn't a pretty site to watch them burn but, thank goodness, they go fast. All that's left are the bones and we buried them in different graves from their skulls. But I watched as Dan put a stake through a little boy's heart. That kid couldn't have been more than ten years old. He was a little skinny thing, not much to him. The sound that stake made will stay with me until the day I die. I hope you never hear that sound or have to watch someone get staked."

"Is it bloody? What does it sound like?" she asked.

"It's bloody some of the time, depending on whether they ate the night before. The sound, please don't ask." Jacob answered, a grim look on his face.

"Guess I better get started with lunch." Cassy said. She got up and headed to the kitchen. Jacob waited expectantly to hear her humming one of her favorite songs, which is what she always did when she was cooking. Today, the kitchen remained silent.

A little over an hour later, Warren pulled up in a motorhome conspicuous by the bright advertising painted on the sides and back. Ty and Krys were right behind him and parked close to the RV.

When they walked in the front door, they were pleasantly surprised to see that Cassy had the table set with paper plates and plastic utensils. In the middle of the table stood a platter filled high with sandwiches, along with a tea pitcher and a bowl of ice. She then brought out the bowls of leftover macaroni and potato salads from the night before.

"Just in time," Cassy said, smiling as she sat down next to Jacob.

After everyone had washed up and they were all seated at the table, Cassy asked if she could say a short prayer. They held hands around the table as Cassy began…

"Thank you, Lord, for this food. Let it nourish our
bodies and strengthen our reserve as we venture
forth. Amen."

Amen was chorused around the table, then everyone began grabbing sandwiches and passing around the salads and tea.

"We forgot about breakfast." Krys commented as she poured her tea.

"No wonder I'm so hungry." Ty said, grabbing another sandwich.

When lunch was over, everyone continued to linger over their tea.

"So, Warren, what's the plan?" Jacob asked as he handed Warren his papers on the parks and truck stops.

"I'm going out this afternoon and drive through some of the parks, just to scope them out. If anything looks suspicious in any way, I'll go back out tonight."

"Me and Krys will go with you this afternoon. Save Jacob and Uncle Andy for tonight with their bows." Ty said.

"Sounds good to me, six eyes are better than two. I'd also like to take Mickey, if she'll come with us." Warren stated, looking at Jacob.

"She'll go." Jacob said. "She loves to ride. At home, when it was just her and Andy, she always rode inside his truck."

"Well, guess we'll get going and see if we can find anything." Warren stated as he stood up from the table and headed toward the front door.

Jacob followed close behind, walking out the door onto the patio with Warren and Ty.

"I've circled two of the parks I think you might want to check out first. One is just down the road. I figured if Rick could sense Blake, then Blake could very well sense Ty and you and might want to be close by. The park circled in red is the closest park to Cassy's house and to all of us."

"Thanks, Jacob. We'll go there first. I knew you'd come through with some ideas. You can't be engrossed in that computer that long without coming up with something. Thanks again."

"No thanks needed. Just find Lisa and then we'll all find Blake."

Krys had stayed behind to help Cassy clear the table but Cassy told her that Jacob would be more than willing to help her and that Krys should catch up with Warren and Ty.

Warren walked down the steps to the RV, turned when he reached the driver's door and called for Mickey. She had been out romping in the yard with Bright Eyes. She immediately turned and ran toward Warren. He patted her on the head and said "up", she jumped into the RV. She walked around the driver's seat to the back of the vehicle, sniffing everything as she went. When she reached the back of the RV, she jumped up on the couch and sat, looking out the side window.

Ty and Krys followed Warren down the steps but went around the other side of the RV and came in through the side door. Krys walked to the back of the RV and sat down next to Mickey. She was carrying a small paper sack. She reached inside and came out with a dog bone. Mickey sat waiting patiently. Krys gave Mickey the bone and she laid back down and started chomping on it contentedly.

Ty had walked to the front of the RV and sat down in the passenger seat. When Warren got in behind the wheel, he handed Ty the papers Jacob had printed out. He told Ty about the one circled in red and that they would drive through the second one a little further out and then try the closer one on the way back to Cassy's.

"Navigate," was all Warren said as he started the RV. He let it warm up for a few minutes, then drove out onto Colfax. It had already started to snow. At first, it was only light flakes that melted as soon as they landed on the street and sidewalks.

By the time they reached the first RV park, which was only about ten miles from Cassy's place, the flakes had gotten much bigger and heavier and started sticking to the grass and trees.

The park was huge but only held a dozen motorhomes and fifth wheels. Warren stopped at the office and went inside. When he returned, he told them that only two of the motorhomes were occupied, both by elderly couples who would usually be gone before the snow fell. They stayed the summer months but went to Arizona for the winter every year.

"Okay, mark that one off the list." Ty said as he pulled a pen out of his pocket and made a big "X" on the map, then drew a line through the park on the papers from Jacob.

By the time they drove back to the second park, the snow had deepened to at least half an inch. Warren drove through the gates and parked in front of the office. Once again, he got out and entered the park office. When he returned, he informed Ty and Krys that two motorhomes were occupied. One had been there for a couple of days and belonged to an older couple. The other one had come in after hours the night before, had left cash in the registration box. The name on the registration card wasn't legible, all he could make out was a "P" for the first name and what looked like a "B" or an "R" for the last name.

Ty sat listening to Warren, noting that the more he talked, the more excited he got.

"Do you think we could be lucky enough to find them our first time out?" Krys asked from where she was now standing behind Ty's seat.

"We can only hope." Warren said as he put the RV in drive and slowly pulled away from the office. The park was a series of parallel streets that ran off of one main road that dissected them all down the middle. The permanent RV was parked on the first street, directly across from the now closed and covered swimming pool.

Warren drove down the main road past the first street, then turned left onto the second one. The door to the trailer was slowly opening. An older gentleman came down the steps, then turned to help a little white haired lady down. He shut and locked the trailer door before once again holding her hand and walking toward their pickup. He said something to the woman who stopped walking to look up toward Warren's RV. They both smiled and waved at Warren, who smiled and waved back pleasantly.

"Guess that eliminates that one." Krys said from her seat by Mickey.

"Yeah. One to go." Warren said as he drove down the third street heading back toward the main road.

"I'm going to drive down here, then double back, make it seem like we're just looking for a good spot."

Ty was looking past Warren at the motorhome in question. It had to be at least a 48 footer, it was huge. It had dark curtains at all the windows. The outside was a bright metallic gray and brown.

The motor home had backed into the spot. Ty also noted that it was parked close enough to the fence, backed up to a grassy hill, that even he couldn't hike around in back of it to read the plates. The front did not have a plate visible.

Warren drove to the end of the street, made a U-turn and headed back down the last street toward the RV. As they approached, a young man came out the side door. He looked around, spotted the RV coming down the street and quickly backed up the step into the motorhome, closing the door behind him.

As Warren cruised past the front of the RV, Ty noticed the curtains across the front window of the cab were fluttering. They were pulled apart an inch or two, the same young man was peering out at them.

Ty waved at him, smiling, but the man quickly closed the curtains, disappearing from sight.

Krys walked to the front of the RV and suggested they stop and let Mickey out for a minute or two. It would look as if the dog needed to go and shouldn't be that suspicious. Warren pulled over as far as possible off the street. Krys opened the side door and called to Mickey, saying "out".

Mickey immediately jumped off the couch, trotted across the floor and jumped out the door onto the ground, paws never touching the step.

As Krys watched from the door, Ty went to the back of the RV to also observe the dog's behavior. Mickey continued to walk across the grassy patch near the other RV. He got to the end of the grass to the small cement patio that was parallel to the RV.

When he reached the patio, he stopped dead in his tracks, raised his head and sniffed the air. He stood perfectly still. Then he tucked his tail between his hind legs, lowered his ears and started growling. It came from deep within him, but it was loud enough for Krys to hear from the doorway.

"He's growling at the RV," Krys whispered up to Warren, who was still seated behind the wheel.

"Call him back." Warren said anxiously.

"Mickey, here." Krys said just barely loud enough to be heard by Ty or Warren.

Mickey stood a few moments more, continued to growl, the hair on his back standing straight up. His tail now stood up in the air and the hair on it also stood on end.

His tail slowly lowered, he turned and walked back to Krys. He jumped up into the motorhome, walked back to the couch and jumped up on it next to Ty. He sat there, looking out the back window at the RV and growled again. He didn't move when Ty got up to go back to the front or when Krys came back to sit next to him. He continued to stare at the RV, not acknowledging anyone or anything else.

"That speaks volumes." Warren stated, having turned his seat around to face the inside of the RV. "Think we need to get out of here before we become too obvious."

"We're coming back, aren't we?" Ty asked.

"Oh, yeah. You can bet on it." Warren stated.

He swiveled back around in his seat, put the RV back into drive and then drove slowly to the other end of the street. He made another U-Turn back down the third street. When he got back to the main drive, he turned right, drove past the office and out onto the main road.

"It's time to make plans, before we move again." Warren said. He then fell silent and remained quiet all the way back to Cassy's house.

Ty sat, a million thoughts going through his head. He hoped they had finally found Blake and he intended to be there tonight. He had made a promise that if Blake was found, he would stake him personally. He felt it was his duty to get rid of Blake and stop all the madness.

Krys sat with Mickey in the back of the RV. Her thoughts were on Ty and her fear that they had found Blake. She had seen his power over people when he had controlled her movements once before, putting her in harm's way. She only remembered waking up as if from a bad dream and screaming. Ty had not been able to help her or to stop Blake and that scared her more than she would ever admit to Ty.

Blake had written Ty a letter when he left him the truck and trailer stating that Ty would never be harmed. "You and yours" were Blake's exact words. Ty believed that meant Krys as long as she was with him. But Krys wasn't as optimistic as TY. She didn't trust Blake, never had and never would. She would never believe he meant her no harm.

By the time they reached Cassy's, the snow was falling heavily and the entire yard was now pure white, the only disturbance in the snow being paw prints from Sam and Bright Eyes.

Warren got out of the RV, called Mickey out and then stood watching the animals romp in the snow. It reminded him of how much help the snow would be when they went back to the RV park. If there was any kind of movement outside the RV, they would see the tracks in the snow.

Of course, Warren realized that both Blake and Pat could actually levitate and glide over the snow without making any tracks. But their friend in the RV couldn't. Even one set of foot prints in the snow was all Warren would need.

He knew it would be dangerous to return after dark, when Blake and Pat would be out and about. But he prayed they would be gone from the RV doing their evil deeds and he and Ty could get inside and hopefully find Lisa. He could picture her in his mind's eye, scared for probably the first time in her life. He had watched her at work when they were tracking a child molester up in Kalamazoo. After working with her for only a few days, he had realized how fearless she was. She never backed down.

But now it was an entirely different situation. He couldn't begin to imagine what she must have been going through over the last month or so with Blake and Pat. He didn't want to even think about it. All he wanted was for her to be safe and back in his arms. This time he swore she wasn't going back to Kalamazoo. She was going home with him.

CHAPTER 22

West on I-70, the 76 Truck Stop was anything but quiet that night. A dozen or more truckers had been on the CB while driving into town. When they were all parked, they congregated inside the truck stop, moving tables together conference style.

A trucker with a Swift cap on took the seat at the head of the tables. His jacket had the name John embroidered on it. After everyone was seated and two waitresses had taken their drink orders, John stood and asked for their attention.

"My name is John Anders. We've all been on the CB and we all know what's going on. Never thought I'd be standing in a truck stop talking about vampires, but it is what it is. You can call the loony bin for me if you want to, but I believe we all know it's for real."

"We'd all be going to the loony bin if that was the case," one of the truckers chided.

"How many of you are packing?" John asked.

To his surprise, all twelve at the table raised their hands.

"Okay, then. I think it's time to take a walk."

"Outside? Are you crazy? Our bullets won't hurt them."

"They will if we have one of those priests sitting in a booth across the restaurant bless then with some holy water."

"Holy water?", another trucker asked. "Just where will you be getting this holy water?"

"Watch and learn, grasshopper." John said, smiling broadly.

Everyone at the table had turned and looked across the restaurant to where John had pointed. In a booth along the opposite wall sat three priests. They had been talking but were now staring back at the truckers who were, in turn, staring at them.

As one, all twelve truckers stood up and, with John in the lead, walked over to the priests. Some of the truckers were huge football type guys, including John. There was only one female trucker who had joined them, but she looked as menacing and determined as the men.

The priest who sat at the end of the booth rose to meet John, holding his arm out to shake hands. He was the oldest of the three, the two still seated in the booth looked more like altar boys than full-fledged priests.

"Hello, Father. My name is John Anders. These with me are my fellow truckers. We'd like to ask a favor of you."

"You want me to bless your bullets." The priest stated, much to the surprise of everyone standing there. A shocked look came over the faces of the other two priests.

"How? What?" John stammered.

"Just because I'm wearing this collar doesn't mean I'm living in a clustered monastery. I watch the news and, believe it or not, I also monitor the CB."

"So you don't have a problem blessing bullets?" asked the lady trucker who had stepped up beside John.

"Although the church won't allow me to participate in what you're about to do and, in fact, won't even acknowledge the existence of vampires, no one has actually said I can't bless objects."

"Wow!" the lady trucker exclaimed. "I used to be Catholic but I never met a priest who seemed so, so human before."

The priest laughed then grabbed her hand and held it in his.

"Young lady, I'm not different than most other priests I know."

The priest let go of her hand, looked at the truckers standing silently behind her and John.

"My name is Father Behrendt, everyone calls me Father B. I'd like to bless your ammo but I would also be honored if you would let me bless each one of you individually also."

Father B then turned around and grabbed two glasses of water off his table, handing them to John.

"Could you please hold them out in front of you?"

John did as he was told. Father B made the sign of the cross over the water, then said a prayer in Latin while holding both hands over the two glasses.

"Okay. That takes care of that. You can put the glasses back on the table."

John opened his jacket, took out a Colt 357 magnum from a shoulder holster, spun the chamber and gathered the bullets in his hand. He stuck his hand out toward the priest who dipped three fingers into the glass of water and sprinkled the bullets while again saying a prayer in Latin. He then made the sign of the cross and gently touched John's forehead.

The lady trucker opened her jacket to reveal a holster clipped to her belt. She unsnapped the holster and pulled out a small but lethal looking 22 pistol. She spun the chamber and soon had a hand full of 22 bullets. Father B repeated his incantation.

As the lady trucker stepped back next to John, she looked up at him, smiled and said, "I'm Sharon Keller".

"That's a mighty small gun," John commented as they both stood reloading their weapons.

"I don't need a big gun, I know what I'm doing," she replied, still smiling.

The truckers got in line, each one producing bullets from their guns. The last trucker in line pulled a long box out of his coat pocket and gently emptied its contents onto the table.

"Buckshot?" Father B asked.

"Buckshot." Was all the trucker said.

Father B finished his blessings and everyone had either reloaded or put away their bullets.

"If you would gather around, I'd like to say a prayer for your entire group."

"In Latin?" one of the truckers asked.

"Not this time." Father B answered.

The truckers formed a circle around the priest, the two young priests stepping out of the booth to join the group.

Father B folded his hands in prayer, bowed his head and then began.

"Heavenly Father, please bless these men and this woman as they venture out on a very dangerous mission. Protect them and do not let any harm come to them. Look over them as they vanquish their enemy, the enemy of all mankind. In Jesus name, amen."

Amen echoed from the truckers as well as numerous customers who had been silently watching all that had been happening.

The truckers thanked Father B in unison, then turned as a unified group, heading towards the exit door. As they walked past the table where they had originally been sitting, each one threw a bill on the table, the smallest being $5.00, the largest $20.00.

They were only a few steps from the exit when the doors were opened and a man stepped inside. He stood silently, looking from one trucker to another but not attempting to move and let them pass.

"Excuse us," John spoke up, "but we're trying to leave."

"Not until you allow me to talk to you first." The man said in a low voice.

"We're in kind of a hurry here," Sharon spoke up.

"It isn't smart to hunt them after dark, you know. That's why we're here, to help you".

"You look like you could use our help, as pale as you are." One of the truckers spoke up, slowly moving forward menacingly.

"I see you all are armed. Do you realize that guns have no effect on them?"

"Wrong," Sharon spoke up. "Our bullets are all blessed with holy water."

"That's a good start." The stranger said. "But I still need to talk to all of you. Is there a private room here?"

A waitress had walked over to the group and told them they could use the dining area. She led them through a door to a more private area, then left, closing the door behind her.

"If you'll all take a seat, I'll make this quick."

The men sat at the down at the tables but Sharon remained standing, as far away from the stranger as she could get, a worried look on her face.

"Would you like to take a seat, miss?" The stranger asked, looking directly at Sharon.

"Not until you tell me why you're so pale and why you're so interested in what we're doing here." She replied.

"I'm pale because I was bitten several months ago."

Before he had completed his sentence, the truckers at the table nearest to him had all drawn their guns and sat with them pointed directly at him.

"That won't be necessary," a deep male voice said from the doorway.

The truckers turned around in their chairs to see a very tall man standing just inside the once again closed doors, smiling as if welcoming them to a party.

The room remained deathly quiet as the new stranger walked across the room to stand beside the other man.

"My name is Larry Moore, I'm Chief of Police here in Denver. This gentleman here is Rick Cartier. And, yes, he is a vampire. Only difference between Rick and what you want to fight out there is that he doesn't crave your blood or your life. A doctor and some scientists have developed a serum that he's been taking. He has been a great help to our department."

"How can he possibly help the police?" one of the truckers asked.

"Not everyone infected got that way willingly. They can be talked down and convinced to take the serum and live a normal life." Larry told them.

"And he can do this how?" John asked.

"I explain to them how the serum works and that they can be entirely normal. The only limitation, no sunlight. Yet." Rick spoke up.

"And if they would rather not take your serum?" Sharon asked.

"Then our backup takes care of them." Larry said.

"So," Rick spoke up, "if I can't convince them that my way is much better than what they have now, you all can use your blessed bullets and dispose of them."

The room remained silent, each trucker in turn contemplating what they had just been told. A few made faces as if either not understanding what had just been said or just not believing it.

"Now," Larry said, "are we all in total agreement that Rick is given the opportunity to talk before you shoot?"

The truckers looked from one to another and finally shoot their heads yes in unison.

"Okay, then," Larry said, "it's dark outside. If you're ready, let's get going."

Larry and Rick led the truckers out of the dining room and through the front door. Although it was dark, the parking lot was well lit. The trucks were silent, as were the people who were seen walking around, in and out between the trucks, some just standing in the middle of the driveway staring at the trucks and the truck stop itself.

Rick left the group and walked over to a woman who was standing in front of an older Kenworth, silently watching the activity in the lot. Although Rick wasn't very tall, probably around 5' 8", he still stood at least 6" above the woman. She was dressed in jeans, a plaid shirt and cowboy boots, but wore the outfit as if she were a businesswoman, very sophisticated. She stood still, looking up at Rick, listening.

As the truckers watched in amazement, Rick took her hand in his and walked her over to a motorhome parked at the curb alongside the restaurant. He opened the side door, spoke to someone inside, then helped the lady up the steps, closing the door behind her.

When he had walked back to the group, he said "Dr. Boykolov will take care of her." He then walked back to the parking lot.

Larry motioned to the truckers to split up and walk behind Rick.

As they watched, Rick slowly approached a trucker who was exiting a truck. They talked for a minute or two, then shook hands. The trucker climbed back up into his truck and disappeared into the sleeper. Rick turned and gave the thumbs up sign, then moved on down the lot.

When Rick had walked past two more rigs, he was approached by a very large man who appeared from out of nowhere. Although at least 6' or more and weighing right at 300 pounds, he moved so fast it was as if he flew

As fast as the man had appeared, Rick moved much quicker. He stood about six feet away from the stranger. They talked for only a few seconds when it became obvious that they were now arguing.

The trucker pointed to a newer Mack truck parked behind him. He raised both arms above his head, hands fisted in a threatening manner. Rick stood, not moving, letting the man rant and rave.

Meanwhile, Larry motioned with his hands behind his back for some of the truckers to slowly move forward toward Rick, encircling him in a protective manner. As they got close, the trucker could be heard.

"Why should I go back to day labor? What's wrong with traveling at night? You talk about being normal again. Normal is boring. What I do now is exciting and very fulfilling. Now I have men and women obeying me. They do what I say. And I say attack."

Rick quickly backed up another four feet and pointed at the trucker. Larry fired once and the trucker immediately burst into flames, the only sound his bones hitting the pavement.

"Holy shit." Was heard from one of the truckers.

"Oh my God, do they always do that?" another one was heard to say.

Before anyone could say another word, people started appearing from in between the trucks.

There had to be 20 or more men and women congregating in a group. No one talked. They just stood silently staring at the truckers, who were all standing with guns aimed.

"Close ranks," Larry shouted.

The truckers moved slowly back into their own little group, never lowering their guns.

"All you have to do is hit one, hit him or her anywhere." Rick whispered. He had walked up behind the truckers.

"You don't want to talk to them?" the trucker standing next to Rick asked.

"I'll let my gun do the talking this time. Way too many of them to talk to." Rick answered.

The standoff seemed to last an eternity but after less than a minute, the group by the trucks moved as one and casually began walking towards Larry and his group.

Larry was the first to fire his gun. He hit a large man close to him. The man stopped dead in his tracks, staring at his arm which burst into flames. Within seconds, his entire body was engulfed and as he fell to the ground, his bones scattered.

The two men who had been flanking that trucker looked in his direction, then continued to walk forward, only at a much faster pace.

"Fire." Larry yelled and the truckers let loose with a barrage of bullets. The vampires in the lead were soon ablaze, lighting up the parking lot.

Larry noted that there were more men and women walking out from between the semis to join the original group, which now numbered only six.

The truckers continued to fire their weapons. The only sounds heard, besides the whooshing of the flames, were the guns firing and a few new clips being quickly jammed back into them.

Suddenly, the lot became deathly quiet. No one stood in front of their group, only the bones and skulls and some smoke still lazily rising into the night.

Suddenly, the silence was shattered by screams from behind them. Larry turned to see two of the truckers on the ground, fighting for their lives.

Rick acted quickly, pulled a sharp stake out of his belt and in a movement impossible to follow, was suddenly standing over the closest man. He raised his arms high in the air and brought the stake down, driving it into the back of the man on top. He then grabbed the man by the arm and threw him over the heads of the truckers onto the lot, adding his body to the bones. He disposed of the second vampire in the same manner.

Rick lowered his arm to the second trucker, held out his hand and helped him to his feet. The other truckers had helped the first man up.

"Come with me," Rick said as he turned and started walking toward the motorhome.

Sharon slowly walked away from the group towards the bones. Without a word, she emptied her gun into the bodies of the two men on the ground, then stood watching as they also burst into flames.

John stood next to Larry, both of them staring at Sharon.

"She yours?" Larry asked.

"Not yet." John answered, looking over at Larry, smiling, then looking back at Sharon, who was now walking back to their group.

"Didn't want to leave the job half done." She said as she continued to walk back to the truck stop restaurant. The men turned and followed her in. All except one who headed back to the parking lot and soon climbed into a new Kenworth.

Larry made a quick phone call and when he hung up he told them that the clean-up crew was on its way.

"What about their trucks?" John asked.

"We'll get it all sorted out, don't worry. And we'll have proper burials." Larry answered.

The group walked into the restaurant and immediately turned into the private dining room. They took the same seats as before. Everyone sat, no one spoke.

The trucker who had gone to his truck soon appeared, carrying a large paper bag in his arms. Immediately behind him came two waitresses and the busboy, all carrying glasses of coke.

"Before you all say anything, the glasses are only partially full for a reason." He opened the bag and pulled out a large bottle of Jack Daniels, then a bottle of Bacardi Rum.

The waitresses and busboy handed out the cokes, then the trucker walked around the table either pouring the Jack or the Bacardi into each glass.

As he poured some Jack into Larry's glass, he smiled and said, "Don't panic, I don't drink and drive. These were for my brothers back home, missed their birthdays. But don't think they'll mind if just a little bit is missing from each bottle, considering the circumstances."

Larry stood up and raised his glass in the air. "A toast to you all. Not only do you keep the wheels turning and keep America moving but you also stop the vampires in their tracks. Salute."

The truckers clinked their glasses, then took a drink.

Rick walked into the room but only one of the two truckers accompanied him.

"I believe Don and I could each use one of those," Rick said. "Don is just fine, no scratches or bites. The other trucker, Pete, was bitten. We've injected him and he's resting comfortably in the motorhome."

"Yeah," Don added. "Pete said you had all better start driving more hours at night so he has someone to talk to. Says he's a preacher and he does like to talk."

Everyone laughed along with Don, the tension slowly dissipating.

John looked at Rick questioningly.

"How do you do it? If they don't cooperate and you have to kill them? Aren't you more or less killing your own kind?" John asked.

"Not even close," Rick answered. "I was very lucky. I got help before I could get near another person and drink their blood. The cravings were there and the pain was excruciating. But I survived. They can too. Pete will lead a perfectly normal life' He'll just learn to drive at night now."

Rick paused for just a second, then continued to address the truckers.

"But those out there, they're not my kind. They're monsters, as far as I'm concerned. They don't have any more humanness in them than a rabid dog. They need to be disposed of as soon as humanly possible."

"What happens if they've been a vampire for a long time?" A trucker at the opposite end of the table asked.

"The longer they've been infected, the harder it is to convince them it isn't the kind of life they want to live. They realize they will live forever but they think they are invincible. Some actually enjoy their new-found power. But some retain a modicum of morality, they don't really want to continue to harm people. Once they decide to let us help them, it works no matter how long they've been infected."

"Isn't it hard to no longer be able to be out in daylight? Sharon asked.

"I have special coverings over my windows at my home, so I can still look at my garden, the birds and the squirrels. But it is really hard and I miss long morning walks and barbecues and, believe it or not, shopping at the mall at Christmas time."

"Will it always be like this for you?" the trucker sitting next to John asked.

"Hopefully, no. Dr. Boykolov and his associates are working on the serum, improving it so that eventually we only inject once a year. And they're working even harder to enable us to be out in the sun. As soon as that serum is perfected, I'm going swimming in my pool from sunrise to sunset."

There were smiles among the truckers, some quiet laughter and a few who actually laughed out loud. Larry was grateful that they had accepted Rick and talked to him on a one-to-one basis, no one leery of him, no one keeping their distance. If more people got to know him and the others who were like him, it would make his job and his life so much easier.

A patrolman poked his head through the door and announced that the cleanup was complete.

"Well, that's my cue to get back to work," Larry announced. "You are all welcome to stay and relax, unwind, just don't drive, okay?"

As Larry walked toward the door, each trucker caught up with him, one by one, shook his hand and told him thank you.

Rick was the last to shake hands with Larry. "See you tomorrow night."

"I'm out of here too. Dr. Boykolov is going to stay here with Pete overnight to make sure the serum has no side effects and explain his new life to him. He'll be fine though. Don't worry. All of you, thank you for your help."

With that, Rick turned and walked out the door. Soon the rest of the truckers excused themselves and headed for their respective rigs.

CHAPTER 23

John and Sharon were the only two truckers still seated at the table. They sat in silence until John finally spoke.

"Where's your rig parked?"

"Back of the lot but just the truck. Got to work this morning and no loads, not even an empty trailer on the lot. Which seems to be happening more and more lately."

"I'm second row, first rig." John told her.

The silence seemed to hang in the air, both sitting expectantly.

Finally, John spoke again. "I'm not really sure I like the idea of you in the last row."

"Why, because I'm a woman?" Sharon asked defensively.

"Not even. I saw how you handled yourself out there."

"Then what?"

"I just have a feeling. Not of danger, though. Kind of a feeling I can't describe."

Sharon looked at him questioningly.

"Are you married?" John asked.

"Do I look stupid?" She answered him with her own question. "No. I'm not married."

"Would you like to be married for the night?" he asked, his cheeks getting slightly flushed.

"If I were to get married, it would be longer than a night or even a week, month or year." She said, smiling.

John looked at her, not sure if she was serious or just kidding with him.

"Don't look so shocked," she said. "I'm what you'd call an independent woman. We are getting more and more numerous every century or so."

"Okay. So, we're both adults and no strings attached. Would you feel more comfortable staying in my rig with me tonight than being alone in yours?"

"Sure," was all she said.

John offered his hand to her. She took his hand, they stood up and walked across the room, out the door and across the parking lot to his truck.

"Nice," she commented when she saw the new Freightliner. He took her around to the passenger side, opened the door and politely waited while she stepped up into the truck. When she was seated, he closed the door and walked around the front of the truck to the driver's door. As soon as he was seated, he closed and locked the door.

"So, how long have you been driving?" Sharon asked casually.

"Started when I was seventeen, driving one of my dad's trucks. Now, about twenty plus years, minus four years active duty in the Navy and then another two to play football, I'm still driving."

"Football?" She asked.

"Yeah, no big deal."

"High school, college, professional?"

"Yeah," John said.

"Yeah to what?"

"To all of the above."

"Okay, I know how to pull teeth. What team and what position did you play professionally?"

"Deodorant for the Denver Broncos."

"You're telling me you played right guard for the Denver Broncos?" Sharon said, disbelief heard in her voice.

"Yeah, that's what I'm saying. Played the same year my cousin played quarterback."

"Only a year?" She asked.

"Only a year. Personal things happened and I got traded to the Miami Dolphins. Didn't get to play for them, got cut early."

"I won't even ask about your personal life. Too bad you didn't get to play more though."

"You're the first one to not ask and I appreciate that."

"So, why are you driving?" he asked, more curious about her than he wanted to admit.

"Well, I've worked secretarial for a long time. Also waitressed in truck stops a few times. Loved the truckers. Unfortunately, I met the wrong ones when it came to that part of the job. Promises became one-night stands. I decided rather than continue to put up with them, I'd become one of them. Be my own person."

"You sound pretty adventurous." He commented.

"Not so much. Sheltered most of my life, made wrong decisions when it came time to get married. Too many mistakes that kept me down. At one point, I was convinced I couldn't make it on my own. Then circumstances made me prove to myself I could. And I did just fine." She said as an afterthought.

"I was very impressed with how you handled yourself tonight. I don't know any other women, truckers or not, who could have or would have stood with the rest of us like you did."

"I look at it this way, vampires have always been of interest to me, but always in the movies or in books. Now that they're real, I look at them differently. Kind of like a rabid dog. If a dog was foaming at the mouth and attacking me, I'd put him down without any qualms. So why not vampires?"

"That's one way of looking at it, sounds like a smart way to me." You also sound like a very well-educated woman. Got college in your background?"

"Some, no degree. Took three years of English composition, wanted to be a writer. Took a semester of creative writing. I just love to write. I have so many ideas in my head that I've already put in writing. Have a book I wrote strictly about truckers and the things that can happen on the road. What about you?"

"I got a degree in engineering, always wanted to build my own house, even have the blueprints for it. Also went to trade school to become a plumber. Used the plumbing in Vegas for a while. Nothing ever came of the engineering though. But then, I know doctors and lawyers who are now driving truck for a living."

"When did you get this truck?"

"Last year. Got tired of making money for the companies."

"Don't blame you. This is the third time I've come in to work only to be told there are no loads. Can't pay bills if I'm not driving."

"How long have you been driving?" John asked.

"Not long. Went to school here, drove doubles out of Modesto for a year til the company went belly-up and stranded all of us. That's when I started driving for this local company, LTL from her to New Mexico, Arizona and then California."

They sat in a comfortable silence for a short while when John swiveled his seat around and stood up.

"I don't know about you, but I'm beat. I've got to go to bed. Join me?"

Sharon didn't answer. John went back into the sleeper, stripped down to his shorts, crawled into bed and scooted to the back against the wall.

Sharon sat in the seat, staring out the window at the parking lot. Her mind went back to her firing her gun and setting the two men on fire. She had grown up with a good knowledge of guns and enjoyed target practice with her dad and her uncles back on her grandpa's farm in North Dakota. She had hunted for elk in the mountains with friends but she had never shot a human being, even when threatened. It bothered her to think of what she had done. She knew it was necessary but the impression it had made on her wasn't a pleasant one.

She slowly rose out of her seat and walked back into the sleeper. She sat on the edge of the bed, took off her boots and socks, then stood and got out of her pants and shirt. She lay down on the bed but almost jumped back up when John threw a blanket over her.

"As tired as I am," John whispered sleepily, "cuddling is the only thing I'm even able to think about right now."

"Okay," she answered. She turned over onto her side, then backed up against him. His body was comfortably warm. He put his arm around her waist and they were both soon sound asleep.

The morning sun burst through the truck windows, waking Sharon. She felt very rested and was surprised she had slept so well after the events of the evening before. She slowly rolled over on her left side, facing John, who was laying there, eyes wide open, smiling at her.

"You're awake," she said.

"Have been for a while."

"Why didn't you wake me?"

"I was just enjoying laying here quietly, listening to you breathe."

"You mean snore?" She asked, laughing.

"No, just breathe."

Without another word, Sharon slowly brought her hand up to John's cheek and caressed it softly. He leaned forward and she met him halfway, kissing lightly. Soon the kisses became more and more passionate.

At first, they were both tentative, but then their passion overtook them. John was adept at unfastening her bra snaps in back and the feel of her body next to his, so warm and yet so strong. Soon she released all his inhibitions. She found herself helping him remove her panties as well as his shorts.

His lovemaking was nothing like she had ever experienced before. He caressed her slowly, rubbing her shoulders, then moving down to her breasts. He was gentle yet he aroused in her a passion that totally surprised her. He kissed her breasts, nibbling tenderly. By the time his hand had wandered below her waist, she was ready to scream, wanting him so badly.

She had been exploring his body as well and found that, although he was a big man, he was still hard muscled. When her hands found his manliness, her eagerness was unbearable.

"Please, now," she whispered. John carefully moved her to the center of the bed and then tenderly rolled over on top of her, keeping his weight on his elbows, staring at her eyes, kissing the lids, then her mouth.

All inhibitions were dissolved in their lovemaking. They both climaxed and then John rolled off of her and lay back beside her, breathing heavily.

Sharon rolled over and laid her head on his chest, her arm around his waist. He enfolded her in his arms and they lay in silence, a comfortable silence.

"That was amazing." She whispered. "I've never felt like this before."

"It's called love at first sight." John told her.

"I don't believe in that."

"Guess I'll just have to convince you otherwise. Let's start with breakfast and then a long discussion as to why you should quit your job and partner with me."

CHAPTER 24

After Warren returned to Cassy's, he called Andy and told him what had transpired in the nearby RV park.

"Put your phone on speaker so I can hear what you all decide. When do you plan on going back to the park, before or after sunset?" Andy asked.

"Not sure. When are you coming back to Cassy's?"

"I'm on my way right now."

"If we go now, we only have his familiar to deal with." Krys said.

"And what's a familiar, pray tell." Cassy asked her.

"A familiar is someone who wants to be a vampire but isn't yet. Blake will have him do all the things he can't do in daylight, like drive the RV, get food for Lisa. The familiar probably filled out the registration card and that's why Warren couldn't read the name."

"Why didn't I think of that before?" Ty asked as everyone looked at him, puzzled. He looked at Warren. "Remember the letter Blake wrote me? He has perfect penmanship. That card had to be filled out by someone else."

"Of course. Lisa and Pat are both well educated women. They wouldn't have written so sloppily, not even intentionally." Warren added.

"So it had to be the familiar." Krys said. "Now what?"

"Now, we strike immediately, while it's still daylight. The familiar is the only one who can fight back." Warren stated.

"When do we leave?" Andy asked Warren.

"Now works for me." Warren stated.

"I'll be there in five minutes or less. This nice cop who's driving just put his flashers and siren on, so don't anybody get alarmed when we pull in. Never mind, he said he'd come in quiet."

As Jacob turned to the door, he said "come". Mickey got up off the floor and trotted over to the door, standing next to Jacob, waiting.

"I'll get the weapons out of the truck." Ty said as he pulled on his jacket and headed out the door. Without a word, Krys grabbed her jacket and followed Ty.

Warren pulled the keys to the RV out of his pocket. "Keep Sam and Bright Eyes close to you," he told Cassy. "Blake's closer than I thought he'd be. Stay safe." He hugged Cassy, giving her a kiss on the top of her head.

"You don't have to worry about us." Cassy told him as he headed toward the front door. "We'll all three be safe here."

Warren and Jacob walked out to the RV. Ty and Krys soon joined them, stakes and hammers in hand. Before they had time to get inside the RV, a Denver patrol car pulled up and Andy jumped out the passenger side.

As the car pulled alongside the RV, the young patrolman lowered his window.

"I'll put a call in to the Chief. I hear he's going out to a truck stop, something about some vigilante truckers. He's afraid they'll get hurt, or worse."

"Thanks", Andy said, then got in and sat down in the passenger seat. Warren got in behind the wheel. Ty, Krys and Jacob sat on the couch by the back womdpw, Mickey lay on the floor up front between Andy and Warren.

The snow continued to fall heavily. Warren ran the windshield wipers while the RV warmed up before heading out. Although it looked like a winter wonderland, the streets were still clear, not yet icy or dangerous.

Warren drove slowly and it took a good fifteen minutes before they reached the park. He pulled in by the office.

"Oh, shit." Warren exclaimed.

"What?" Ty cried out as he rose and quickly walked to the front of the RV. He bent over to look out the front window.

"It's gone." He cried out, the disappointment evident in his voice.

"Drive up to the spot where the RV was parked. Let's see if they left any clues behind." Andy said.

Warren drove slowly up the center road to the third street. He turned right and then made a U-turn at the end of the street to come back down the fourth road. He parked on the street directly in front of the spot where the motorhome had been parked. It was evident that they had pulled out just minutes earlier. The spot where they were parked was still dry, even though the snow had been getting heavier over the last hour or so.

Ty jumped out of the RV, stood staring at the spot where the rig had been. Warren put the RV in park and exited out the driver's door. He joined Ty on the cement pad. They stood there silently while the others slowly joined them. Everyone stood scanning the area around the parking space, looking for any movement or any clues as to when they had left or where they headed when they drove off.

Mickey suddenly appeared next to them. He stood staring at the fence line, growling low but didn't move.

"I don't know what's wrong, but something is. He jumped out even though I told him to stay." Andy said, puzzled.

Mickey stood for another minute, sniffing the air, then whining.

"Go." Andy said loudly, commandingly.

Mickey ran across the patio and into the snow-covered grass. He ran straight for the fence. There was a mound by the fence. Mickey howled once, then started digging at the mound.

"Oh, my God." Warren cried out. "Lisa."

Warren ran the 15 yards to where Mickey was digging. The dog had uncovered a white sheet and was pulling on the corner of it. Warren picked up the end of the sheet and pulled it back.

There, on the ground in the fetal position, lay Lisa. She wasn't moving. Warren couldn't tell if she was breathing or not. He did note that her left wrist was handcuffed to the fence.

When Warren knelt down in the snow beside Lisa, he immediately noted that she had her free arm wrapped around a bundle covered in another sheet.

Warren carefully removed Lisa's hand from on top of the bundle. He pulled the sheet back and suddenly gasped. Beneath the sheet lay a small boy. He was maybe 5 or 6 years old, curled up with his back up against Lisa. He looked so small and so pale.

Krys, who had come up and was standing behind Warren looking over his shoulder, immediately came around to his side. She knelt down and felt the boy's neck for a pulse. Without a word to anyone, she gently picked the boy up, cuddled him in her arms and quickly walked back to the RV.

In the meantime, Warren reached out to take Lisa's hand in his. He felt for a pulse.

"She's still alive," he said, "but she's so cold.

"Let's get her back to the RV." Andy yelled.

"We can't. The bastard handcuffed her to the fence." Warren cried out

"No problem." Jacob said. He walked around Warren and knelt down by the fence. He pulled a small knife out of his jeans pocket. He then released a small tool that he used to work on the handcuff. In less than a minute, he had the handcuff opened and he was gently removing Lisa's wrist from it. He laid her arm back on her side.

Warren very gently picked Lisa up in his arms and started walking back to the RV. She moaned slightly when he started walking and he held her more tightly.

Ty ran ahead and when Warren reached the RV, he was standing in the doorway, arms outstretched to accept Lisa from Warren. They made the transfer and Ty carried her to the couch and lay her down. Jacob, Andy and Mickey followed Warren into the RV.

Krys was already sitting in the recliner, the boy cradled in her arms. She had removed her jacked and wrapped it around the boy.

"I'll drive," Jacob said as he headed toward the driver's seat.

Warren never heard Jacob, he was so focused on Lisa, rubbing her hands in his trying to warm them up as best he could.

As Jacob started driving down the main road of the park toward the gait, a police car skidded to a stop in front of him. The same cop who had brought Andy back to Cassy's jumped out and ran up to the driver's window.

"Larry gave me orders to stick with you. Did you find anything?"

"We found Lisa and a small boy. She's alive, but don't know how long she's been in the snow." Jacob told him.

The cop pulled out his cell phone and dialed the number three on his speed dial. When the call was answered, he said, "This is Thomas Walker. I'll be on Colfax and County Line Road in approximately ten minutes, escorting an RV. I need an escort to Denver General. And have the staff there put on stand-by. I have a female and a small child who have been exposed to the weather, not sure what else. I want personnel at the door when we arrive at the hospital."

"I'll lead the way," the cop said as he ran back to his car. With lights flashing and siren blaring, he led them out of the park and back down the road toward Colfax. There were two Aurora police cars waiting, lights flashing, traffic at a standstill.

As soon as Jacob reached the intersection, both cars turned on their sirens. One car moved out ahead of the other two vehicles, making sure that traffic would be clear for them to proceed once they got into the heavier populated areas. The second car pulled out but stayed close to the RV. The one escorting them stayed just in front of them.

As they were escorted down Colfax, Warren remained kneeling on the floor, rubbing Lisa's hands and talking to her continuously.

Warren took off his jacket and covered Lisa up. Ty followed suit, handing his jacket to Warren to lay over Lisa's legs and feet.

Ty put his hand on Warren's shoulder. "She'll be fine. She's strong. She lasted this long with Blake, you can't lose her now."

"Blake didn't turn her, she didn't burn up when you removed the sheet." Krys added from over in the recliner. "She'll still be your Lisa."

"No, she won't." Warren said emphatically. "She'll be Mrs. Josiah Warren as soon as she is up and about. This time there won't be any indecision. I won't let her say no or wait ever again."

Ty walked over to Krys, who was still cuddling the child in her arms. He had moaned a couple of times and once actually moved, trying to get even closer to Krys' warmth.

Ty sat on the floor beside Krys, hoping his presence would help insure her that things would be okay.

The RV suddenly slowed down.

"What's wrong?" Warren asked anxiously.

"We're here." Andy called back from the passenger seat.

Ty went to the side door and opened it up. Two male nurses climbed in and immediately took charge.

The first nurse to enter noted Krys with her bundle sitting in the recliner. She told him the child was also found in the snow. He started examining the boy, allowing Krys to continue to hold onto him.

He took the child's pulse and said it sounded strong. He pulled the boy's eyelids back, shone his penlight into his right eye, then his left.

Without a word, he took the boy from Krys, cradled him comfortingly, stepped out of the RV and walked quickly into the hospital.

Warren got up off the floor and stood back a couple of steps. One of the male nurses asked if she had fallen or was there any possibility of broken bones.

"We found her in the snow cuffed to the fence. When I carried her to the RV, she moaned once, but didn't sound like she was moaning in pain."

"Has she regained consciousness at all?" the nurse asked.

"No." Warren said.

"How long has she been like this?"

"About an hour that we know of." Warren told her.

The nurse effortlessly picked Lisa up and walked to the door. He stepped sideways, walked down the two steps and gently placed her on the gurney. He covered her up with warm blankets, strapped her in and wheeled her through the emergency room doors.

"Now what?" Ty asked, not really looking at anyone in particular.

"I'm staying with Lisa." Warren stated. Without another word, he walked out of the RV and trotted toward the emergency room doors. He soon disappeared inside the hospital.

"I'll stay here with Warren." Ty said. He turned to Krys. "Do you want to stay or go back to Cassy's?"

"I'll go with Andy back to Cassy's. We'll bring you dinner later and then I can stay with you if you decide to spend the night." Krys told him. She stepped up to him, kissed him and then turned to leave.

After only a few steps, Krys turned back toward the hospital doors. "Keep in touch. See if you can keep tabs on that little boy, too."

"Okay, love you." Ty said. He walked through the doors and then headed down the hall toward the nurse's station.

Andy was already seated in the driver's seat. Kris joined him up front. Mickey sat down on the floor between the two of them.

"So, Jacob's staying here?" Krys asked Andy.

"Yeah. Says he'll be more help here with the guys, just in case."

"Just in case what?" Krys asked, sure she knew the answer before it was given.

"Just in case Blake is nearby waiting to see if Lisa makes it or not." Andy told her.

Andy started the RV and headed back to Cassy's. As soon as the vehicle started moving, Mickey sat up and put his head on Krys's leg. Krys started petting his ears and head as if she had been doing it for years. It was the comfort that Krys truly needed and appreciated.

CHAPTER 25

The drive through Denver and then Aurora was a quiet one. A few miles from Cassy's house, Andy finally spoke up.

"It was nice of Ty to stay with Warren. Are they that close?"

"We all are, after what we went through in Kalamazoo. But that's not the reason he's staying."

"Really?"

"Yeah. In Kalamazoo, Lisa shot an intruder. The man was taken to the hospital and put under police protection. That night, Blake showed up on Lisa's back patio along with others like him and the man Lisa had shot. Blake said the man didn't bring Lisa to him like he was ordered to and, because of that, he had to suffer the consequences. Blake stood there staring at the guy who was kneeling on the patio. The man began scratching at his eyes, screaming in pain the whole time. He scratched his own eyes out, then lay down and bled out."

"So Ty wants to stay with Warren in case Blake comes after Lisa again." Andy said. "That explains why Ty was wearing Warren's over-sized coat."

"I hadn't even noticed."

"Under the coat, Ty has a crossbow and quiver." Andy explained.

"That sounds like Ty." Krys said.

When Andy pulled up outside Cassy's, he and Krys stepped out of the RV. Mickey followed Andy out the driver's door. Andy pointed to the yard and said "go". Mickey ran into the yard. Bright Eyes came from around the back of the house and together they ran across the snow and were soon out of sight.

Cassy greeted them at the door and immediately asked where Ty and Warren were. Jacob pulled her into the dining room and filled her in on all that had taken place.

Andy came over to the dining room table to join Jacob, Cassy and Krys. When Jacob finished telling Cassy what had happened, Andy spoke up.

"Do we all want to go to the hospital?" Cassy asked.

"In a little while." Andy said.

"I promised to bring TY and Warren some dinner, so maybe we can pick up something on the way down there." Krys suggested.

"That'll work," Cassy told her. "There are a lot of fast food and drive-through restaurants on Colfax. We'll find something we all agree on."

"Let me go check the truck and I'll be ready to go." Krys said.

"I'll go with you," Jacob volunteered, "can't be too careful."

After Jacob and Krys left out the door, Cassy asked Andy what he thought had happened to Lisa.

"She looked pretty pale but that's probably due to being out in the snow."

"Not because of any other reason?" Cassy asked.

"No. If she had been turned, she would have burned up when Mickey pulled on the sheet that covered her. Warren pulled the sheet completely off her when he realized it was Lisa. Even though it was snowing, it was still daylight and she still would have burned up. Besides, Mickey would never have approached her like he did if she was a vampire."

"Mickey didn't growl at her at all?"

"Nope. He's the reason we found her. She was covered in a white sheet and then the snow covered that. If it weren't for Mickey, none of us would have ever spotted her out there."

Jacob and Krys came back into the house.

"It quit snowing." Jacob announced.

"Are we ready to go?" Cassy asked.

"I've got Warren's keys," Krys said, "so if Andy wants to drive the pickup, we can all ride together."

"I want to go in my Jeep. That way, if you all decide to spend the night or stay late, I can get back home to Sam and Bright Eyes. And Mickey if he's staying here with them."

"Okay then." Andy said. "You lead, we'll follow.

"And when you find a good place, we'll stop and I'll get dinner for everyone. We can all eat together at the hospital." Krys volunteered.

Cassy and Jacob rode in her Jeep, Krys and Andy followed close behind in Warren's pickup.

Cassy stopped at a fast-food Chinese place that didn't look like much of a restaurant. It was strictly a to-go place, no tables or chairs anywhere in sight. Cassy got out and went in with Krys close behind.

"This place is much better than it looks. I've eaten here since I was a little kid." Cassy told Krys.

They ordered a little bit of everything along with extra egg rolls and sweet and sour sauce. When it was all bagged up, the owner added two extra to-go boxes with fried rice and noodles, then included extra plates, silverware and napkins.

They arrived at the hospital within the next twenty minutes, found parking spots next to each other close to the ER. They walked up to the desk and asked where the waiting room was located.

The nurse at the desk asked if they intended to bring the food into the ER. Andy politely told her no, they were bringing it into the waiting room.

The nurse grudgingly directed them down the hall, second door on the left. When they entered the room, Krys went immediately to Ty, who was sitting on a couch near a window. Warren was pacing the floor. When Krys was done saying hello to Ty, she walked over to Warren and hugged him tightly.

"Come and sit down, we brought supper."

"I'm not that hungry." Warren told her.

"Don't care." She said as she pulled him by the arm across the floor toward the rest of the crew.

Cassy pushed the coffee table over in front of the couch, Ty and Jacob moved chairs over to the table. Cassy and Krys took the food out of the bags and set the containers on the table along with the plates and silverware.

When they opened the boxes, the aromas made everyone, including Warren, realize how hungry they were.

Before they were through eating, Larry walked into the room.

"Couldn't wait for me?" He asked. "I'll remember each and every one of you the next time you're driving one mile over the speed limit out on the highway."

"If you'd stop jacking your jaws long enough, you could sit down and eat with the rest of us." Andy told him.

"Okay." Larry said. He grabbed a chair and squeezed in between Andy and Warren.

"Any news yet?" he asked.

"Nothing." Warren responded. "I told them we're engaged and she doesn't have any other relatives. That didn't seem to impress any of them."

"So, anything new on the home front?" Andy asked.

"I guess," Larry said. "Just got back from the 76 Truck Stop across town."

"Trouble out there?" Cassy asked.

"Nothing me and about a dozen truckers couldn't handle. When I got there, they already had all their bullets blessed by a priest who happened to be there eating dinner. They were headed out the door when Rick stopped them. They weren't too receptive but then I showed up and, together, we dispensed about 30 or more vampires."

"Are the truckers okay?" Ty asked.

"Two got jumped, one got bit. But Rick had his RV there with Dr. Boykolov and an assistant and they took care of that trucker. You should have been there, Cassy."

"Why."

"There was this lady trucker there, she fought alongside the men, probably better shot than most of them. Rick dispensed the two vampires who were able to get around the truckers and attack two of them. He threw them on the pile of bones and ashes. She walked up to those two and fired point blank into both of them, set their asses on fire. Never seen anything like it."

"That's one woman I'd like to meet up with, on her good side though," Krys said, chuckling under her breath.

"Wow," was all Ty said.

Larry ate a plate full of egg foo young and fried rice while everyone else talked about unimportant things, trying to keep Warren's mind averted.

Larry finished his plate, got up and excused himself. Approximately five minutes later, he returned with a sullen looking doctor in tow.

"This is Dr. Asher. He's in charge and has news for you, Warren." Larry said as he urged the doctor ahead of him into the room.

"We got Lisa warmed up and were able to give her a thorough exam. We weren't exactly sure what we were looking for. She doesn't have any scrapes or scratches except at the wrist where the handcuff was in place. She has an old bruise on her face, what's left of a black eye. We wrapped her wrist. We did check for sexual abuse, which is standard procedure, but none was evident. She's a bit malnourished and so we have an IV going."

"Will she be okay?" Warren asked anxiously.

"Why don't you ask her that yourself." Dr. Asher said.

"You mean she's awake?"

"She was when I left her a couple of minutes ago." Dr. Asher answered. "She's in the first cubicle, I already cleared you to go in."

"Thank you. Thank you so much." Warren said, shaking the doctor's hand energetically.

Warren walked through the waiting room entrance, then stopped and turned back.

"How do I get there?" he asked, looking lost.

Dr. Asher volunteered to show Warren the way.

Warren followed the doctor down a short hall to a set of double doors. They went through the doors, then the doctor turned immediately to his right. He walked through a set of curtains, then stopped short. Warren almost ran into him.

"You have a visitor," the doctor said as he stepped aside.

Warren walked through the curtains, not certain what to expect. Lisa was sitting up in bed. When she saw Warren, she started crying uncontrollably.

Warren quickly walked over to the bed, sat down on the edge and took her in his arms. She continued to cry, long choking sobs, as he held her. Warren sat stroking her hair, telling her she was going to be okay.

They sat like that for what seemed a very long time before Lisa finally stopped crying and started to relax somewhat. She finally sat back in the bed.

"I must look a mess." she said, rubbing her eyes.

"You look beautiful to me," Warren told her. "You've always looked beautiful to me and always will."

"Not so much now," she protested. "How did you ever find me?"

"With the help of a lot of people and a very special dog."

"A dog?"

"Yeah. His name is Mickey, he's the biggest Collie I've ever seen. You'll meet him when you get out of here. As well as Jacob, Cassy, Bright Eyes and Sam, the bobcat."

"Sounds like I've got a lot of catching up to do." Lisa said.

"Me too. And so does Larry, the Chief of Police here in Denver. But we won't rush you. Besides, I have a couple of people who have been chomping at the bit to say hi to you."

"Who?" Lisa asked.

"It's a surprise." Warren answered. "Be right back."

"No," Lisa screamed at Warren. "Don't leave me."

"Okay." Warren said as he sat back down on the bed. "I'll call them."

Warren took out his cell phone and quickly scrolled down to the number he wanted. When the person on the other end answered, he gave directions to Lisa's cubicle.

Less than five minutes passed before the curtains were parted and Krys stuck her head into the room.

"Hey, girl." Krys quipped.

"Oh, my God." Lisa exclaimed. "You're here."

Warren got up from the bed as Krys and Ty walked into the cubicle. Krys almost ran to the bed. She and Lisa hugged for what seemed forever.

"So what am I, chopped liver?" Ty laughed when Lisa and Krys finally let go of each other.

Krys moved away from the bed so Ty could give Lisa a big hug.

"When did you guys get here?" Lisa asked.

"A couple of days ago. Had a delivery in Aurora."

"Where are you staying?"

"We're parked out in Aurora at Cassy's, kind of country and so nice and quiet.

Krys proceeded to tell Lisa how they had been in Florida when they were told of some abnormal activity in Colorado. She told her how they had met Cassy, who turned out to be the sister of one of Warren's volunteers back in Hebert. Anyhow, Jacob and Andy were already coming up with Warren. They all met at Cassy's place and had been there ever since.

"You and Ty still sleeping in the truck?" Lisa asked.

"Of course," Ty told her. "It's our home away from home."

"It's where we're the most comfortable." Krys added.

"Were you there when they found me?" Lisa asked.

"Where else would we be?" Ty answered.

"Warren said a dog found me."

"Mickey. He's Andy's Collie. Andy brought him up here because he was so good at finding vampires back in Hebert." Krys said.

"Did Mickey think I was a vampire?"

"No. If he had he would have been growling like he did earlier at the RV." Warren told her.

"You were there earlier? Why?"

"Krys figured out early in the game that Blake was probably traveling in an RV instead of a semi like before." Ty said.

"And," Warren added, "I rented an RV to go through the different parks. You know, in disguise."

"We came through the park just as the snow started. A guy came out of the RV or started to. When he saw us, he scooted back in. Then he was peeking out the front curtain at us. I waved and he backed up into the RV and closed the curtains."

"So," Krys interrupted Ty, "Ty got out as if looking at another space. That's when Mickey jumped out of the RV. He stood staring at your RV, just growling. That's when we knew we'd found something. We didn't know if it was Blake, but we knew it was something."

"We went back to Cassy's, got weapons and came back. But the RV was gone." Warren added.

"And the dog found me." Lisa repeated.

"That was a miracle." Krys said. "You were covered with a white sheet and then the snow was on top of that. There were no tracks in the snow."

"Blake must have put you out there before it snowed too heavy. You were out there for a while then." Ty commented.

"Chad must have knocked me out because I don't remember getting cuffed to the fence."

"We'll talk about all of this later." Warren said. "Right now, you need to rest."

"But we won't be far," Krys announced. "We'll be in the waiting room with Jacob, Cassy, Andy and Larry. You'll be well protected."

"Thank you, all of you." Lisa said. "You know I love you guys."

"We love you too," Krys said as she and Ty turned to leave.

CHAPTER 26

Meanwhile, back in the waiting room, Jacob and Andy had gotten up from their seats to greet a stranger who had just walked into the room. They both immediately realized what he was.

Jacob lunged across the coffee table, scattering the food and boxes still sitting there.

Larry's instincts kicked in within seconds of seeing Jacob's reaction. He pulled out his service revolver, then stood facing the stranger.

Andy instinctively motioned to Cassy to get behind him. He faced the stranger, realizing he had no weapons but knowing he had to protect his niece.

The man stood silently, looking from one to the other.

Suddenly, he opened his mouth wide to expose long fangs. He made a hissing sound, then screamed in pain as one of Jacob's arrows pierced his chest and punctured his heart. Before he fell halfway to the floor, he burst into flames.

Jacob looked over at Andy, a shocked expression on his face that immediately turned to bewilderment.

"It isn't sunny in here." Jacob said. "Why'd that happen?"

"It might have something to do with the fact that I rubbed holy water all over the arrows." Andy said.

"Damn." Larry exclaimed. "Do they always do that?"

"I'll explain later." Andy told him.

The fire alarm had sounded several seconds after the man burst into flames. Suddenly, they heard several doors closing throughout the ER. They knew why the alarm had been set off but were still surprised by the immediate response from the hospital security system.

Dr. Asher appeared in the doorway. He stared down at the skull and bones spread out on the floor, still smoldering.

"What happened here?" he asked, looking from one to the other of the four people in the room.

"A vampire happened here." Larry told him.

"I see. So you destroyed him? That's too bad."

"Excuse me?" Larry said, giving the doctor a quizzical look.

"I said that's too bad. Too bad he didn't get the job done. Because that just makes my job that much harder."

"Why is that?" Larry asked, trying to keep the doctor's attention on him while Jacob reloaded his bow.

Larry continued to hold his revolver out in front of him, now aimed at the doctor. He took one step forward, blocking the doctor's view.

"Ralph was supposed to take care of you all so I could finish Lisa and Warren. Blake was very disappointed when the weather didn't finish her off."

"But you're a doctor." Cassy said, having come out from behind Andy, now standing beside him.

"I still am a doctor. I'm just on the night shift now. Many more patients to take care of, one way or another."

"You can still do your job properly, if you wish to." A voice said from just past the doorway.

Suddenly Rick walked into view. He strolled up to Dr. Asher.

"It doesn't need to end like this, there is an alternative." Rick said, slowly closing in on the doctor but moving ever so slowly so as not to alarm him.

"And what would that alternative be?" Dr. Asher asked.

"We have a serum, a cure for what ails you, so to speak. It's a preventative medicine. You take it instead of taking someone's life."

"What if I enjoy what I'm doing more?" the doctor asked.

"Then you die like the vermin you are." Rick said, now standing within a few inches of the doctor.

Dr. Asher stood staring into Rick's eyes for a good minute.

"I think not." he said.

The doctor turned quickly toward the room of people. Everyone was too startled to move. He took half a step into the waiting room when Rick caught him, wrapping his arms around the doctor's head and neck.

Suddenly, a loud cracking sound was heard. The doctor stood for a few seconds, his eyes wide with shock. Then he fell limp in Rick's arms, where he was held upright.

"Finish him, Jacob." Rick said, keeping the doctor's body upright.

Jacob immediately fired an arrow. As soon as the arrow punctured the doctor's skin, Rick let go and stepped back. The body burst into flames before it hit the floor. The body turned to ashes, the skull and bones intertwined with those of the first vampire Ralph.

"Well," Rick began as he walked further into the room, "guess we can't win them all."

"Thanks, Rick." Larry said, turning back to the others.

"Where are Lisa and Warren? Is she okay? Are Ty and Krys with them?" Rick asked.

"Ty and Krys just joined Warren in Lisa's room." Andy told him.

"And all the doors will be locked because of the fire alarm." Cassy added.

"Well, we'd better see what we can do about that." Rick said. He turned and started walking out of the waiting room door. Andy took Cassy's hand in his and, along with Jacob and Larry, followed Rick out of the room and down the hallway.

Back in the ER, Ty and Krys were exiting through the curtains when the fire alarm sounded. The doors shut and locked. Ty looked at Krys, surprised, then worried.

Warren was already coming through the curtains. They met outside the room, each reaching for weapons, alert to any strange sounds. All three realized instantly that they had not brought any weapons into the room with them.

"What's up?" Warren asked.

"Fire alarm. Doors are all shut up tight. Don't think this is a drill." Ty answered.

Without a word, Warren walked to the double doors to check them. They were indeed locked. Ty started walking in the other direction. Krys went back into Lisa's room.

When Ty returned, Warren was still standing outside the curtains.

"No exits?" Warren asked.

"Nope. Everything's shut up tight. There's one other patient, a nurse and two orderlies."

"Are they all okay?"

"The patient and the nurse were okay. But I'm not so sure about those two orderlies. They were acting pretty peculiar."

"Peculiar? How?" Warren asked.

"Neither one would look me in the eye, they both kept their backs to me the whole time I was down there."

"We'd better get prepared." Warren said, looking down the hallway in the direction Ty had just returned from.

"I'm not seeing anything useful out here." Ty said.

"I know." Warren stated, turning back into Lisa's room. Ty followed close behind, scanning the entire room looking for anything useful.

Warren walked past Krys to the head of Lisa's bed. He unceremoniously swept all the items on top of the small bedside table to the floor. He picked up the table and held it in the air over his head, then slammed it to the floor, shattering it. He kicked at the rubble, then bent over and picked up two of the legs, handing one to Ty.

Without a word, they silently walked back to the curtains. Ty parted them a fraction of an inch and peered out.

"They're coming," he whispered. Out of the corner of his eye, he noted that Krys had walked around to the other side of Lisa's bed, picked up the other two table legs. She handed one to Lisa and then stood protectively beside her bed, the wooden leg held in both hands, ready for whatever came next.

Ty turned his attention back to the curtains. As he and Warren watched expectantly, a hand reached around the curtain in front of Warren, grabbing hold but not attempting to open it. A second later, another hand appeared and grabbed the other curtain which had been shielding Ty.

Both men stood, their weapons ready to strike, when the curtains were suddenly pulled apart. The two orderlies stood there. They both made a sound like a snarl. Before they could move, both Ty and Warren made jabbing motions with the wooden legs.

Warren's table leg struck true, piercing the vampire's heart. The man looked shocked, then fell backward onto the floor, no longer moving.

Unfortunately, Ty's table leg was too blunt to pierce the man's skin. It made a thumping noise against the man's chest but did no damage. The man grabbed Ty by his jacket and threw him into the hallway. The sound of Ty's body hitting the wall seemed to echo through the small cubicle.

Warren backed up at an angle so that he was outside Lisa's room and his back was up against the hallway wall. He yelled at the orderly in an attempt to lead him away from the women. The orderly turned toward Warren.

Warren walked slowly backward down the hallway, continually looking for anything to be used as a weapon but also keeping his eye on the orderly who was following him.

Suddenly there was a wild banshee like scream from behind the orderly. Krys literally flew down the hallway, a wooden leg raised high over her head. When she was a couple of feet away, Warren stepped forward and grabbed the orderly's arms, keeping the man's attention focused on him.

Krys brought the table leg down as hard as she could. It pierced the man's back and continued to travel through his body. Warren released the man's arms when he saw the tip of the leg protruding out of the middle of the man's chest. Without a sound, the man silently slid to the floor, where he lay completely still.

Without a word, Krys and Warren immediately ran back to TY. He was lying on the floor, his back against the wall. He was moving but groaning loudly. As he tried to sit back up, he yelled "shit" and sat back down.

Krys reached Ty first and quickly knelt on the floor next to him.

"Are you okay?" she asked, the worry evident in her voice.

"Nothing broken that I can tell." Ty answered. He tried to stand up again and, with help from Krys, made it this time. He stood for a minute, then shook his head as if shaking off spider webs.

"Man, that son of a bitch was strong." he said.

"Is everyone okay?" Lisa asked, standing in the doorway of her cubicle.

Warren sprinted over to Lisa. She was holding her gown against her arm.

"What are you doing out of bed?" Warren asked.

"I took out my IV, I'm applying pressure to stop the bleeding."

"You what?" he asked, incredulous.

"You getting deaf in your old age?" Lisa asked. "I said I took out my IV. Now help me find my clothes and let's get out of here." She said, turning back to the room to search for her clothes.

"But you need nourishment and rest." Warren protested.

"A good meal is nourishment. And rest, where better than in your arms?"

"That's my girl." Warren laughed.

They found her clothes in the closet but they were still soaking wet. Krys said she's find some scrubs. When Krys returned from down the hall, she was carrying some green scrubs and some footies, as well as a jacket.

"The nurse and the patient are both okay, they were hiding in a closet in one of the rooms. The nurse gave me the jacket, said it belonged to one of the orderlies. It's going to be way too big for you, but I figured it would be better than nothing. And I don't think he'll be needing it anymore, anyhow."

While Warren and Ty waited patiently outside the cubicle, Krys stayed in the room with Lisa while she got dressed.

"Green becomes you." Warren said when Lisa walked out of the cubicle.

"What about Scotty?" Lisa asked.

"Scotty?" Warren inquired, a puzzled look on his face.

"Yeah, Scotty. I remember holding him in the dark, trying to keep him warm."

"The little boy who was with you in the snow." Krys stated.

"Was he the other patient you said was okay?" Lisa asked, looking over at Ty.

"No. That was an older guy." Ty told her.

"We've got to find Scotty." Lisa insisted. She turned and headed down the hallway toward the nurse's desk. Warren looked at Ty and Krys as if to say here we go again. The three of them turned and followed Lisa.

When they reached the nurse's station, neither the nurse nor the other patient were anywhere to be seen. Krys walked around the desk and started leafing through the charts that were stacked beside the computer terminal.

"He's in Cubicle 12. Krys announced.

Warren and Ty led the way down the opposite hallway from where Lisa had been. They reached the cubicle but the curtains were drawn together. Warren motioned for the girls to wait in the hall.

He opened the curtains and he and Ty entered the cubicle. Ty closed the curtains behind them.

They could see a small mound under the blanket on the bed. The figure was completely covered and not moving.

Warren walked over to the right side of the bed. Ty followed and stood on the opposite side. Slowly, Warren took hold of the top of the blanket and started pulling it toward the foot of the bed. Underneath the blanket was a red sheet. Warren thought at first that the red sheet just meant it was for a kid, since all kids liked bright colors.

Suddenly, Warren realized the sheet was soaking wet. It wasn't a red sheet, it was a sheet soaked in blood.

Warren looked over at Ty and knew that he had come to the same conclusion.

Slowly, Warren pulled the sheet back, then both he and Ty gasped in horror.

"Oh, my God." Ty exclaimed.

"What is it?" Lisa asked as she came through the curtain.

Ty immediately blocked Lisa's view, took her by the arm and led her back out into the hallway.

"What's wrong?" Lisa insisted, trying to break loose from Ty's grip and go back into the cubicle.

"Just wait out here." Ty told her in a commanding voice.

"Is Scotty sleeping?" Lisa asked.

"Yeah." Was all Ty said. He gave Krys a look. She immediately took hold of Lisa, turned her back toward the nurse's station and started walking down the hall.

Krys and Lisa had stood by the desk for only a few minutes when Ty and Warren joined them. Warren's face was ashen and Lisa knew immediately that Scotty wasn't sleeping. He was dead.

"How?" Lisa asked Warren.

"You don't want to know." Warren told her.

"Yes, I do." Lisa insisted.

Warren took Lisa's hand in his but she pulled away from him.

"Tell me or I'll go see for myself." Lisa said.

Warren sighed, knowing that Lisa meant what she said.

"He's gone. That's all you need to know." Warren said.

Lisa took a step toward the hallway leading back to Scotty's cubicle.

"Okay. Okay." Warren said. "He's gone. They tore him apart. You don't need to see him. It's something no one needs to see. And it's something I'll carry with me until the day I die."

Without another word, Warren took Lisa's hand in his and started walking back toward her cubicle. This time Lisa didn't pull away from him. Krys and Ty walked silently behind them.

When they were about ten feet from the double doors, the short rings of the fire alarm finally fell silent. They could hear the clicking noise of the double doors ahead of them as the locks disengaged automatically.

When Ty pushed the door open, standing on the other side were Andy, Jacob, Cassy, Larry and Rick.

"This must be your Lisa," Rick said as he took a step forward, his hand outstretched, ready to shake Lisa's hand.

Lisa immediately shrunk away from Rick, grabbing Warren's arm and backing up behind him, putting Warren between her and Rick as a shield.

"It's okay," Warren told her, "he's on our side."

"But, he's…" Lisa began.

"I know." Warren said soothingly, "but not like Blake."

"We all have a lot of questions and a lot of explaining to do." Larry stated. "By the way, Lisa, I'm Larry Moore, Chief of Police here in Denver. I'm glad to make your acquaintance."

Lisa moved to Warren's side, then stuck her hand out to shake Larry's.

"And this is my good friend, Rick Cartier. It's because of him we knew you were still alive."

Lisa remained wary and no one pushed her any further.

"Do we need to get Dr. Asher's permission so that Lisa can leave?" Warren asked.

"I don't think that will be necessary." Larry told Warren. "Our Dr. Asher is now ashes on the waiting room floor."

"You're kidding. Is that what caused the fire alarm?"

"Nope. It was the first vampire I shot with one of my arrows." Jacob volunteered.

"Since when does a wooden arrow cause a vampire to go up in flames?" Ty asked.

"Since I rubbed holy water over all of them." Andy spoke up.

"So the good doctor wasn't so good after all?" Warren mused.

"He was good enough to fool all of us; that is, except for Rick." Andy informed Warren. "He broke the doctor's neck slicker than shit."

"By the way," Andy continued, "thanks, Rick." Andy took a step forward, then shook Rick's hand exuberantly.

"You all go ahead and get Lisa out of here. I'll take care of cleaning up this mess. I'll be out at Cassy's in the morning to take Lisa's statement," Larry told them.

"Come on." Warren stated to everyone, "Let's get Lisa back to Cassy's. Is there a store open this late so we can get her some clothes?"

"There's a big Walmart on the way home." Cassy volunteered.

"Oh boy, shopping." Krys laughed.

"By the sound of her voice, you all should realize that Krys hates shopping." Ty said.

"I never would have guessed." Andy laughed.

"Anyhow," Ty said, "three women shopping for clothes together is a major accomplishment. Hope you guys aren't tired. It's gonna be a long, long night."

CHAPTER 27

The girls spent almost two hours in the store shopping. Ty had given Krys his credit card and told her to make sure everyone was taken care of. Krys took Ty at his word and, when the girls came out of the store, each one was pushing a buggy full of bags. Lisa's buggy had a suitcase on top of the bags. They were all talking and laughing as they came across the lot. Jacob and Ty helped unload the bags into the RV.

"Any place open for dinner this late?" Ty asked Cassy.

"There's a Big Boy and a Pancake House down the road." She told him.

"Which one has the better food or steak?" Warren asked.

"The Pancake House. They've got a good variety of food."

"That's it then. We all celebrate at the Pancake House." Ty stated.

Cassy, Jacob and Andy piled into her jeep. Warren helped Lisa into the passenger seat of his truck, then went around and got in through the driver's door. Ty and Krys were already seated in the back seat. When everyone was settled in, Warren followed Cassy back down Colfax. They were soon pulling into the parking lot of the Pancake House.

There were only two other cars on the lot, so Warren took up a space near the door, not caring if it was a handicap spot. They all walked into the restaurant together.

The hostess greeted them, told the waiters they needed a table for seven, then offered them seats on the couches by the door while the tables were being set up.

It only took the waiters a few minutes and then one of them appeared by the hostess's station and led them to the tables they had arranged to accommodate their party.

As soon as they were seated, the waiter gave them menus and took their drink orders.

Five minutes later, he brought them their drinks and took their orders.

"I didn't realize I was so hungry again." Jacob commented.

"Guess that's what fighting vampires will do to a person, even a skinny little brother like you." Cassy said, poking Jacob in the arm.

They all talked about the weather and other news-worthy items, everything except what was really on their minds.

"Warren," Andy began, "you and Lisa can take the guest room. Me and Jacob will crash in the craft room tonight."

"You don't have to do that." Warren protested.

"Yes, we do." Jacob countered. "We want to be closer to the front door so we can keep track of the animals, especially Mickey."

"You don't think Blake would hurt him, do you?" Cassy asked, the worry evident in her voice.

"Blake will hurt anyone or anything that gets in his way." Lisa said emphatically.

"What about Sam and Bright Eyes?" Cassy asked, getting more and more anxious about her pets.

"Unfortunately, neither one of them would be a match for Blake or any of his kind." Andy said, putting his arm around Cassy, trying to reassure her. "Don't worry. We won't let anything happen to either one of them."

"Who is Sam and what is Bright Eyes?" Lisa asked Cassy.

"Sam is Sam Elliot Minsky, my bobcat. Bright Eyes is a Husky mixed with wolf that I rescued from a shelter. You've got to see them to believe how well behaved they are and how great they get along with each other. Sam goes with me in the semi when I'm driving, he loves to ride." Cassy explained.

"I can't wait to meet them. They sound very special." Lisa said.

The waiter returned with a tray full of plates, followed by the other waiter with another tray. They distributed the meals, asked if everyone was okay on their drinks, then once again left them to their meals.

Cassy said a short prayer and they all dug in. The food was actually very good and the waiter returned frequently to refill their drinks and to take away any empty plates or bowls.

Everyone turned down dessert but lingered over their drinks.

"Time to get home." Cassy announced.

Ty grabbed the check. Everyone left a sizeable tip and then they all headed toward the door. Once they were all seated in their respective vehicles, Cassy headed back onto Colfax with Warren following close behind.

The moon was full and looked so close to the ground, it seemed to be almost touching the street ahead of them. It was bright and seemed to light their way home.

It had been a very long but prosperous day. Everyone realized how tired they were and how much they were looking forward to a good nights sleep.

CHAPTER 28

Lisa and Warren slept in the guest room. Warren had helped her remove tags, fold clothes and put them away in the suitcase.

"Will they all fit?" he asked.

"Of course. I didn't buy that much, just enough for a few days. I didn't want to take advantage of Ty's generosity."

"What about the other girls?"

"Cassy just got a couple pairs of jeans and a couple shirts. Krys bought a few new outfits and a couple of sexy negligees."

"So many bags for so few clothes?"

"Krys got some things for each of you guys and some toys and treats for the animals. She bought some groceries too. Said they had been mooching off of Cassy's kitchen far too long already."

"That explains the full buggies. Did you get a sexy negligee too?" Warren asked hopefully.

"Me? No. Not yet."

"What do you mean not yet?"

"I'm going to wait for our honeymoon, then I'll get the sexy stuff." Lisa told him, smiling, then moving closer to hug him tightly.

Not knowing what to say but being happier at that moment than he had ever been before, all Warren could do was put his arms around her and hold her tightly to him.

They sat down on the bed, continuing to hold each other, neither one of them saying a word. When they parted, Lisa got up and stripped out of the scrubs. She put on a pair of panties and a matching bra.

"You lied to me." Warren said.

"I lied? What did I lie about?" Lisa asked, puzzled.

"You said you didn't buy anything sexy. What do you call that outfit?"

"Comfortable. I call it comfortable. But if it bothers you, I can put the scrubs back on."

"Oh no you don't." Warren laughed. "Sexy to me may not be sexy to you. But you won't be changing out of that outfit any time soon."

Warren stripped down to his boxers and they got into bed. They lay there holding each other until they fell into a restful sleep.

CHAPTER 29

The next morning, the sun was bright and the sky was clear blue with just a few wispy clouds scattered here and there. Cassy was up early, had coffee brewing and was starting to cook some side pork. Soon, Lisa walked out from the bedroom and Krys came in the front door, both ready to help.

By the time the men arrived at the dining room table, the side pork was fried and eggs were being whipped up. The men sat quietly at the dining room table drinking their coffee.

Suddenly, Mickey stood up from beside Andy's chair, walked across the living room and stood by the doggy door whining but not attempting to go through it to get outside. Both Sam and Bright Eyes stood silently behind Mickey, as if to back him up.

"Something's wrong." Andy whispered to Jacob.

Warren looked up from his coffee as Andy motioned for him to follow.

Andy walked quietly across the living room, past the three animals. He slowly opened the door and had his hand on the screen door when he stopped dead in his tracks.

"What the hell?" Andy asked loudly.

The girls came out of the kitchen.

"Stay in there." Andy told the girls, motioning for them to stop, then waving them back into the kitchen.

Jacob and Warren came up behind Andy and stood staring out at the deck.

"Not again." Warren said as he moved to follow Andy out the door.

The deck was covered in blood along with pieces of flesh and clumps of hair. They knew immediately it was an animal but did not recognize what it could have been because not one piece was more than an inch in diameter. It looked as if it had been put through a shredder. All they could determine was that it was a fairly large animal.

"Thank God all of our animals were inside last night." Jacob commented.

Warren went back into the house. All three animals continued to stand by the front door, none of them attempting to leave the house. As he turned to walk back outside, Bright Eyes moved up closer to the door, sat down and started howling.

Cassy ran into the room, thinking her dog had been hurt somehow. She immediately knelt down on the floor and consoled Bright Eyes. He eventually calmed back down but then lay down with his nose near the door, not moving.

"Keep them all inside for now." Warren said as he stepped back out through the door. When he walked back onto the deck, Andy and Jacob were still standing in place, staring at the mess.

"Look over there" Andy said, pointing to a corner of the deck.

Written in the blood were the words "Mickies next."

"Must have been Blake's familiar guy. He still can't spell worth a shit." Jacob said.

As they stood staring at the gruesome sight, Ty came walking toward the house from his truck.

"Oh, shit." Ty exclaimed when he came up the steps and saw what the guys were staring at. "This is fresh, had to happen in the last 10 to 15 minutes."

"How do you know that?" Jacob asked.

"Because Krys left the truck about 10 to 15 minutes ago to go into the house. If it had been here then, she would have screamed out. This could have very well been Krys and not some poor animal." Ty said, turning pale and looking very disturbed. His cheeks soon turned red and the others knew how mad he was getting, neither of them commenting but letting him get his anger over with.

"Do we clean it up or do we wait and let Larry see what's happened?" Jacob asked.

"Let's clean it up." Warren said. "The girls don't need to see this. We can keep the remains in a garbage bag in case Larry wants to take it to the precinct."

"At least it's an animal this time." Ty commented.

"What do you mean, this time?" Jacob asked Ty.

"The last time it was human entrails and feces all over Lisa's front door, porch and window." Ty explained.

"Was a message left that time too?" Andy asked.

"Yeah, it said 'Lisa, you're next'."

"And look what happened to her." Andy said, looking around the porch at the mess.

"Just keep Mickey close to you. When we go back out later in the RV, we'll take him with us. None of us will let Blake get his hands on him." Warren stated.

"Andy, you and Warren go on inside and keep the girls and the animals in there. Me and Jacob will clean this up." Ty said.

"Not until I take pictures." Jacob said as he headed toward the front door. "Let me get my digital. I'll be right back."

Andy and Warren went into the house and sat at the dining room table, continually talking to the girls in the kitchen about everyday things.

Jacob got his camera from a bag in the living room and went back outside. After he took the pictures, he went down the deck steps, around the deck toward the back of the house to Cassy's shed. He came back out with a long garden hose which he hooked up to a spigot on the side of the house. He then removed one of the hardy panels from the house and turned the water back on. He had a garbage bag which he proceeded to cut into pieces.

"What's that for?" Ty asked.

"You don't want to pick this stuff up with your bare hands, do you?"

"Point taken." TY took some of the strips from Jacob and proceeded to pick up animal pieces off the deck and stow them in the garbage bag, Jacob working beside him as they made their way across the deck. When they were done, Ty carried the filled bag to the bottom of the stairs and set it on the grass near the bottom step. Jacob then hosed the deck down.

When they were done, Jacob turned the water off and closed up the hardy panel. He then rolled up the hose and returned it to the shed.

"We'll leave the bag down there so the girls don't see it and it'll be handy if Larry wants to take it in and find out what kind of animal it was, not that it matters now anyway." Ty said.

"It might matter to someone if it was their pet." Jacob pointed out. "And I think it mattered to Bright Eyes. Did you see how he reacted when he got a sniff of that mess. I have a feeling it was an animal he knew."

"I understand about it being someone's pet. I just assumed it would be a wild animal and not one that belonged to anyone else. I never thought of it being a pet."

Ty and Jacob finally went back into the house. They both noticed immediately that Bright Eyes was still lying on the carpet by the door, his nose as close to the door as he could get without getting it hit when the door was closed.

"What was it this time?" Lisa asked.

"You don't want to know." Ty told her.

"Yes, I do." Lisa insisted.

Ty described to her what they had found on the deck.

"It's all gone now, all cleaned up." He told her.

"At least he killed an animal this time instead of another human being." Lisa said.

CHAPTER 30

"Knock, knock." Larry called from outside the screen door.

"So come on in, already." Cassy called out from the kitchen.

"Bacon smells good. Got any coffee to go with it?" Larry asked as he took a seat at the table.

"You must have woke up on the right side of the bed this morning, Larry." Andy noted. "You're sarcastic as ever."

"So, why is your deck all wet?" Larry asked.

Without a word, Jacob showed Larry the pictures he had taken.

"Okay. Is this something Blake does often?" Larry inquired.

"He was nicer this time," Lisa said. "Last time it was human intestines with blood and shit."

"Nice guy." Larry commented. "By the way, we had officers go through the hospital after you left last night. They eliminated a nurse and one more orderly."

"Seems to me that Blake's been pretty busy since coming to Denver." Andy commented.

"I talked with Kee, back in Kalamazoo, and he said there it was mostly homes, not big businesses like a hospital" Larry stated.

"In Hebert," Warren interrupted, "it was all houses, either inside or underneath."

"You want to get started?" Lisa asked, looking directly at Larry, as she walked into the dining room.

"If you don't mind." Larry said. "I'd like to record your statement. I just need your permission."

"Fine with me." Lisa told him.

Larry pulled out a small recorder from his shirt pocket along with two extra tapes. He checked the recorder to make sure the tape inside was wound back to its beginning. He set the recorder on the table, turned it on and started the interview.

"This is Larry Moore, it is Tuesday, December 15th and I am interviewing Lisa King, a detective from Kalamazoo, Michigan. Okay, Lisa, if you'll start from the beginning."

"My name is Lisa King. I am from Kalamazoo, Michigan. Approximately six weeks ago I was at my residence. I was sitting in the kitchen with a cup of tea when I heard a loud crash in my living room. I was still in uniform. I pulled out my service revolver and walked from the kitchen to the living room doorway. My front picture window was shattered. There was a man getting up off the floor by the couch. He looked at me, then ran to my front door. I yelled at him to stop. He opened the door and said "Come in". I fired once, he turned to face me, made a move toward me and I fired again. He fell where he stood."

Lisa paused for only a second to take a sip of her coffee.

"When I looked up, Blake was standing inside my house and Pat, my sister, was walking through the doorway. I just stood there, not believing my eyes. I had put a stake through my sister's heart, she should have been dead."

Lisa stopped once more, this time to wipe a tear from her eye. She then resumed her story.

"Blake said 'Hello, Lisa'. I saw Pat swing at me, she was so fast I didn't have time to react. The next thing I knew, I woke up in the motorhome handcuffed to the kitchen table leg. It was still dark out, so I just assumed we were still in Kalamazoo. I was alone for about an hour or so before Blake and Pat came back into the RV."

Lisa stopped to take another sip of her coffee.

"Blake explained to me that I had a choice. I could either drive the motorhome during the day to whatever destination he desired, or I could become like Pat and drive at night instead. I figured I'd play along with him until I had a chance to run. Of course, he kept my ankle cuffed to the driver's seat during the day and then I was cuffed to the table leg at night."

"Did you stop often on the trip from Michigan to Colorado?" Larry asked.

"I drove only six or seven hours a day. He would have the route all planned and had me stop in truck stops or rest areas."

'You didn't stop in any RV parks?"

"Not until we got to Denver. He said if he and Pat turned the truckers, he could create an army all over the states and it would increase that much more rapidly. Every time I'd stop, he'd let me cook myself some supper and give me time to clean up afterward. Then he'd handcuff me again and they'd go out for an hour or two."

"How did you get away a few nights ago at the truck stop here?" Larry asked her.

"Pat put the cuffs on me but then was distracted when Blake demanded she hurry. She didn't lock the cuff to the table leg. I waited about half an hour before I ran out of the RV. It was parked near the back of the truck stop parking lot, in between two other trucks. I knocked on one of the truck doors but no one answered. I ran across the lot and into the restaurant and started screaming for help. Unfortunately, Blake and Pat came in right behind me. Pat held me while Blake made sure no one there remembered me ever being in there. He carried me back to the motorhome and cuffed me to the table leg again. But how did you know about that night? I thought he had hypnotized everyone in there to not remember anything."

"A trucker was in the bathroom and he witnessed it all. But it was our bad luck that he didn't witness what you all left in. He was busy yelling at the other customers because they didn't attempt to help you. He got very angry at them for ignoring what went down. He's the only one who remembered any of what happened. And he was very remorseful for not trying to help you out. He came down to the station and made a statement for us."

Larry stopped to change the tape in the recorder.

"Go ahead, Lisa." Larry urged.

"After that night, he had me park in rest areas and then in the RV park where you found me."

"What about the other guy in the motorhome. Who was he and where did he come from?"

"He recruited Chad in a truck stop but I never knew his last name. From all I could gather, Chad had either walked away from his truck or got fired. He was looking for a ride and, of course, Blake offered him one."

"After that, Chad started driving and I just stayed cuffed to the table. Chad never questioned me or talked to me or otherwise acknowledged my presence."

Lisa stopped as tears started rolling down her cheeks. Warren put his arms around her protectively. Larry turned the recorder off.

"If this is too hard, we can finish it later on." Larry told her.

"No. I want to get this over with now."

Larry turned the recorder back on and motioned to Lisa to continue.

"The night before we pulled into the RV park, we were in a rest area. Blake and Pat went out as usual but when they came back in, Blake was carrying Scotty. He carried him under his arm like a sack of potatoes. I was lying down on the fold-down bed in the kitchen. Blake threw the boy at me and said, 'Here's a present to keep you company. Don't get too used to him, neither one of you will be here much longer."

"Scotty immediately cuddled up in my arms, he was so small and so scared. I held him close and talked to him softly, trying to calm him down, he was shaking so hard. We both finally fell asleep."

"The next morning, Chad took my cuff off and had me make breakfast for the three of us. I got Scotty to eat some eggs and drink some orange juice. When we were done, Chad cuffed me back up and started driving.

I got Scotty to talk a little bit. He was in the rest area with his mom and dad. He went to the bathroom with his dad. He was washing his hands when Blake walked through the door. Blake walked right up to Scotty's dad, pushed him back into a stall. Scotty stood staring at Blake's back and heard his dad scream one time. Then he heard the sucking sounds. He was so scared, he just stood there, couldn't move. When Blake came back out of the stall he just stood staring at Scotty."

"Scotty said he tried to look around Blake to see if his dad was coming out too. All he could see where his dad's lower legs and feet on the floor. Blake picked him up and walked out of the restroom. Scotty said there was a lady waiting outside of the lady's bathroom and she had blood on her mouth and chin. They walked back to the RV. Scotty kept looking back to see if his mom and dad were coming but they never showed up."

"The next day, Chad drove around the country side most of the day and then, just before sunset, he pulled into the RV park. He and Blake had a long conversation. Pat walked past me on her way to the front of the RV. She stopped and looked at me but there was no emotion in her at all. She told me it was almost over. That's all she said. Later that day, Chad must have hit me from behind because the next thing I remember is waking up in the hospital."

Lisa took a long breath, then looked up at Larry expectantly. "Okay?"

"Okay." Larry said. He turned the recorder off, then reached across the table and patted Lisa on the hand. "You did good."

"Do you think you can remember some of the places you stopped at each night?" Larry asked.

"I can pull up maps from Michigan to here in Denver, if that would help." Jacob volunteered.

"It would help," Lisa told Jacob. "Thank you."

"Alright." Larry said, "now down to the real reason I'm here."

Everyone looked over at Larry, expecting some kind of bad news by the way he talked.

"What's that?" Andy asked.

"Breakfast, of course." Larry said.

Cassy served a crustless quiche, fresh side pork, homemade biscuits and fresh fruit for breakfast. Everyone ate with relish. After breakfast, they all lingered over their coffee.

"So, what's next?" Andy asked Larry. "And don't say lunch, okay?"

"Now, we go after vampires that Rick can't convert."

"Are you going to enforce a curfew?" Warren asked, thinking about Hebert and the curfew they had to enforce when they were fighting their own vampires.

"I really don't see how it would be possible to have a curfew here in Denver. We're just too big." Larry answered.

"True." Warren agreed.

"So, what do you want all of us to do?" Andy asked.

"For today, relax and get some well needed rest. Tonight, I want Jacob and Ty to accompany me and Rick on a tour."

"A tour? Of what? Ty asked.

"Of downtown Denver. Rick suggested we get together in the area around the hospital, especially since we found so many working inside last night."

"Why just the two of us?" Ty asked.

"Jacob because of his crossbow and arrows. Ty because of your experience and knowledge of Blake. Rick to try and convince them to do it his way. Me for backup."

"Don't you want the rest of us to come too? More backup?" Warren asked.

"Not really. I believe you, Andy and Lisa are better off here. Cassy hasn't been involved in any of this before, so she's really a rookie. She might freak out if she sees us eliminate one of them."

"Did you forget where I was last night?" Cassy spoke up. "I saw that doctor and that other man eliminated, as in bursting into flames. I didn't freak out then."

"But you're not a hunter yet." Larry reiterated. " Seeing it happen and making it happen are two different things."

"Well, I'll be a hunter by tonight. Me and Jacob are going to be doing some target practicing out back. I'll be as good if not better than him before the day is over." Cassy said, looking straight at Larry the entire time.

"Okay." Jacob interrupted. "So what time do you want to meet and where?"

"I'll pick you up after 8 p.m. There'll be one more going with us tonight. But he'll probably arrive before I can get out of the station. You'll hear him coming before you see him. Be nice, he's one of ours." Larry said.

With that, Larry stood up and walked across the living room and out the door. He picked up the bag that Ty had put at the foot of the stairs, threw it in the back of his pickup and left.

"So, what do we do, twiddle our thumbs all day?" Lisa asked Warren.

"After the incident on the deck this morning, I believe Larry's thinking about keeping you safe. Maybe, just maybe, he feels that me and Warren can keep you that way." Andy said.

"I've known Larry a long time," Andy continued, "and I'm with him in so far as I believe he needs to assess the situation downtown before anything drastic happens. He needs to plan ahead but knows that there's not much time for a lot of planning."

"Larry's thinking like a cop. If there's a nest where all of this is basically originating from, find that nest and eliminate it. Then all the fledglings that have flown the nest will be easier to find and get rid of." Warren added.

"Well, Larry needs to know that keeping me out of this is not a forever thing." Lisa insisted. "I want Blake disposed of as much as TY does, maybe even more now. And this time, I'm not stopping anyone from disposing of Pat permanently."

"Let's not forget Rick. You don't think he'll be able to talk Pat into taking the serum?" Warren asked.

"Not really. She follows Blake around like a little lost puppy. Plus, she showed no emotion or even recognition towards me. The only time I saw her smile was when she'd come back to the motorhome after being gone a couple of hours or so during the night. Then she'd be covered in blood. It was then and only then that she seemed happy at all."

"So, are you okay with Pat being eliminated completely?" Ty asked.

"Yes. Now I am." Lisa answered with conviction.

"Well, I feel confident that Warren, Andy and Krys can keep both of you safe out here." Jacob said. "I know that Sam and the dogs will let you know if anything is going on outside of the house. But I think I'd keep that doggy door of yours locked up tight once darkness falls."

"I intend to, little brother. I know that Sam and Bright Eyes, and even Mickey if it came to it, would defend us with their lives. I just don't want it to go that far."

"Well, Larry has been having more crossbows and more wooden arrows made over the last two days." Andy said. "So, if you don't mind, Jacob, would you leave yours here with us?"

"No problem. I know how accurate you are with it, I've watched you get better and better before we left Hebert. And knowing Cassy like I do, I'm sure she'll be just as accurate before the day is over."

"Better, little brother." Cassy said, smiling. "Better."

"Oh, and Ty. Before you leave out tonight, would you mind getting us some stakes and hammers and, of course, holy water out of your truck. I don't want Krys trying to retrieve that stuff after you're gone and I know I'm not going out after dark." Warren said.

"On my way," Ty said as he walked quickly out the front door.

Krys had silently gotten up out of her chair and followed Ty out the door. When she caught up with him at the bottom of the patio steps, he took her hand and they walked across the lawn together.

"It seems so strange to see so much love come out of such a horrendous situation." Lisa said, looking directly at Warren.

"Nothing in this world could ever be more amazing as far as I'm concerned." Warren told her as he leaned over and kissed her.

"Okay, you two," Andy interjected. "Let's not get all sentimental over this."

"That's right. No sentiment." Cassy added. "Just find me a man and find a girl for Jacob, and we can all get kissy, kissy like you two."

"Oh, my goodness." Lisa said. "I really do believe we've started something, Warren."

"Start anything you like," Cassy said, smiling, "just make sure we all get set up before this is all over, okay?"

"Okay." Warren said, smiling at Cassy, then turning to Lisa and giving her a long, long kiss."

"That's our cue, Sis," Jacob said as he got up from the table, "to get to work outside practicing."

"Not a problem. It's nice and sunny out and I'm ready to show you up."

"Good God, now I have to listen to this too." Jacob said as he picked up the bows and started for the door. "So, make yourself useful, already, get the arrows and come on."

"I think I better go referee." Andy said as he grabbed his cup of coffee and headed toward the door. "Old rivalries die hard. Come on, Mickey, let's go."

Andy walked out the door with Mickey close behind, following Cassy and Jacob. Warren and Lisa could hear the two young ones still teasing each other as they walked down the steps of the patio and then headed toward the back of the house.

"Think they left on purpose?" Warren asked.

"Of course they did." Lisa told him. "You want to take advantage of that?" She took Warren's hand and led him down the hallway toward the bedroom they were sharing.

Warren followed Lisa down the hallway. They entered the bedroom and he closed the door quietly behind them.

CHAPTER 31

The day seemed to drag for those at Cassy's house. But downtown at the police station, it was anything but quiet.

Larry arrived early to his office, having come directly from Cassy's. He brought the sack full of remains from the porch with him. He told his secretary to have one of the boys from the lab pick it up as soon as possible and get back to him with the results by this afternoon. He explained his only question was what it had been, what kind of animal.

He finished filling out the incident report regarding the hospital the night before. He always had paperwork at his apartment for just such occasions too. He told his friends that that was why he wasn't married, his job hours were 24/7.

He took out another incident report from his file cabinet and started filling it out. It was a short report since he had only seen the pictures and had word of mouth from Ty and Jacob as to the mess on Cassy's deck.

The man from the lab came up to collect the garbage bag. Two hours later, he called Larry to report it was the remains of a very large wolf. They estimated it was an alpha male by the amount of pieces, age and length of the hair.

Larry called out to Cassy's and asked to speak to Andy. He explained the results of the lab work.

"I want you to know," Larry continued, "why I chose Ty and Jacob to go out tonight."

"You don't have to explain." Andy told him. "They're younger guys and get around better."

"No, that's not it. Tonight is like a foraging expedition. I basically want to scope things out, try to figure out if Blake is coming downtown and approximately how many of these things we're dealing with. And if Rick is going to be able to convert any of them or if we will have to dispose of them."

"And…" Andy prompted when Larry stopped talking.

"And I want you and Warren out there with Cassy and Krys, and especially with Lisa. If Blake sent his guys after Lisa in a public place like a hospital, I'm pretty sure he won't have any qualms about coming out to the house, especially when it sits in the middle of nowhere. And I can't think of anyone more qualified to fight Blake than you, Warren, Lisa and Krys."

"Okay, point taken." Andy said. "So, who else is coming out here to help protect us?"

"Like I said before, you'll hear him before you see him and that's all I'm going to say. Except, I've changed my mind about one thing. I'm going to have him stay out there with you tonight instead of going back to the hospital with us. Since we're just going to be observing tonight, I really feel he'll be more helpful out there than downtown. See you later. Bye."

With that, Andy sat listening to the dial tone.

"Well," Andy said out loud to himself, "at least he said bye."

CHAPTER 32

The morning went by slowly. For lunch the girls went out and got hamburgers. Everyone took turns in the shower except Krys. She was able to lounge in Cassy's garden tub with lots of bubbles.

Jacob spent the later part of the afternoon on the laptop. He was very secretive regarding what he was up to. No one bothered him, knowing that whatever it was he was working on, it would benefit them one way or another.

Around 4 o'clock, Jacob stood up and blurted out, "That's it." He stretched elaborately, then joined the rest of them in the living room.

"Okay, little brother, "Cassy said, "what did you do now?"

"Hopefully, I just got us a lot more help finding Blake." Jacob said as he sat down on the couch next to Andy.

"Are you going to spill the beans or not?" Andy asked.

"I constructed a web page that extends out to Facebook, Twitter and a dozen more social medias."

"Internet?" Cassy asked.

"Yeah, internet. Now, Ty and Krys, answer one question for me. How many truckers out there have computers in their trucks?"

"A lot." Ty answered. "But mostly they use them to interact with their dispatchers for loads and directions and that sort of thing."

"Do you have one?"

"Krys has a laptop but I don't use it."

"Okay, Krys." Jacob continued, turning his attention her way." What do you do on your laptop?"

"I'm mostly on Facebook talking to my cousins up in North Dakota."

"And if you were on Facebook and got an emergency post for truckers, would you open it and read it?"

"Of course I would."

"Good. Then that tells me that other truckers would look at it too. That's what I was hoping for."

"So, if I open up your post, what exactly is it going to say?" Krys asked.

"I printed it out so you could all read it." With that, Jacob stood up, walked over to the dining room table, picked up some papers and proceeded to hand them out around the room.

> *"ATTENTION ALL TRUCKERS: THROUGH THE CHATTER ON THE CB, I'M SURE YOU'RE AWARE OF THE PROBLEMS INFECTING THE U.S. IT AFFECTED THE SMALL TOWN OF HEBERT, ILLINOIS AND CLOSED THEIR TRUCK STOP FOR A SHORT WHILE. THE ORIGINAL OWNERS WILL NEVER BE ABLE TO RETURN TO THEIR DREAM; THAT IS, SERVING YOU TRUCKERS.*
>
> *THEN KALAMAZOO WAS A TARGET CITY. THE PROBLEM WAS ELIMINATED BY THE POLICE DEPARTMENT WITH THE HELP OF VOLUNTEERS FROM HEBERT AND ALSO SOME TRUCKERS. CHICAGO ALSO GOT ITS FAIR SHARE OF PROBLEMS.*
>
> *NOW, DENVER IS BEING TARGETED. THE PERPETRATORS, BLAKE AND PAT, HAVE BEEN IN THE DENVER AREA FOR AT LEAST A WEEK OR MORE NOW.*
>
> *THEY ARE TRAVELING IN A WINNEBAGO JOURNEY MOTORHOME. IT IS THE NEWER COPPER COLOR WITH SILVER SWIRLS. NO EXTENSIONS.*

THE RV IS BEING DRIVEN BY AN APPROXIMATELY 30 TO 35-YEAR-OLD MAN NAMED CHAD. HE IS AROUND 6 FEET TALL, VERY THIN WITH SHAGGY BROWN HAIR.

BLAKE IS OVER 6 FEET TALL, BLACK HAIR AND PALE COMPLEXION. HE HAS NO QUALMS IN ADMITTING TO BEING OVER 100 YEARS OLD. HE LOOKS TO BE AROUND 50, UNTIL HE FEEDS. THEN HE CAN PASS FOR 40. HE WALKS WITH A REGAL STEP AND DEMANDS TO BE HONORED BY ALL WHO MEET HIM. HE CAN LOOK YOU IN THE EYE AND EITHER YOU END UP INFECTED OR YOU DO NOT REMEMBER HIM OR ANYTHING THAT HAS HAPPENED AROUND YOU. THIS CAN BE VERIFIED BY THE SAPP BROTHERS TRUCK STOP HERE IN DENVER.

PAT IS TALL, APPROXIMATELY 5' 7", A THIN BEAUTY. SHE HAS LONG STRAIGHT BROWN HAIR AND BROWN EYES. HER HAIR LACKS THE LUSTER OF LIVING HAIR AND HER EYES ARE VACANT. SHE CAN BE VERY SEDUCTIVE AND IS AS BIG A THREAT AS BLAKE.

IF YOU'VE BEEN MONITORING YOUR CB, YOU ARE AWARE OF THE FACT THAT I'M TALKING ABOUT ***MODERN DAY VAMPIRES****. BLAKE ORIGINALLY TRAVELED CROSS COUNTRY BY DRIVING A SEMI AT NIGHT. HE MAY STILL REVERT BACK TO THAT MODE OF TRANSPORTATION.* ***BE AWARE****.*

IF YOU SEE THEM OR THEIR MOTORHOME IN OR AROUND THE DENVER AREA, DO NOT APPROACH THEM. THEY CAN AND SHOULD BE CONSIDERED EXTREMELY DANGEROUS. THEY HAVE NO EMOTIONS, NO MORALS. BLAKE INTENDS FOR THE U.S. TO EVENTUALLY CONSIST ENTIRELY OF HIS FOLLOWERS WITH HIM IN CHARGE. HE HAS NO RESPECT FOR THE HUMAN RACE, CONSIDERS US CATTLE TO BE HERDED AND, AS HORRIFIC AS IT SOUNDS, RECRUITED OR DISPOSED OF AT HIS LEISURE.

PLEASE, IF YOU SEE BLAKE OR PAT, OR ANYONE ELSE WHO ACTS SUSPICIOUS, CALL THE DENVER POLICE AT (303) 333-3333.

WE TRUCKERS NEED TO UNITE TO ERADICATE THIS VERMIN. IT'S TIME TO BE THE HUNTERS, NOT THE HUNTED."

"So, what do you all think?" Jacob asked when everyone had finished reading and put the papers down.

"I think you're as long-winded as ever." Cassy began. "But I also think you've pretty much covered it all."

"What about you, Ty?" Jacob asked hopefully.

"I'd read it and I'd believe it. But then I've also lived it." Ty answered.

"If I was on Facebook, I'd read it." Krys interjected. "And I'd believe it. It's been all over the CB. There can't be many truckers out there who don't know what's been going on."

"Well, it's posted. So hopefully it will help us find Blake." Jacob added.

"What about this Rick fella?" Ty asked.

"What about him?" Warren responded.

"Do you think he can do any good just talking to them?"

"Guess you and Jacob will find out tonight." Warren said, looking from Jacob over to Ty, then back to Jacob.

Cassy got up and headed toward the kitchen, Krys and Lisa following close behind.

"How about soup and sandwiches for supper, something light?" Cassy asked the other two.

"Canned soup?" Krys asked.

"No, homemade chicken soup."

"My kind of cook. What can we do?"

"I've already got the broth cooked. You can chop up the leftover chicken pieces for chicken salad sandwiches."

The girls got to work and half an hour later, everyone was seated at the kitchen table enjoying the meal. After dinner, the girls told the guys to go relax and they'd clean up.

Everyone seemed a little bit more on edge, now that the sun had set and darkness was descending. The animals, who had all been peacefully sleeping, had picked up their heads and perked their ears, more attentive now.

Just as the girls finished in the kitchen and were headed into the living room, there was an earth-shattering noise down the street from Cassy's house. All three animals were immediately up off the floor and making a beeline for the doggy door. They quickly disappeared outside. The noise became almost deafening as it got closer to the house. Then, all of a sudden, it was quiet again.

Cassy ran after Sam and Bright Eyes, frightened for their safety after this morning's episode on the deck. When she exited the door, followed by the rest of them, she stopped short, realizing it was now totally dark.

Sam, Bright Eyes and Mickey were at the curb surrounding a man who was kneeling beside a huge black motorcycle. He was laughing loudly as Sam licked his face and both Bright Eyes and Mickey were nuzzling him, trying hard to get his attention.

"Sam, Bright Eyes, here." Cassy commanded.

Both animals reluctantly turned and slowly walked back to the deck. They sat on either side of Cassy but continued to look back down the walkway toward the man.

The biker walked up onto the deck, Mickey walking close beside him.

"Hi, I'm Mike. Larry sent me." He held out his hand to Cassy.

"Wait." Jacob yelled, coming up behind Cassy.

"It's okay." Cassy said as she shook Mike's hand.

"I'm Cassy. This is my brother Jacob. And standing back there staring are Uncle Andy, Krys, Ty, Lisa and Warren."

"Pleased to meet all of you. Larry sent me to help out while Jacob and Ty are in town."

"Sounds like Larry, covering all his bases." Andy commented.

"Would you like to come in?" Cassy asked. "We're trying to keep the animals inside tonight."

"Me and Jacob are going to leave now." Ty announced. He turned and kissed Krys, assuring her that they'd be okay and they'd be back soon. He also told her to keep safe.

Warren handed Ty the keys to his pickup and wished him and Jacob good hunting.

Everyone stood on the deck as Ty and Jacob drove off.

Suddenly realizing how cold it was outside, they turned in unison and headed toward the door, walking back inside the house one by one.

Mike was the last to enter. As soon as he closed the door behind him, he locked it and then locked down the doggy door.

CHAPTER 33

Warren sat in the recliner and Lisa stretched out on the floor, sitting in between his legs. Warren could feel Lisa tensing up and was determined to keep her close.

Krys sat on the couch with Andy, both watching Mike, their suspicious natures evident in their mannerisms.

Cassy pointed to the love seat and after Mike sat down, she joined him. She was curious about this man and anxious to talk to him. She had a lot of questions she felt she needed answered.

"Anyone want a drink? I've got coffee, tea, beer or water." Cassy offered, looking from one to the other and finally at Mike.

Everyone turned down her offer.

"If I'm not being too forward, what's it like." Cassy asked Mike.

"Different. It happened five days ago. At first I was completely confused. I felt like I'd die without blood."

"Do you still crave it?" Lisa asked from across the room.

"No, not at all. Larry introduced me to Rick's doctor the night after Pat got me. I started taking the serum that night and there haven't been any more cravings, thank the Lord."

"Where did you meet Pat?" Warren asked when he felt Lisa's body go rigid at the mention of her sister's name.

"I was staking out a drug house on my bike that night and she walked past me. I couldn't help but watch her. She looked so out of place in the neighborhood where we were."

"How so?" Warren asked.

"I wasn't exactly in the best of neighborhoods. She was in a long gown and she seemed to just float past me. She's a real beauty, as you all know."

"Did she talk to you?" Lisa asked.

"As a matter of fact, yes. I kept staring after her. She turned around and came back to where I was sitting on my bike. She asked me what I was doing, said I looked out of place in that neighborhood. Kind of like the pot calling the kettle black."

Mike paused for just a minute, watching Lisa's reaction to his story. He could see her body going tense and wasn't sure if he should go on or not.

"You can go ahead," Lisa said, as if reading his mind. "It's okay."

"We talked for about ten minutes about nothing in particular. I kept thinking how it was a good cover for my stake out, not so conspicuous as just me sitting there. She was really very charming. When she said she had to go, she bent over as if to kiss me on the cheek and that's all she wrote."

"How did you find Rick?" Krys asked, making polite conversation.

"I didn't. I don't remember the rest of that night and I must have slept all the next day. I woke up the next night in an abandoned house about a block from where I had been the night before. I walked back and couldn't believe my bike was still there and still in one piece. I drove back home and immediately called the Chief. Half an hour later, he was knocking on my door with Rick, Rick's doctor and the serum."

"And now?" Cassy asked.

"And now I'm the hunter, not the hunted."

"Can I ask what you and Pat talked about?" Lisa asked him, anxious but also dreading the answer.

"It was very weird. She asked me why I was there and who I was. I told her I was a cop and I was on a stake out. Don't know why I compromised my cover like that, but I did. Every time I'd ask her a question, she would turn it around to be about me again. All I ever learned was her name."

They all sat in silence. Lisa was naturally thinking about her sister.

"While I was held captive by Blake and Pat, she never held a conversation with me. She never spoke more than a couple of words. I can't get over the fact that Pat talks to everyone but me."

"It might have been because Blake was always right there in the motorhome with the two of you." Warren suggested.

"It might also be because they knew you and what they intended to do with you. They knew you would fight them all the way and never concede to becoming one of them." Mike added. "I believe Pat asked me so many questions, probably at Blake's command, so she would know what kind of person she was infecting and how it would serve their cause. I'm a cop, imagine me infecting the rest of the police force and putting them all at Blake's disposal?"

Lisa sat pondering. She didn't know if she believed that Blake was the reason Pat could be more verbal with everyone but her. She felt she would never get any answers because sooner or later they would destroy Pat. The only consolation being that when they found Pat this time, they would hopefully also find Blake and destroy him once and for all.

CHAPTER 34

Ty and Jacob met Larry outside the police station on East Clay. Larry joined them in Warren's truck, saying it would be less conspicuous than a police vehicle, and then directed them across town to Denver General Hospital.

"We've gotten a lot of reports of strangers walking around the hospital at night. After our encounter last night, we felt it was a good place to start." Larry stated after they had been sitting in the parking lot facing the emergency room entrance for only a few minutes.

"Do you think they'll try to get inside again?" Ty asked.

"Don't know." Larry answered. "I hope not."

"Can you imagine the havoc if they did get inside with all those helpless patients?" Jacob said.

"Even worse, those patients wouldn't be so helpless afterward. They could infect the entire place and then spread out to their families, neighbors, friends, who knows how many others."

They sat watching the door for another ten minutes when they noticed a tall lady walking down the sidewalk toward the doors.

Ty immediately recognized her as Pat, Lisa's sister. Before she could reach the door, Rick appeared as if out of nowhere, stopping her in her tracks.

As they sat in the truck watching, they were close enough to see that Rick was talking quickly to Pat. Ty was shocked when he realized that Pat was actually listening and not attempting to continue into the hospital or to turn away from him.

Jacob reached over the seat for his bow and quiver.

"Wait." Ty whispered.

Jacob turned to face Ty, not understanding why Ty would stop him.

"That's Pat, Lisa's sister." Ty said. "And where there's Pat, there could be Blake."

They continued to watch Rick. At one point, he actually stood there holding Pat's hand.

All of a sudden, Blake appeared as if out of nowhere. With a sweep of his arm, he sent Pat flying across the small patch of grass and into the side of the building. She fell to the ground, motionless.

Ty grabbed the bows and handed one off to Jacob. They both exited the truck and started running toward Blake and Rick, Larry close behind with his service revolver drawn.

As they drew closer, Ty could see Blake clearly. He was facing Rick, had moved closer and was actually snarling at him.

The three men stopped abruptly when Rick raised his right arm in a gesture for them to not come any closer.

"Do you treat all your followers so gently?" Rick asked, never faltering from his position, not backing up or averting his eyes from Blake's.

"If they don't obey me, they answer with consequences." Blake answered, still staring directly at Rick.

In the background, they all heard Pat moaning in pain. None of them moved toward her, they all stood their ground. Their main objective was Blake and none of them would be deterred from that objective.

"But she was your one true love, forever." Ty interjected from where he and Jacob were standing.

"Love? What is Love?" Blake said, turning to face Ty. "Is that not one of your emotions, a human thing?"

"So why did you go back to Kalamazoo if not for her?" Ty asked, wanting Blake to continue to face him and hopefully not pay any attention to either Jacob or Larry.

"She interested me at the time. That interest is lost when she doesn't obey and do as she is told."

Out of the corner of his eye, Rick watched as Pat picked herself up off the ground and walked back to the sidewalk. He smiled slightly when she stopped next to him, listening to Blake as he talked to Ty.

"It is time to go." Blake said, looking back at Pat.

"I think not." Pat whispered.

"You would disobey me again?" Blake asked, taking a step toward Pat.

Rick quickly stepped in between the two of them.

"Even vampires have a free will, they just need a little push in the right direction. In Pat's case, we'll call it a big shove." Rick said. He faced Blake, his right hand behind his back. He gave the boys the thumbs up sign.

Jacob already had his bow cocked. He slowly brought it up, aimed directly at Blake.

Rick showed three fingers, then two, then one, then none. When his hand had formed a fist, he ducked to the right, grabbing Pat as he fell to the ground.

Both Ty and Jacob pulled the triggers on their bows and their arrows shot true, straight at Blake.

With one motion, faster than either Jacob or Ty could follow, Blake caught both arrows in midair, inches from his chest. He held them by the shaft, careful not to touch the arrow heads.

His hand began to steam and he quickly dropped the arrows to the ground. Both Jacob and Ty instantly realized that Andy had sprinkled more than just the arrowheads with holy water.

Larry had been standing observing all that was happening. He was in his firing stance and started to fire rapidly. The bullets seemed to bounce off Blake, no matter whether they hit him in the chest, shoulder or even the head.

"You puny humans. I give you credit for your efforts, no matter how fruitless they may be." Blake laughed, an evil sound that sent chills up their spines.

"Keep trying. It truly does amuse me." He told them as he turned his back to them and slowly walked away. When he was approximately 20 feet away, he disappeared completely, as if blending with the darkness.

Rick stood back up on the sidewalk. He offered Pat his hand. She took it willingly, letting him help her up off the grass. She stood beside him, still holding his hand.

"I'm going to take Patricia to my place. I have the serum stored there." Rick told them.

"Okay." Larry said. "We'll continue to stake out the hospital for a while longer."

Rick turned and walked down the sidewalk, still holding Pat's hand. She walked beside him willingly. They disappeared slowly into the night.

Larry, Jacob and Ty returned to Warren's truck.

They had been seated back in the truck for only a few minutes when Larry whispered "over there".

He pointed to his side of the truck. Walking across the parking lot toward them were three men, all looking like weight lifters, muscles exaggerated by the tight shirts they wore. They were approximately 120 feet away but continued to walk directly toward the truck very slowly. Their intentions were obvious.

Ty and Jacob jumped out of the pickup and took a stand side by side, both aiming their bows at the two men closest to them.

Larry jumped out the opposite side, then ran around the front of the truck to stand next to Ty, his Glock aimed at the man who was walking directly toward him.

When the three men had closed the gap between them, standing only approximately 20 feet away, Larry shouted, "Stop or I'll shoot."

The three men continued to advance, although slower than before, more cautiously.

Simultaneously, Ty and Jacob took aim and fired. Their aim was true. When their arrows hit, the man on the right and the one in the middle both fell to the pavement, engulfed in flames.

The third man continued to walk toward the truck, veering slightly toward Larry, not even glancing down at his companions.

"Stop!" Larry shouted again.

The man never wavered but kept advancing on Larry.

Seconds passed, Larry fired. The man was hit in the upper chest. As he fell to the pavement, he also burst into flames.

Both Ty and Jacob looked over at Larry, astonished but puzzled.

"Andy is very generous with his holy water." Larry said, turning to get back into the truck, leaving both Ty and Jacob outside, speechless.

When the flames had died down, Jacob and Ty turned back toward the truck. Larry was sitting nonchalantly behind the wheel, watching the emergency room entranceway, not paying the least bit of attention to the two men outside the truck still staring at him.

When Ty and Jacob finally got back into the truck, Larry looked over at Ty and said, "Oh, by the way. I called in a couple of men on the cleanup crew. We wouldn't want those ashes to clog up the sewer, now. Would we?"

"Okay," Jacob began, looking directly at Ty, "why didn't Larry's bullets set Blake on fire?"

"I don't know." Ty answered. "I just don't know."

CHAPTER 35

Both Lisa and Krys remained leery of Mike, not quite trusting him. They continued to sit across the room while Cassy sat next to him on the loveseat, continuing to have a civil conversation with him.

"So where do you go from here?" Cassy asked him.

"Right now, I'm working the night shift. We're trying to find their lair. If Rick can't talk them down, I take care of them. And now we have Ty and Jacob helping, so we'll either convert them or destroy them."

Warren's phone rang and everyone grew quiet.

"Hello, Larry," Warren answered. "What's up?"

Everyone in the room sat watching Warren's expressions, especially when he said, "You're kidding. That's great." He listened a while longer before he hung up.

He looked down at Lisa, who had turned completely around on the floor, listening to his phone conversation expectantly. He took her hands in his.

"They encountered Pat and she was actually listening to Rick until Blake showed up. He hit Pat hard enough to send her flying up against the building. Ty and Jacob tried to take Blake out but he caught their arrows in midair, laughing at them the whole time. Larry said he rapid fired his gun but to no avail. Blake was still laughing when he turned around and left them all standing there."

"What about Pat? Is she okay or not?" Lisa asked anxiously.

"Pat is fine. She left with Rick. They're on their way to Rick's house where he can administer the serum."

"Oh, my God. She left Blake?" Krys asked.

"I'd say they left each other." Warren said. "Larry said Blake was furious with Pat and he thinks Blake's actions actually woke Pat up."

"Can we go see her?" Lisa asked.

"Tomorrow night. Rick's working with her right now." Warren told her.

"I can't believe Blake." Krys said. "What happened to partners for life, the forever bit?"

"Guess that was just an act to get under your skins. He said they were to be together forever, then he just and walked away." Warren stated.

"So now what happens to Pat?" Lisa asked. "Will she be my sister again?"

Mike turned to face Lisa.

"One of the biggest differences I've noted between the so-called real vampires and us is that, although we still can't be out in sunlight, we are basically human, we still have feelings. We can still love or be sad. We're still ourselves just night people now."

"I never thought I'd get my sister back. I can't believe it." Lisa commented.

Before anyone could say anything else, there was a commotion outside as if someone was banging on the patio with a big stick.

Sam walked over to the middle of the living room, the hair on his back standing straight up. He stood motionless, staring at the door, growling like a dog. There was nothing feline about him at that moment.

Both Mickey and Bright Eyes made a beeline for the front door. Mickey tried to go out through the doggy door. When he couldn't get it open, he backed up and stood next to Bright Eyes, both dogs growling loudly.

Mike was the first to reach the door, having gotten up off the loveseat in one motion and then seeming to fly across the room.

"You girls hold onto the dogs. Cassy, you handle Sam. Warren, Andy, do you have bows?"

"We're ready." Andy announced from halfway across the room, Warren next to him, both heading toward the door, bows in hand.

Cassy sat on the floor with Sam. Krys held onto Mickey and Lisa held Bright Eyes by his collar.

Mike unlocked the door, then slowly pulled it open. He stood looking outside for less than five seconds when he motioned to the other two to follow him out.

He stepped through the door onto the deck, Warren and Andy close behind.

Standing in the yard were four men. Two of them were holding 2x4 boards about 3 feet long. They continued to bang on the patio railing.

When Mike stepped through the door, the pounding stopped immediately.

Now all four men stood staring at Mike. It was as if there was a connection between the five of them, as if they actually knew each other.

They were staring at Mike, not actually noticing Warren or Andy, who had crept up on either side of Mike.

"What are you boys up to tonight?" Mike asked.

The two men on the outside of their line continued to stand motionless, silent. The two in the middle looked at each other, then back to Mike, also silent.

"We're here for Lisa." The older of the four spoke up.

"Sorry. You can't have her." Mike answered.

"And who can stop us?" The older man asked.

Mike had been quickly sizing up the four men. The two on either end would be the biggest threats. They were both young and well built. Of the two in the middle, the one talking to him was the oldest. He looked to be around 60, thin but not skinny. The fourth one was maybe 40 or a little older, seemed to be a follower, not a leader.

"The three of us will stop you." Andy said before Mike could reply.

"Seems like we outnumber you right now." The older man said, looking from one to the other of his companions and smiling confidently.

"That depends." Mike said, a smirk on his face, no fear evident.

"Depends on what?" The man on the right spoke up.

"On whether you want a chance to live semi-normally or if you want to die tonight. I mean truly die."

"How do you describe semi-normal?" The older man asked.

"Living like a human should, only at night. But no more sucking necks."

"And where's the fun in that?" The man on the right end asked.

Mike stood, watching the men silently. They were only around three feet from the porch, could rush it quickly. But he believed that both Warren and Andy were mentally and physically prepared to counteract any attempt those two on either end could make to rush the house.

Suddenly, the musclebound man on his right made his move. He leaped up into the air, landing on the railing. He stood there, staring straight ahead at Warren. Before he could make a move of any kind, Warren pulled the trigger on his bow. The arrow was a direct hit. It entered the man's chest and knocked him off the railing. He burst into flames before he hit the ground.

The other three had moved a foot or two to their left, staring at what was left of their companion, no emotions evident, as if not comprehending the enormity of what had just happened. The flames died quickly, leaving only ashes and bones.

"Impressive." The older man said. "Your two friends have their weapons. But what do you have?"

"Me." Mike answered.

Before the man could reply or make a move, Mike leapt over the railing. As he came down toward the man, he produced a stake from out of nowhere. He held the stake up over his head. He landed on the man, knocking him backward. He brought the stake down and pushed it through the man's chest. When the man hit the ground, the stake was imbedded in the grass and dirt beneath him.

Before the other two could retaliate, both Warren and Andy let loose with their arrows and eliminated them.

Mike stood back up and with a leap that neither Andy nor Warren detected, was again standing on the deck.

He pulled his cell phone out, dialed a number and told the person on the other end to send out a cleanup crew to Cassy's address.

"Well, looks like we make a pretty good team." Mike said when he got off the phone.

Warren walked forward and stood face to face with him. He put out his hand and shook Mike's. Andy had been standing behind Warren but soon walked around him and also shook Mike's hand.

"Trust me now?" Mike asked, smiling broadly.

"Oh, yeah." Andy answered.

"Hell, yeah." Warren reiterated.

The three men walked across the deck and through the door into the house. The girls were all still holding onto the animals but now let them go and stood up.

Lisa ran over to Warren and wrapped her arms around him, hugging him tightly.

Krys was hugging Andy, who stood motionless, blushing bright red.

Cassy walked over to Mike and, to everyone's surprise, gave him a hug also. At first he stood rigid, surprised by her actions. Then he relaxed and put his arms around her, actually enjoying the contact.

She pulled back and looked up at him, as if surprising herself by her action.

"Sorry about that. Guess I got caught up in the moment." Cassy apologized.

"We need more moments like that." Mike said, smiling as she blushed an even brighter shade of red. "Let me see if I can order up some more vampires."

"That's okay." Lisa said. "I think we've had enough for one night. What did they want, or do I even have to ask?"

"You." Mike told her.

"Why?" Krys asked, looking directly at Mike.

"Only Blake can answer that question." Warren told Krys.

"It just doesn't make any sense." Krys said. "If he was so enamored of Pat but could throw her away like he did, why would he want Lisa back. Didn't he basically throw you out too?"

"Totally." Lisa said.

"He's always talking about having no emotions, that those are what humans suffer with." Krys continued. "Then he shows rage or affection. He loves Pat forever, then throws her against a building and walks away, as if she never meant a thing to him. He cuffs you to a fence in the snow, evidently hoping for a slow death, but now he wants you back. I don't get it."

"I truly believe he's breaking down." Lisa noted. "His power over us puny humans is coming to an end. And in so far as I'm concerned, maybe he's upset because I didn't die. Maybe he feels that the job isn't finished and he can't stand to leave things undone."

"So, for short, "Andy added, "we're finally getting under his skin, confusing the situation and maybe, just maybe, beating him at his own game."

"Maybe. Hopefully. "Krys said.

"Guess we'll know if he stops pursuing Lisa." Warren said.

"Let's hope he doesn't." Mike told them.

They all looked at Mike as if he had turned into a full-fledged vampire, under Blake's rule.

"No, listen." Mike continued. "If he continues to focus on Lisa, that means he isn't focusing on ruling the entire United States. And that also means that he'll become emotionally caught up in his pursuit of Lisa, that he'll mess up. When that happens, we've got him."

"Well, I just hope it happens soon." Lisa said. "Cause I'm sure getting tired of constantly looking over my shoulder every time the sun goes down. I'm ready to get on with my life and leave all of this behind me."

"I'll second that one." Warren said, holding Lisa just a little tighter, smiling just a little broader.

"Well, working together like we did tonight, you know that is going to frustrate him even more. He keeps sending more and more of his vampires to get Lisa and they keep failing. If he gets angry enough, he'll eliminate most of them for us. Don't think he takes too kindly to failure."

"Hopefully that's it for the evening and we can all relax for the rest of the night. Remember, I said hopefully." Krys said.

"We'll see." Mike told them. "Meanwhile, I'll stay here until Ty and Jacob get back. Just call me backup."

"I prefer to call you Mike, if that's okay." Cassy said, smiling at him, then walking back to the love seat.

CHAPTER 36

Cassy brought everyone a can of Millers from the frig. They had no more than sat down when there were footsteps on the patio.

Cassy got back up off the loveseat, heading toward the door, but Mike caught her by the arm, saying "Let me."

He walked across the living room and, without hesitation, opened the front door. In walked Larry, Ty and Jacob.

Krys immediately got up and ran into Ty's arms.

"Are you okay?"

"A little disappointed but okay." Ty told her.

Cassy had been hugging Jacob until he finally squirmed out of her grasp. He backed away and stood staring at her, a puzzled look on his face.

"What's wrong? Can't a sister be glad to see her little brother?"

"I guess. It's just that you've never hugged me before."

"Nerd." Cassy teased and punched him in the arm playfully.

"Okay. The real Cassy is back. Glad to see you too, sis." Jacob laughed.

Once they were all settled in, Larry spoke up.

"Tomorrow night we start hunting in earnest. Our main objective will be Blake. What I need is help from all of you."

"Anything you need." Andy said.

"Lisa, I want you to visit with your sister as soon as the sun goes down tomorrow. She should know where Blake is hiding out. And I know you're more than anxious to see her."

"You can't know how much I want to see her back to her old self. I'm praying that, with Rick's help, I'll get my real sister back again."

"I'll give you Rick's address and Cassy can drive you out there. Take Bright Eyes with you."

"Okay." Was all Lisa could say. She sat back down, imagining what her reunion with her sister would be like.

"And the rest of us?" Warren asked.

"The rest of you will be going with different teams to hunt Blake and his people. Some of Rick's crew will join you in the patrol cars. Four to a car."

"You do know that Blake is my top priority?" Ty asked him.

"I know. That's why I've partnered you up with special S.W.A.T. people and Rick. I'll have Lisa and Cassy keep in contact with you directly in case Pat can remember anything of importance in order to track Blake down."

"You sure are organized." Krys commented. "In Kalamazoo, we were forever having morning conferences. So much time was lost."

"I've talked to Kee quite a few times. I can't fault him or his department for the way they handled things. It was the first big city and it was a trial and error situation. They learned from Hebert and we learned from both towns. But I do have to admit that they did get the job done."

"But they didn't have Rick or his family working with them." Jacob added.

"That's very true." Larry commented. "But we all learn from other peoples' mistakes. Every time a new town gets infected, that Sheriff or Chief will have all of us to fall back on, get a better perspective of what's happening and how to stop it."

"Plus, in Kalamazoo we didn't have any idea where Blake was staying during the daylight hours. Now we at least know he's in a motorhome and it can't be that easy to hide." Ty added.

"And we also didn't have Jacob's genius on our side either." Larry said. "I love your wooden arrows and your blog to the truckers."

"How did you know about that?" Jacob asked. "I just posted it this afternoon."

"I'm not totally in the dark ages." Larry answered. "And I've got a few friends who drive truck. That helped a lot."

"But now, I'm out of here." Larry continued. "We'll meet tomorrow at sunset at the station. We'll have specific routes written out for each unit to follow. Some will be stationed at a specific spot. Others will be on the road going from one spot to another, basically hunting."

"So, our hunt begins again." Warren said, looking from one to the other of the people in the room.

Warren was relieved that Cassy would be with Lisa and not out in the thick of things. She was still new to the hunt. And he knew that Andy and Jacob both felt the same way. They had been in Hebert and volunteered there to help eradicate the vampires. They knew how gruesome it could get and he was sure they wanted to spare Cassy the more gruesome parts of the hunt.

Warren looked over at Krys and Ty, they were a couple who were meant to be. It was just too bad that they had to be brought together under such dire circumstances. He prayed they would find Blake and eliminate him so that Ty and Krys could get on with their lives. He knew as long as Blake was out there somewhere, Ty would never rest, never stop hunting him. Ty felt responsible for a lot of what was happening, even though it was something that could not have been avoided. If it hadn't been Ty driving that semi during the day, then some other unsuspecting truck driver would have been doing Blake's dirty work. At least Ty, with help from Krys, finally figured it out and was willing to help stop all the madness. He gave Ty a lot of credit for all the hard work he had done so far in Kalamazoo and knew Ty would not stop until there was no more Blake.

Warren sat in Cassy's overstuffed chair with Lisa on the floor, sitting between his legs, using his knees for arm rests. He wanted this to all end quickly and knew that when it was over, he and Lisa would only be starting. She had intimated numerous times since they had found her that she intended to finally go back to Hebert with him. He didn't know if there would be a place for her on the police force there, but there would always be a place for her in his home and in his life.

Warren gave Larry credit for believing in what was going on and taking the necessary steps to eliminate the problem. When they were in Kalamazoo, Warren didn't think Kee ever believed in the vampire theory, was just going along with the scheme of things to eliminate whatever it was that was devastating his town. But here in Denver, Warren felt he had an ally in Larry. Although he could be very abrasive at times, his heart was in the right place, along with his mind. He accepted the fact that there were vampires in Denver and that they needed to be eliminated once and for all. Larry had been working closely with Rick before Warren and the rest of them got involved in it. He had an open mind to the situation and Warren truly appreciated all his help.

CHAPTER 37

The next morning, Larry arrived in his office a few minutes after 7 only to find Mayor Bob Upchurch sitting in his chair behind his desk.

"You been promoted?" Larry asked as he walked through the door, threw his jacket on top of his coat rack and then motioned for the mayor to move out of his chair.

Mayor Upchurch slowly rose and walked around the desk to sit in the chair in front of it. His movements were such that anyone looking into the office would have thought it was the mayor's idea, voluntary, not ordered.

The tension in the room could have been cut with a knife. The office personnel, as well as all the officers working with Larry, knew what Larry thought of the major. There was no love lost between the two of them.

Larry considered the mayor a pompous ass who wasn't fit to run a garbage truck, much less the city of Denver.

The mayor tolerated Larry because, above all else, Larry got the job done, was well liked in the community and respected by everyone in the police community. He also felt threatened by Larry because more than once he had been proven wrong by the man.

Larry walked around his desk and then slowly sat in his chair. After rifling through a few papers, he looked up at the mayor.

"So, what can we do for you today?"

"I came in about the situation we have here in our city."

"Situation?" Larry interrupted.

"Yes, situation. That's what we're calling it. We don't need to be more explicit or cause any rioting. We wouldn't want to scare anyone."

"Are you so high and mighty you can't admit our situation involves vampires?" Larry asked sarcastically.

"That's not a word we need to put out there at this time." The mayor shouted, his voice dripping irritation.

"So, what now? Deny we have a real problem?" Larry asked.

"Works for me."

"Well, it doesn't work for me." Larry said, banging his fist on the top of his desk for emphasis.

The mayor jumped up from his seat, glared at Larry but eventually sat back down.

"What exactly are you doing about our situation?" the major asked.

"All of our officers are on alert. We also have hunters here who are experienced in eliminating the vampires, having fought them in Illinois and again in Michigan. We're monitoring and putting extra patrols at the hospital and all the local truck stops. We're taking care of our situation just fine."

"Not fast enough to suit me," the mayor replied.

"Sorry for you." Larry said, snickering under his breath.

"What about your friend Rick? How do you figure he's helping? He's allowing the vermin to continue to live in our city."

"Rick isn't letting so-called vermin loose in your precious city. He's giving them an alternative."

"An alternative? Are you kidding me?" the major yelled, his face turning a dark red with anger.

"Whether you like it or not, he's doing a hell of a lot more to solve our situation than you are."

"Enough," the mayor shouted. "I'll not sit here and be insulted by the likes of you."

"The likes of me? Just who in the hell do you think you are?" Larry shouted back with a voice that could be heard down the hall all the way to his secretary's desk.

"I am the mayor." Mayor Upchurch shouted as he rose up out of his chair. "And I'm in charge here."

"You may be in charge at city hall but you are definitely not in charge of me or my department." Larry told him as he stood up from his desk, squaring off.

"We'll see about that." The mayor said as he turned to leave.

"Meaning what?" Larry asked.

"Meaning I've called in the National Guard and we will eliminate these vermin, and I mean all of them. We start tonight."

Larry was stunned.

"Tonight? That shows just how ignorant you really are. They're more powerful after dark. You'll have a massacre on your hands."

"That's exactly what I'm talking about. You may call it a massacre but I call it eradication."

"I'm not talking about a massacre of the vampires. I'm talking about a massacre of the National Guard. You can't send those soldiers in after dark."

"Watch me. I can do whatever I deem necessary to protect this city. I've already cleared it with the Governor. There's no turning back now."

Larry continued to stand behind his desk, staring at the mayor in disbelief.

"Then do me one favor," Larry said.

"What's that?"

"Lead the soldiers. Be the first in line."

The mayor huffed loudly, then turned and stormed out the door. Larry stood listening to him stomping down the hall, yelling for people to get out of his way.

Larry finally sat back down. "Idiot" he shouted at the empty door.

CHAPTER 38

Larry sat behind his desk, still fuming, when his cell phone rang. He picked it up and looked at the ID.

"Hi, Rick. What's up?"

He listened to Rick for only a minute before Rick asked if he could come over to his house in a half hour or so with a couple of the volunteers.

Larry then called Cassy's and asked for Warren.

"Can you, Andy and Jacob meet me at Rick's in half an hour or so?"

"Sure. Send the address to my phone and we'll head out."

Larry sent the address, then left his office, letting the desk sergeant know he'd be gone for a while but could be reached on his cell phone if an emergency came up.

Larry arrived before the other men and was relaxing in Rick's family room, a cup of hot tea on the side table, his second cup, when the front doorbell rang.

Rick ushered the three men down the hallway to the family room. Larry stood up to greet everyone. Rick offered them tea, coffee or soda.

While Rick disappeared out the door to get their drinks, Warren and Andy seated themselves near Larry. Jacob stood in front of one of several floor-to-ceiling book cases silently reading some of the titles.

Andy silently pointed at Jacob and the three men sat watching him as he kept moving sideways, one step at a time, continually reading titles.

Jacob suddenly stopped in front of one section, put his hand up to tenderly touch the jacket of one of the books.

"It's a first edition," Rick said from the door.

Not only Jacob, but both Warren and Andy jumped at the sound. No one had heard Rick enter the room.

Jacob turned away from the bookshelves, walked over to Rick, took his soda off the serving tray, then took the cup of coffee for Andy. Rick served Warren his coffee.

When the three men were once again seated, Rick finally sat down in an old- fashioned wood rocking chair near his piano.

"I know it doesn't match the décor," Rick stated, "but it was my grandma's. I can still remember her rocking me in her arms. She could soothe a lion with an abscessed tooth in this rocker, she was that good."

"So, why are we all here?" Andy asked, looking from Rick over to Larry.

Jacob sat smiling. He knew Andy so well and wasn't surprised by his directness. Andy wasn't one to beat around the bush, never had been. It was just one more reason Jacob loved the old man like a father.

"I'm about to have a big problem on my hands," Larry began, "the mayor."

"Again?" Rick spoke up. "Now what is our favorite S.O.B. up to?"

"He's calling in the National Guard."

"Why is that a problem?" Warren asked. "Can't we instruct them and quickly train them to help us?"

"If you knew our mayor, you wouldn't ask that question." Rick spoke up.

"He's a pompous ass. He doesn't work well with people, especially people like us. He considers us lowly peons." Larry added.

"By way of a better explanation, Larry and Bob have had an ongoing feud for years now, ever since Larry made a big drug bust and our beloved mayor, who was then a lawyer, got the scumbags off on a technicality. Then, all of a sudden, he had all the money he needed to campaign for the mayor's office."

"Our problem is that he intends to use these soldiers to hunt the vampires at night." Larry interjected.

"At night?" Jacob asked. "Do they even know what they're up against?"

"No." Larry stated emphatically. "He refuses to even say the word vampire. All he ever says is that we have a situation and he will massacre the vermin."

"Isn't there anyone who can talk some sense into him? He'll get those young folks all killed." Andy asked.

"No one can talk to our beloved mayor. For one, he doesn't listen. And two, he thinks he's always right and everyone else is always wrong." Rick told them.

"So, what can we do?" Jacob asked.

"Maybe I could go in ahead of them." Rick suggested.

"Bob wouldn't allow it, Rick." Larry said. "He thinks of you as vermin like the rest of them. He feels that you are promoting their behavior and have an agenda to flood his city with them."

"I can see where your opinion of him comes from," Warren spoke up.

"Now what?" Rick asked, looking directly at Larry.

"I just don't know." Larry said, shaking his head. "I don't have the authority to stop him. If I could make a phone call and stop the guard from coming in, I would. Unfortunately, I can't do that. He's got permission from the governor and he's determined to go ahead with his plans. I can't over-ride his orders."

"What happens if we just show up?" Andy asked.

"Where?" Larry responded. "He's being very closed lip about what, where or when. All I can figure is maybe some of the empty warehouses downtown. But which ones or even which areas, I have no idea."

Everyone sat, quietly contemplating what, if anything, they could do to prevent the inevitable, the slaughter of a unit of young inexperienced men and women.

"We have to do something, anything." Jacob spoke up.

"I don't know what to do." Larry said. He had become uncharacteristically emotional and his voice quivered when he spoke.

"When is he planning on this happening?" Rick asked.

"I'm not sure. At one point, he said tonight. But can he get all of this organized by tonight? I don't know. He's being otherwise very secretive about all of it. Everything will be coming from his office and I'm not privy to any of it."

"Well, I hate to be the voice of doom," Rick began, "but I really don't see where we can do anything until something happens. I realize that means we're looking to have fatalities, but maybe, just maybe, we can be there afterwards and at least save some lives."

"I know how you feel right now, Larry," Warren began, "it's called helpless. I felt it back in Hebert at the beginning, when I didn't understand what was going on in my town. I can't begin to imagine what it's like to feel responsible for a city this size. But, you have to know you are doing everything possible to solve the problem."

"And if this raid the mayor is planning falls through, it's on him," Rick added. "If it all goes wrong, and I'm sure it will, then we do whatever we can to make it right. And in the process, we make sure he never has that kind of authority again."

"I know what you all are saying. It's just hard thinking of what can happen and how many lives will be affected needlessly. It makes me sick." Larry said.

"So, what sarcastic thing did you say to him when he left, because I know you wouldn't let him leave your office without saying something." Rick asked.

"I just told him he needs to lead the troops, be first in line." Larry told him.

"We can only wish he takes your advice. That would solve a lot of our problems." Rick said.

"Sounds like this meeting of the minds is over," Andy spoke up. "We'll be heading back to Cassy's."

"Before you go, Jacob," Rick said as he got up out of the rocker and walked over to the bookshelf. He took down a book, the one next to the book Jacob had been admiring.

"The one you liked so much is the first book ever printed, this is the second. I want you to have it with my blessings."

"I can't...." Jacob started to say.

"Yes, you can. You'd insult me if you didn't take it. You don't want to insult a vampire now, do you?" Rick stated, smiling broadly.

"But..." Jacob stammered.

"No buts. Enjoy."

Jacob took the book, cradling it in his arms as he walked out the door and down the hall.

When Warren and Andy exited the house and climbed up into the pickup, Jacob was already sitting in the back seat, still hugging the book close to his chest.

"Okay," Andy said once they were on the road again, "don't keep us guessing. What book is so precious you can't quit holding on so tight?"

"Yeah," Warren added, "you're holding onto it like it was a long-lost girlfriend you just got back,"

"It's better than a girlfriend," Jacob said as he put the book down onto his lap, rubbing the cover tenderly. "It's Dracula by Bram Stoker, dated 1897."

"Other than the fact that it's that old, what else makes it so valuable to you?" Andy asked him.

"In this original, he portrays Dracula differently than he's portrayed in other books or in movies. In this original transcript, Dracula is a centuries old vampire and a Transylvania noblemen who claimed to be a Szekely descended from Attila the Hun. He inhabits a decaying castle in the Carpathian Mountains near the Borgo Pass. He exudes aristocratic charm. He reveals himself as proud of his heritage and nostalgic about the past."

"Sure doesn't sound like Bela Lugosi to me." Warren commented.

"No. In the book he's portrayed as a soldier, a statesman and an alchemist. He has a deep knowledge of magic. He had a great brain. And his heart knew no fear and no remorse."

"Now he's beginning to sound more like Blake." Andy added.

"He studied black arts at the Academy of Scholomance in the Carpathian Mountains, overlooking Hermannstadt. That's the name of the town in some of the movies where the people are so afraid of him and warn travelers about him." Jacob added.

"You sound almost like you admire him." Warren said.

"In a way I do. Not the brutality or the savagery, but the education he had and the fact that he used his education. It may have been an education in the black arts and alchemistry, but he was so smart, so wise. He was a man who should have been born 200 years later. Maybe then he would have been appreciated and accepted. Writers wouldn't have had a chance to make him so evil."

With that the truck fell silent. Andy and Warren both sat thinking about what Jacob had said and what difference it could have made, if any.

Jacob sat, tenderly touching the book in his lap. He loved the history of the Count, but never in his wildest dreams did he ever imagine he would own one of the original books by Bram Stoker. He couldn't quit smiling.

CHAPTER 39

As soon as the mayor walked out of the police station, he was quickly surrounded by reporters and cameramen. Questions flew from all directions regarding his stand on the idea of vampires in Denver.

"I'm more apt to believe our problem is with gangs or insurgents." He answered, posing for the cameras, smiling broadly.

"What about the dead rising and walking within 24 hours?" a very tall and muscular reporter asked, raising his microphone close to the mayor's face.

"Pure conjecture. You know how rumors get started and then escalate."

He tried to push forward, able to see his limo only 20 feet or so in front of him, the driver holding the door open for him.

"You have to excuse me, I have a meeting and wouldn't want to be late."

"Mayor, are you getting involved in this hunt? The sheriff seems to be progressing in eliminating the vampires." A lady reporter standing next to him asked. His escape was blocked by the larger reporter who had previously asked him a question.

The mayor stopped dead in his tracks, looked menacingly at the woman. He then yanked the microphone out of her hand.

"The rumor that these are vampires has not been substantiated to my satisfaction. As far as Larry Moore is concerned, I don't believe he has this under control, much like everything else he has done during his term in office."

"What about Rick Cartier?" a voice in the background asked.

"Mr. Cartier is no better than the hooligans we're hunting. I believe he is in some way encouraging our problem and increasing the numbers of these hooligans."

"You're making some serious accusations," the large reporter said. "It's no secret that you and Mr. Moore are not on the same page very often…"

"Never would be more accurate." The mayor interrupted.

"So what are your plans to take care of our problem?" the lady reporter asked, leaning into her microphone that the mayor was still holding.

"My plan is to eliminate our problem. Now, excuse me," he said as he threw the mic back at the reporter. He then pushed another reporter aside and quickly made his way to his limo. The reporters and cameramen followed him to his car but his driver shut the door behind him, then trotted around the front of the vehicle and got in behind the wheel. The limo had been running and within seconds the driver pulled away from the curb, scattering the reporters who stood close to the street.

"Back to my office." The mayor demanded from the back seat.

The driver smiled as he looked back through his rearview mirror at the angry reporters, many of whom were giving him the bird.

CHAPTER 40

The mayor's limo drove through the gate into a private underground parking garage. The driver pulled up in front of the elevators, got out and opened the door for the mayor.

The mayor walked quickly to the first elevator, pushed the up button and only had to wait a matter of seconds when the door opened and he entered. The elevator seemed to move slower than usual, maybe because he was in such a hurry.

When he reached his floor, he stepped out and rapidly walked to his private office, slowing down only long enough to tell his secretary to get the governor on the phone, hold all other calls and cancel any appointments he had for the rest of the day.

As soon as he sat in his chair, his phone rang.

"Hello," he answered briskly.

He listened to the reply, then said. "I want you to declare a state of emergency."

As he listened to the reply, he frowned and banged his fist on his desk.

"No excuses, Governor. This isn't your call, it's mine. I'm not asking, I'm ordering."

After a short silence, he loudly responded, "I just made me in charge, that's what. Larry is living in a fantasy world, talking about vampires. Whoever is in charge of the National Guard is scheduled to be in my office in the next two hours, no later. I'll give him his orders at that time."

With that, he hung up the phone, then sat back in his chair, smiling evilly.

"Take that, Larry." He said out loud. "This time the ball is in my court."

CHAPTER 41

Two hours later, the mayor's secretary came to his door announcing the arrival of a Captain Randolph Wilkerson.

"Come in, come in," the mayor said. "Have a seat." He motioned to a chair in front of his desk.

Captain Wilkerson, carrying his hat under his left arm, stuck out his arm to shake hands.

"No time for niceties," the mayor announced. "How many men can you produce for a raid tonight?"

The Captain brought his hand back to his side, sat down and frowned at the mayor.

"Well?" the mayor demanded impatiently.

"The only reason I'm here is because the Governor declared a state of emergency and commanded me to come to your office. What is your emergency?"

"Insurgents."

"Insurgents? Sorry, that's not enough information. My men need to know what to expect. They have to be prepared and aware."

"We are going downtown to vacant warehouses. When we come across an insurgent, we eliminate him or her, as in shoot them dead."

"Are you talking about the problem with vampires?" the captain asked.

"No such animal. All we have are some low-lifes causing mayhem. They will be eliminated."

"And when do you propose this expedition?"

"Tonight." The mayor responded.

"Impossible."

"Nothing is impossible. I'll expect you and your men to be outside this building by 6 p.m. tonight."

"Mayor, I really don't believe..."

"Dismissed." The mayor shouted. He picked up the phone and dialed a number, completely ignoring the captain who was still standing, speechless.

"I said dismissed. I shouldn't have to repeat myself."

The mayor sat listening to the phone ringing on the other end. He watched as the captain turned and left the room.

"George, we're going out with the Guard tonight. Get geared up." With that, he hung up.

CHAPTER 42

Around 5 p.m., the mayor returned to his office from an early dinner, George following close behind.

"Is everybody ready?" the mayor asked.

"Yes, sir. The captain said he'd be back by six. I have to go get my gear on." George answered.

"Go ahead. I'll wait for the captain."

At 5:30, Captain Wilkerson walked into the office. He was in camouflage and armed with a 9 mm in a holster on his belt. He didn't bother to greet the mayor, didn't attempt to sit or shake hands. He stood at attention just inside the door.

"You're early." The mayor commented, stacking some papers on his desk, never looking up at the captain.

"Didn't dare be late," the captain answered. "Just came in for our orders."

"Your orders, captain, are to follow me and my bodyguard. We'll lead the way."

"That's highly irregular, sir."

"Irregular or not, that's the way it's going to be."

"Fine, then. I'll be downstairs with my men."

"See you in a bit." The mayor told him, never once looking up.

Captain Wilkerson took the elevator down to the first floor, then walked through the lobby and out the front door. He joined his men, some of whom were still in the troop transports, some standing on the sidewalk, smoking or talking, passing time.

When the captain came out the door, the men on the sidewalk promptly stood at attention and saluted.

"At ease," Captain Wilkerson commanded. "All weapons checked and extra ammo on board?"

"We're all good," a young boy standing close by answered.

"Everyone relax. We have to wait on the mayor." The captain told them.

Ten minutes later, the mayor and his bodyguard, George, came out the door. The mayor had changed into a pair of jeans and a Denver Bronco sweatshirt. He was carrying his jacket but no weapons were in sight. He made note that there were three transport trucks idling in front of the building.

George, on the other hand, was dressed entirely in black. Holstered to his belt was a 357 Magnum. Strapped over his shoulder was a repeating rifle. Across his chest, an ammo belt.

"Okay, captain, follow us." The mayor commanded as he walked to his car. George held the door open for him and once he was in, shut it quickly, then ran around to the driver's door. He pulled his rifle off and threw it across the inside of the car to the passenger seat, got in and started the limo.

Captain Wilkerson gave the command for his men to load up into the transports. He then climbed up into the cab of the first truck and instructed the driver to follow close behind the limo.

The limo drove west toward the setting sun. After eight blocks, it stopped in front of a huge warehouse. The paint was faded and in some spots had peeled off completely. There were no signs on the building to indicate what had once been housed inside. The street level windows were all boarded up. The windows on the second story were nonexistent.

Captain Wilkerson stepped out of his vehicle and started walking up the sidewalk toward the double doors at the front of the building. The soldiers stepped out and silently followed in double file close behind him.

The mayor's limo sat directly in front of the building. The mayor had his window down and George was standing outside the driver's open door.

The captain didn't acknowledge their presence as he continued toward the building.

When the captain reached the door, he tried the knob and found the door to be unlocked. The men had silently now formed four rows behind the captain. With a gesture only, the captain indicated the two outside rows should cover the perimeter of the building, working their way around to the back doors. In unison, the two teams quickly separated from the rest of the unit and began their surveillance across the front of the building and then disappeared around the opposite corners.

The captain only waited another three minutes before walking through the door, gun drawn. The inside of the warehouse was dark, but he noted no movement. As the last soldier entered through the door, the captain heard a soft click and immediately dozens of fluorescent lights came on revealing the inside of the warehouse to be completely empty.

It was evident that the building had been empty for quite some time because the floor was covered in a thick layer of dust. The dust was not disturbed; no footprints, no evidence of anyone having been in the building for some time.

The captain heard the back door hit the wall when it was pushed open but no other sound. Soon, the rest of his unit walked out of an inside door and across the warehouse to join forces. The first soldier simply shook his head no to indicate that they had not encountered anyone.

The captain told the men to spread out and check behind the closed doors and the second level. They soon returned to report that the entire building was vacant.

The captain led his men back outside. While they climbed back into their vehicles, he walked over to the limo.

"Empty. Has been for a long time. Where to next?"

"Follow us," the mayor said as his window slowly closed.

Captain Wilkerson turned his back on the limo and stomped back over to his transport.

"Just follow the S.O.B." he ordered his driver.

They searched two more warehouses with the same results.

It was now around 9 p.m. and they were finally heading back down Huron when the limo suddenly pulled into a parking spot at the side of a building.

The captain pointed to the limo and his driver pulled in parallel to the sidewalk, taking up five spaces. The other two trucks pulled around the block and parked on that side of the building.

The captain exited his vehicle and walked over to the limo.

"Why are we stopping here?" he asked George who was already standing outside by the passenger door.

"Saw movement inside and what looked like candlelight upstairs."

"Is it supposed to be an empty building? I see the for sale sign on the window by the door."

The back window rolled down. The mayor didn't attempt to get out or even move from his seat. A laptop was open on his lap.

The captain leaned into the window.

"The building has been on the market for over a month. It is for sale but completely furnished. Check it out." The mayor said, never taking his eyes off his laptop.

"Yes, sir," the captain said as he saluted, a salute with his middle finger extended.

As at the other buildings, the captain and half his men approached the front door while the other half split up once more and walked both sides of the building around to the back.

The building itself was a newer office building. With the streetlamps throwing light on the building from both sides, the soldiers could see shadows of furniture in the various rooms; desks, file cabinets, even pictures on the walls.

There were also shadows that were not stationary but moving toward the center of the building, away from the windows.

The captain raised his hand for silence, tried the front door to find it unlocked. He quietly stepped inside, his men coming in behind him and spreading out along the walls on either side of the door.

Captain Wilkerson walked into the waiting area which was open to other rooms. By the light shining through the windows, he could see couches, chairs, end tables, even some magazines scattered around.

He took a few steps but motioned for the soldiers to stay back. When he was even with the open window into the reception office, he looked in quickly but saw no movement.

Suddenly, there was a big bang from the back of the building. Instincts told the captain that the back door had evidently been locked, which didn't stop the other half of his unit from entering.

He motioned for his men to proceed through the building. Within minutes, they met up with the rest of the unit, finding themselves in front of a flight of stairs that led to a small landing, then more steps on the other side of the wall leading up to the second floor.

The captain motioned for the men in front of him to search the second floor. They proceeded up the stairs and swiftly disappeared.

Before the captain could take another step, he heard a voice that sent chills up his spine and made the hairs on the back of his neck tingle.

"Good evening, captain."

Captain Wilkerson stopped dead in his tracks, turned toward the stairway. Standing on the landing was a very tall man. He was dressed in dark clothing which made him look like a shadow of a man, somehow not real.

"Who are you? What are you doing in here?" the captain asked.

"Why, I'm living here temporarily."

"You mean trespassing."

"It isn't trespassing if I'm only here for minutes at a time," the stranger reasoned.

"Who are you?" the captain asked again, losing his patience quickly.

"My name, sir, is Blake."

The captain immediately aimed his gun at Blake's chest. His men followed suit.

"You really don't believe those weapons are going to protect you, do you?" Blake asked, laughing menacingly.

"They have so far." The captain said.

"Well, they won't this time."

Suddenly, there was movement all around the room. The soldiers instinctively formed a circle around their captain, guns drawn and aimed into the darkness.

From the second floor, gunfire was suddenly heard along with shouting and then screams of pain. It was impossible for the captain to know if the screams were coming from those attacking his men or from his men. They were blood- curdling and he could almost feel their pain.

Before the captain or his men could fire their weapons, the shadows became men and women, some silent but others hissing and screaming.

The soldiers started firing at the men and women. Each time one was hit, he or she stopped as if they had been poked or slapped lightly. Then they would continue moving forward.

In a movement unseen by the soldiers, the advancing people literally flew at them, landing on top of the soldiers, who toppled to the floor, covered by the aggressors.

It quickly became a massacre. The vampires tore at the soldiers' throats, their faces, anywhere there was exposed skin. The entire scene was as if a red wave was moving across the floor. The captain realized the movement was from those on top as they gorged themselves and then proceeded to tear the bodies beneath them apart. Body pieces were seen flying in every direction.

The captain suddenly realized that only he and Blake were still standing. He was still firing his gun at Blake, but now only the click from empty chambers could be heard. He didn't know how long he had been firing an empty gun.

Blake slowly descended the stairs until he stood inches away from the captain.

"You were never told that your weapons were not going to save you?" Blake asked in a whisper.

Before Captain Wilkerson could answer or make a move, Blake took his head in his hands, tilted it to the right and ripped a chunk of flesh from his neck. He held the captain's head in his hands for a few seconds more, then said, "Goodbye, Captain."

He then let the captain's body fall to the floor where it was immediately covered and savaged by two women.

CHAPTER 43

Meanwhile, George had been standing outside the limo by the mayor's door. The mayor's window was down. The two of them had been listening to the gunfire and then the screaming. Now all was quiet.

"Check it out," the mayor commanded.

George looked at him as if he had just lost his mind.

The mayor promptly closed his window, leaving George staring at it.

Slowly, George turned toward the building which was once again silent and dark. He drew his gun and walked onto the sidewalk, then through the front door.

"Oh, my God" George exclaimed but, before he could finish his sentence, he was grabbed and pulled into the building. No shots were fired.

Someone had bit down on his gun hand, severing two fingers. The gun dropped and was lost from sight. He was subsequently wrestled to the floor and covered by writhing bodies, each person biting and taking chunks of flesh from his body. George lost consciousness quickly, which for him was a blessing.

The mayor sat in the limo, all the doors locked and the windows shut tight. He was shaking in terror. He was too afraid to get out and jump into the driver's seat. Besides, he didn't even know if George had left the keys in the car or taken them with him inside the building.

He almost jumped off the seat when there was a knock on his window. He looked out but with the tint could only make out a figure.

Suddenly, the window imploded, shattered particles of glass covering the mayor's lap and legs. A hand came through the window, grabbed the door and yanked it completely off the car. The mayor watched as the door flew across the parking spaces, the sidewalk and eventually hit one of the building's windows, shattering it.

The mayor sat in shocked silence, eyes wide, staring at the darkness.

"Mr. mayor, won't you join me?" a gravelly voice whispered.

Before the mayor could move away from that side of the car, the same pale hand reappeared, grabbed him by his suit lapels and none too gently pulled him out of the limo and threw him down on the pavement.

The mayor landed hard on his back. When he looked up, a man was standing over him. There were several more people standing behind the man and up on the sidewalk.

Even in the semi darkness, the mayor could see the blood dripping from the lips and chins of the many people standing silently behind the stranger, staring at him. There clothes looked wet, as if they had been swimming. Then the mayor realized the wet was also blood.

"What happened here tonight is on you, Mr. Mayor." Blake whispered.

"Don't kill me," the mayor cried in a trembling voice, tears running down his cheeks. "Please, don't kill me."

"I'm not going to kill you. Neither are any of these. You deserve to live and face your peers. Face your responsibilities and the fact that you caused this slaughter tonight."

Without a sound, the men, women and children turned in various directions and walked quietly away.

"They won't return. You have nothing to fear from us."

"Why?" the mayor screamed.

"Why? Because you aren't worthy. The men inside fought valiantly while you sat on your ass in your fancy limo. Now, everyone will know what kind of a man you are, a coward. They will realize that you are a thief, a braggart, a liar and now a murderer. They will laugh you out of office and out of Denver."

With that, Blake turned and walked away, soon blending into the darkness.

The mayor finally sat up on the pavement, looking all around him but seeing nothing and no one. It was as if they had all disappeared into the dark night.

Suddenly, there was movement behind him, just shadows. He thought it was the bushes moving in the wind. Then he realized that it was movement coming through the door of the building. Men and women walked out onto the sidewalk and then walked away from the building. Two literally walked close enough for him to smell the blood.

He turned away and loudly vomited his entire supper all over the pavement and himself. He slowly sank back down until he was lying on the pavement once more, staring up at the sky. He remained that way for over an hour, just staring, a frightened look in his eyes and on his face.

CHAPTER 44

For Lisa, the day went entirely too slow. She was anxious to get to Rick's and see her sister. She continually checked her watch only to sigh in frustration when she realized it was only an hour since the last time she had checked.

She kept stealing glances at Warren during the day. She was sorry that she hadn't realized what a catch he was when he volunteered to come to Kalamazoo and help with the Blake problem up there. If she had only left with him then, she would never have been kidnapped or left in a snowbank to die. And she wasn't so sure that Warren would have volunteered to come to Denver if it hadn't been for her predicament.

She was afraid for Cassy and her family, having put them in the middle of all of this. Lisa knew Blake would continue to send others for her, how long that would last she wasn't sure. If he could be eliminated once and for all, she was sure that his followers would stop hunting her, would be more worried about their own lives and where to go and what to do next without their leader. They were all like sheep being led by an evil shepherd.

She had her own feelings about Blake and why he was still after her. She was, after all, the one that got away. He wasn't used to being thwarted in such a manner. He had fully expected her and Scotty to freeze to death in that snowbank. He had, after all, handcuffed her to the fence to make sure she couldn't get away. He had put a blanket over them, not to keep them warm, but to help hide them from anyone who might wander by. Although she had been unconscious when he had her placed outside, she was sure it must have been snowing at the time and with the white blanket and the snow, Blake must have thought it would be their demise.

Why he didn't turn her or just kill her himself, she had no idea. For that matter, he could have ordered her sister Pat to suck her dry, but he hadn't done that either. He had never shown any emotion toward her while she was in the motorhome, no compassion and no hatred. He told her where to drive, how far and for how long, let her fix herself something to eat, then left her cuffed in the motorhome while he and Pat did their thing.

She wondered if the reason he hadn't turned her was because of her rebelliousness, he might have figured that part of her would never change, no matter what. He would have been right. She had been determined from the start to, one way or another, get rid of Blake, whether he turned her or not. She knew in her mind that even if she was a vampire, she would still hunt Blake down and, if possible, kill him.

Warren had been watching Lisa, knew she was thinking about Pat but was also thinking about Blake. He knew what was in store for all of them tonight, but he was anxious about what was in store for her. He hoped and prayed that Pat would once again be herself, would be able to show Lisa the love they had always shared before Blake came into their lives. He thought about Rick and Mike and how normal they both seemed, even though they had been infected. His biggest worry for Pat was that she had been with Blake for quite some time and had tasted blood on a nightly basis. Both Rick and Mike had received the serum before ever tasting another person's blood. Would it work as well on Pat after all this time?

Cassy and the girls fixed a light supper once again, sensing that no one would be very hungry. Cassy could feel the tension in the air and knew what it could do to their appetites. She planned on a big dinner when this was all over. She hoped that that would happen very soon.

She was fearful for her brother Jacob and her Uncle Andy. Jacob had always been a computer nerd, she had never envisioned him out in the dark hunting vampires. Of course, she had never envisioned him hunting anything, daylight or dark. She wasn't aware that he had become an avid deer hunter and fished with a bow. The idea for the bow and wooden arrows was not a surprise to her, his mind never quit inventing things to help people out.

She was more fearful for her Uncle Andy. He wasn't exactly in his prime and she knew he suffered from arthritis in his knees and elbows. She also knew how stubborn he could be and that he wouldn't quit until the job was done.

She envied Ty and Krys, their relationship, even knowing that it had been brought about by Blake. Krys and Cassy had become close friends, being close in age and both driving truck hadn't hurt their relationship one bit. The biggest thing they had in common was their love for the open road. Cassy came from a long line of truckers, she enjoyed basically being her own boss and didn't mind being out in the truck by herself. Of course, she was never truly alone with Sam in the truck all the time.

Cassy was driving in order to pay off her bills and finish college. Her first love was her animals and she wanted to help any and all other animals eventually. She had approximately one year of schooling left that could still be accomplished on the computer. But then, she would have to quit driving and go to college here in Denver. She was driving all the miles she could get in order to get that done and be able to get the rest of her education without having to continue to work the whole time. She wanted to spend her entire waking hours in school or studying, not worrying about having to work and pay bills. If she continued to get the miles she had been getting, in the next year everything would be paid off and she could follow her dream.

After dinner, Larry called and gave Cassy the address for Rick and quick directions.

Cassy and Lisa left for Rick's before sunset. Cassy took Bright Eyes with her, as Larry had suggested. She wanted to take Sam with her too but asked the rest of the crew to let him out before they left, then lock down the doggy door. She didn't want him outside after dark. He was too brave for his own good.

Those left eventually piled into Warren's truck and headed downtown with Mickey sitting in the bed of the truck enjoying the cold air. Everyone remained quiet during their ride to the station, each lost in their own thoughts, dreading what was ahead of them.

CHAPTER 45

Warren, Andy, Jacob, Ty and Krys arrived at the police station just before sunset and met Larry in his office. He took them to a conference room to meet up with their designated teams.

"Before we get this show on the road, I have an update on an incident that occurred last night." Larry began. "Thirty-seven National Guard men and women and the mayor's bodyguard were murdered by Blake and his followers."

Gasps were heard around the room and "I don't believe it" and "Oh, my God" were whispered.

"What the hell happened?" a voice at the back of the room asked.

"The mayor evidently contacted the Governor, declared a state of emergency and called in the guard. He led them around town in his limo checking out empty warehouses. From what I gathered, the warehouses were all empty."

"Then how?" another voice shouted out.

"On their way back toward the mayor's office, he spotted movement in a building that was up for sale and not supposed to be occupied. The guard entered, were attacked and literally torn apart."

"Why didn't they just turn them?" Warren asked.

"Blake wasn't recruiting last night. He was demonstrating his power, his ability to destroy. He was laughing at us and our efforts."

"What about the mayor, the sorry...." The desk sergeant began before Larry cut him off.

"The mayor is no longer mayor, he resigned this morning. From what I've heard through the grapevine, Blake spared him on purpose, wouldn't let any of the others touch him either."

"I'd say it serves the mayor right, now he's got to live with what happened, what he orchestrated. But then he'd have to have a conscience and he definitely doesn't have one." The desk sergeant spoke up.

"At least we don't have to listen to his stupidity anymore." Another voice from within the assembly said.

There were murmurs of assent all around the room.

"Well, now you are going to see an influx of guardsmen on the streets. But at least they'll be prepared and know how to handle any crisis. A couple of our officers have been with them most of the afternoon instructing them and basically educating them." Larry added.

"What did they do last night, go in blind?" the desk sergeant asked.

"Basically. No crosses, no holy water, no stakes. Only their pistols and rifles which were, as you all know, useless. As a matter of fact, from what I've been told, they didn't even have a chance to fire their rifles."

"So, does this change any of our plans?" Andy asked.

"No. Our plans don't change for tonight. There will be more guardsmen on the streets but most of you will be outside the city tonight. The guardsmen are going to be searching outside the downtown area, the rest of us will be back at the hospital, which seems to be their center of activity." Larry answered. "Now, let's get you all assigned and out of here." Larry added.

CHAPTER 46

Andy was paired up with a team of highway patrolmen, Rob and Paul, as well as Rick's protégé Eric, who would accompany them in Rick's place.

Rob and Paul could have been brothers, they looked so much alike. They were both tall and well-muscled. Rob was 35 years old while Paul was only 24, but they both had short brown hair and brown eyes. They were both well-tanned and admitted to liking the outdoors, whether it be camping or fishing or hunting. They commented on the bows that they had been practicing with, Ron saying it was something he wished he had had the last time he went elk hunting up in the mountains. Paul joked with Rob, saying he couldn't hit the side of a barn with an arrow, much less an elk. At that point, Rob reminded Paul that he had out-shot him two to one on the practice range that afternoon.

Eric was a quiet, short, thin man who looked almost sheepish in the presence of the two larger officers. He told Andy that he was an accountant, had not been in the service or seen any kind of action in his lifetime. He was a meek and mild-mannered individual. Andy wondered if Eric could possibly be of any help if they did encounter Blake or any of his followers.

As if reading his mind, Eric looked directly at Andy and said, "You don't have to worry about me, Andy. I'm a lot tougher than I look. And I don't back down from anything, not now, not ever."

Andy looked Eric in the eyes and believed every word he had just said.

"Hope you all like dogs cause Mickey's coming along. She'll sniff out a vampire before we can spot it. She's a necessity."

The three men all agreed that Mickey would be an asset and proceeded to make friends with her.

Eric knelt on the floor, eye to eye with Mickey. As he scratched her ears, Andy could hear him talking to her in a very gentle voice. "Don't worry, girl. We're going to be best of friends. You warn me and I'll protect you, although I bet you can be pretty vicious if you want to be."

Warren was teamed up with two members of the S.W.A.T. Team, Mike and June.

Mike was around 5' 10" tall, on the stout side. He said he was from Michigan but had settled in Denver after spending time in the Army, where he served as Military Police. He had done two stints in Afghanistan before coming back to Denver and going to the police academy. He was soon recruited for the S.W.A.T. Team because of his record for arrests in a timely manner, ones that stood up in court and actually put the criminals away. He was proudly responsible for putting quite a few drug dealers out of business. He had an outgoing personality, said he loved to play guitar and actually had a country band that played different gigs on the weekends. He had always thought he would end up being a DJ, but later on felt what he did was more important.

June was the complete opposite of Mike. She was petite, only 5' 4", very slender. She had a nice smile but Warren immediately sensed that the smile could be very deceiving. She had been responsible for the arrest and conviction of a drug lord, to her credit she admitted it was because she was so charming rather than her ability to carry out the arrest. She was known to be brutal in her determination to carry out the law.

And she was small enough that she could pass for a teenager and infiltrate the drug business in the local high schools.

Warren wasn't sure if she was more deadly than Mike or not, but he was confident in both of their abilities to handle the situation they would be facing tonight.

The extra member of his crew was Jean, a small blond girl who was young enough to be his daughter, maybe even his granddaughter. She carried herself with confidence. She admitted to having been infected by her ex-boyfriend, against her will. When asked about the ex-boyfriend, she just said, "He's an ex and always will be, in more ways than one." Warren immediately felt protective of her and was determined to stay close to her when the situation arose.

Jean stood facing Warren, holding one of Jacob's bows with the quiver draped over her shoulder. She looked more like a modern-day Peter Pan than a Robin Hood. She looked up at Andy and smiled, warming his heart even more.

"I'm much more capable than I look. I've been out on the streets with Rick and he's taught me an awful lot. I can snap a neck as fast as or even faster than you can aim your bow. Either way, the job gets done."

Krys met Sarah and Hank, members of the Denver Police Department. Sarah was tall and lanky but carried herself with a sense of pride. She had been on the police force for 11 years now and had done her share of arrests. She never backed down from a fight and had lost more than one tooth in scuffles with perpetrators. She wasn't what would be considered beautiful but she had a way about her that could draw in any man. She was proud to show Krys pictures of her husband and her two kids, an 11-year-old boy and an 8-year-old girl. The kids were so cute and the husband was what Krys would consider a "real hunk".

"I know I'm older than most of the females here," Sarah told Krys, "but that doesn't mean I'm slower or less deadlier. I know what we're up against and how to handle any situation that should arise." Krys could tell by just that short speech and the look in Sarah's eyes that she should be considered charming but deadly.

Hank, on the other hand, was a sixteen year Veteran on the police force. He had been promoted to detective but couldn't handle the desk and the paperwork. He had asked to be demoted back to the streets and Larry had obliged him, knowing he would be more effective out in public. The first thing Hank did when introduced to Krys was show her pictures of his grandkids. He was proud of his kids but even more proud of his grandkids, which did not surprise Krys in the least.

"I'm one of those grandparents who truly believes we should have had the grandkids first. They're so much more fun than the kids ever were. And we're older and more patient, plus we've probably done everything they're trying to do and can keep one step ahead of them. Except for those damned cell phones. When I got my first upgrade, my 12-year-old granddaughter had to show me how to answer the stupid thing, I kept hanging up on everyone who called me." The smile on his face told Krys how much he truly loved his grandchildren.

Krys was then introduced to Marian, a member of Rick's family and a Kung Fu black belt who told Krys to call her May. She looked like a body builder and Krys immediately wondered how she could have possibly succumbed to a vampire.

Without being asked, May quickly explained to Krys that her husband had infected her one evening in their bedroom. May also explained that her husband was no longer with them. They were now divorced in every sense of the word. May was a very pretty woman, only 24 years old and, even though well-muscled, still had a very feminine way about her.

Krys thought that May was actually a very pretty woman, she could have even been a model. May admitted that she wanted to help out in any way she could to eliminate Blake and all his followers. She had seen a small child who had been infected and was grateful that the child was smart enough to listen to her and Rick when they found him. Although May had no children, she was hoping that some day she would have at least three or four. She loved kids and had always wanted a house full to clean up after. She wanted kids to love not to have to hunt down. But she admitted that she had taken that small boy into her home and was in the process of adopting him. She said if that was how she would become a mother, it worked for her. She could raise a house full of children and didn't necessarily need a husband to do it.

Ty was also teamed up with two Denver Police Department officers, Brad and Tom. When they shook hands, Ty understood why Brad was aboard. His handshake left Ty's hand feeling numb. He was a powerfully built man with a gentle smile. He was 30 years old, married with three kids. He had been a policeman for only a couple of years now, having done a lot of construction work before finally deciding that being a policeman was what he was meant to do. Ty liked Brad immediately but determined that he would not want to go up against him and was glad he was on their side.

Tom was a little over 6 feet tall, average build, long blond hair tied in a ponytail at the back of his neck. Tom laughingly teased Ty about his long braid to which Ty told him at least he figured out how to braid his. They had good rapport immediately upon meeting each other. Tom looked more like a biker than a cop. He wore a biker's jacket and a Harley Davidson bandana. He explained to Ty that he was usually working undercover with the biker gangs and hadn't had time to change before coming to work tonight.

The last member of their team was Phong. He was a short but well-built Asian man. He was an expert in Kung Fu and Karate. He was a trainer with the police force, teaching other police officers the techniques of his art.

Of all the members of Ty's team, Phong was the most likely one to do the most damage when they were approached by Blake or his followers. Ty felt more at ease with Phong along for the ride.

"With a name like Ty, you should look like me." Phong laughed as he shook Ty's hand.

"I've got to ask. A man with your abilities, how did you ever get infected?"

"I've always loved the ladies, but this time I got loved a little too much, if you get my drift."

"Got it." Ty said.

Jacob was introduced to John and Darren, two Highway Patrolmen.

John was still in his uniform and looked to be about Jacob's age. He was of average height and weight but he had a look about him that said "don't mess with me". He spoke with a quiet voice and Jacob determined that he would not want to be stopped on the highway by this man. Although he was quiet, he had a power behind him that commanded respect. He was young in age, but old in experience.

Darren was older, probably over 50. He wasn't very tall, only around 5' 8". He was the kind of person who did not stand out in a crowd, could blend in with people and not be noticed. He had been on the force for over 20 years, coming in fresh out of the Police Academy. Although he had many chances to be promoted, he stayed in the police car on the highway. Jacob could tell that everyone in the room, including Larry, had respect for this man.

Then, Jacob was introduced to Molly, the person Rick had sent to help. She very quickly explained that she had been recruited by Rick after only being infected for three days. She was so thankful to Rick that she had volunteered for this assignment.

Molly was very petite, only 5' 3" tall, maybe weighing 100 pounds soaking wet. But she had a determined look to her. She wasn't nervous about what lay ahead but was ready to face it head on. She carried one of his bows at her side, the tip of which, because of her height or lack of, was dragging on the floor. Although she was so very small, when it was time to leave the room, she carried the bow as if it weighed only an ounce or two. Her confidence was contagious.

"Now that introductions are over and you all have your areas to patrol, all I can say is 'be careful out there' and keep in touch." Larry told them.

With that, all the men and women paired up and headed out to their respective vehicles.

CHAPTER 47

Cassy and Lisa drove in silence, Bright Eyes sitting regally on the back seat of the Jeep. Cassy had rolled down the canvas sides to keep the cold air out, so they were comfortable during the ride.

"Will Sam be okay back at your house?" Lisa asked suddenly.

"He'll be fine." Cassy said. "He won't be happy about being locked inside but it's for his own good.

Although Cassy tried to sound confident in Sam's ability to take care of himself, Lisa could tell she was still very worried about him. Lisa was worried too, knowing exactly what Blake was capable of, but she didn't want to upset Cassy any more than she was already. And the way Blake seemed to know where they all were located, she doubted he would be interested in Sam but more interested in what was going on around town with the police hunting him.

They arrived at Rick's half an hour after leaving Cassy's place. The house sat at the foot of the mountains in Steamboat Springs. It sat back from the road and was hidden by multiple pines and spruces, making it almost invisible from the road.

As Cassy drove up the driveway, she noted that the house was a block long and bordered by large oak trees, now bare of their leaves. The oak was not the normal tree to have in the yard, or anywhere else in the state for that matter. She wondered what they had looked like when fall set in, knowing that they would change to a hundred different shades of yellow, then orange, then red and finally brown.

The house was a large brick ranch style. It seemed to stretch forever. The front door contained an etched glass window which sparkled different colors when her headlights hit it. The house had a very large picture window next to the door that probably afforded a view across the front lawn to the road.

There was a three-car garage at the south end of the house. The garage door on the end was extra-large and she guessed it housed a motorhome.

Cassy knew immediately that they were in the better part of town. Even though it was already dark outside, she could make out the silhouette of the foothills behind the house, stretching up into the mountains and disappearing into the night sky.

The front porch extended the length of the house. Near the front door stood four rocking chairs along with various tables. Cassy parked the Jeep in front of the porch and the girls walked up to the front door, Bright Eyes walking between them.

Before Lisa could knock on the door, it was opened and in the doorway stood Pat.

Lisa didn't move, just stood staring at her sister. Pat was dressed in a peasant skirt with a white lacy blouse and flat ballet type shoes. Her hair was once again styled and shiny, flowing down her back and across her shoulders.

"Oh, my God." Lisa exclaimed, continuing to stand and stare.

"Are you going to stand there in the cold all night, little sister, or are you going to come inside and give me a hug?" Pat asked.

Lisa continued to stand on the porch, staring at Pat in disbelief. After what seemed forever, she finally took a step forward and almost fell into Pat's arms. She started crying uncontrollably, never letting go of her sister.

Cassy watched Lisa's reaction and noticed that while Pat held Lisa, she also starting crying.

Rick appeared out of nowhere, asking the two women if they were going to come the rest of the way into the house and let Cassy come inside before she froze outside on the porch.

Pat and Lisa turned together, Pat leading Lisa down the hallway into the living room. Rick invited Cassy and Bright Eyes in out of the cold and then escorted them down the hall.

When Cassy entered the living room area, the first thing she saw was a roaring fire in a huge fireplace. It seemed to take up the entire wall. The room was refreshingly warm and she immediately removed her coat which Rick took and hung up on a coat tree near the doorway.

Lisa and Pat sat together on an over-stuffed high-backed sofa. All the furniture in the room was old fashioned but exceptionally comfortable looking. Cassy noted a lot of polished wooden tables scattered around the room, some with very expensive looking knick-knacks on them.

"How are you feeling?" Lisa asked Pat.

"I should ask you the same thing, considering what I've been told I put you through." Pat answered.

Lisa looked angrily over at Rick.

"Not me," he confessed. "Larry brought the tape you did over here for Pat to listen to. Pat insisted on it because she didn't remember what had happened in the RV."

"I'm okay now." Lisa insisted. "But, what about you?"

"A lot of the past weeks, even months, I don't remember. I can remember when I met Blake. I was walking down the street with some purchases I had just made, some leotards for the girls back at work. He came out of nowhere. He grabbed my arm and I turned, ready to knock him out for being so presumptuous. That's all I remember."

"What about all the visits to my house every night?" Lisa asked.

"When? What happened?" Pat questioned Lisa, looking bewildered.

"Nothing major happened. What's the last thing you do remember?"

"Picking myself up off the grass at the hospital downtown and watching Blake disappear. Rick holding my hand, then coming here."

"Will you be okay now?"

"Rick says I'll be just fine, I just won't be on the beach tanning any time soon." Pat announced.

"Oh, yeah." Lisa said, looking around the room at Rick and then at Cassy. "Pat's getting better every minute. I'd say she's almost back to normal after that wise crack."

The tension left the room and Lisa sat, holding Pat's hands, just looking into Pat's eyes and smiling.

CHAPTER 48

Andy joined Eric in the back seat of the highway patrol car with Mickey lying on the seat between them.

"If she sniffs out vampires, why is she so friendly to me?" Eric asked as soon as they were settled in.

"She knows instinctively that you aren't a threat." Andy told him.

"That's good to know cause she may look gentle but I wouldn't want to tangle with her."

"Good judge of character." Andy commented.

"We'll be going out on the highway and then through some truck stops and RV parks. Maybe we'll get lucky and find the RV." Rob said from the front seat.

"If we find it, you'll be calling in for backup, right?" Andy asked.

"Yeah. Why?"

"We shouldn't tangle with Blake by ourselves, not unless you want to end up like him or dead." Andy said.

"So you're saying this Blake's a real bad ass?" Paul asked.

"What Andy's saying is that even us four are no match for him. He has so much more going on than you could ever imagine. Your bullets won't harm him, and I'm not sure even these arrows will." Eric interjected.

"That's all he's got going on for him?" Paul asked.

"Not really. He can put you in a sort of trance and make you do stuff you wouldn't do if you were aware of your actions. If you look into his eyes, you might find yourself offering your neck to him without even thinking about it." Eric told him.

"He can literally disappear in front of your eyes, just walk away and blend into the night. I've seen him catch bullets and arrows in midair before they reach him, then laugh as he throws them back at you." Andy added.

"Sounds more like a magician than a vampire." Paul said, sarcasm evident in his voice.

"I know one of the volunteers from Hebert who went up to Kalamazoo, have known him his entire life. He watched a man scratch his own eyes out and bleed to death. That man died because Blake gave him the command to do so without ever saying a word." Andy told them, hoping that Paul would come to realize how serious the situation was, that it wasn't something to joke about.

"Blake has powers you really don't want to get involved with. And he has no qualms in punishing someone severely if they do not do as he commands." Eric added.

"Sounds like we're about to meet our match." Rob said.

"More than your match, unfortunately." Eric told them.

Paul drove onto the highway, heading toward their first destination, the RV park where Lisa had been found. They were hoping that Blake would consider it safe, that they wouldn't expect him to return there. Paul kept quiet the entire drive.

Andy sat in his seat, petting Mickey, trying to stay calm. He hoped that Paul's sarcastic remarks would not be his downfall. He knew Blake's power and was sure that Paul would not know what to do if he came face to face with Blake.

CHAPTER 49

June drove away from the station.

"What's our destination?" Warren asked.

"We're going to Denver General. That seems to be the busy spot for our vamps. Rick will join us there later." Mike told Warren.

"It's my understanding that all of this started in your town, Warren?" Mike asked.

"This phase of it, yes."

"This phase?" June asked.

"According to Blake, he's been around over 100 years. According to Krys, our vampire expert, he's been previously drinking blood and taking it all, leaving people dead. It's only now that he's recruiting and, although he still drinks their blood, he's leaving enough in them to keep them alive and ready to do his bidding."

"What about this Rick fella?" June asked. "I've heard of him but never met him. Is he a vampire too?"

"I've worked with Rick at the hospital a couple nights ago. He is a vampire, but the serum he takes stops him from craving blood. He's an okay guy. He's on a mission to eliminate Blake and help as many of the people Blake and his followers have infected as he can."

"What about this serum he takes?"

"Right now, the serum is working." Jean interjected. "I'm living proof. I still can't go out in the sunlight though, that's the only drawback so far. But I don't crave human or animal blood and I can otherwise lead a normal life. Rick still works for the FBI, only now he's on the night shift, like the rest of us."

"Sounds interesting," June said.

"Let's hope you never have to find out how uninteresting it really is. I can't lead a normal life, none of us can, yet. But we're hopeful that Rick's Dr. Boykolov can perfect the serum. The doctor, along with other doctors and scientists, are working on it and hopefully one day we can all be back to normal, or as normal as we can ever be again. I want to see the sunlight without worrying about being burned up and turned into ashes. You don't know how lucky you are."

"By the way, we won't be the only ones at Denver General. Ty and Jacob and their teams will be joining us. We'll basically be surrounding the hospital. The rest of the teams will join us after they've checked out the closer RV parks and truck stops." Mike told them.

"That young couple working with the DPD, what's their story?" June asked Warren.

"Ty partnered with Blake for three years driving semi, didn't know what he was. He met Krys in Effingham. She's the one who figured out that Blake was a vampire, even though at that time Ty still didn't believe her. They drove down to Hebert and convinced me that my problem with the disappearances and reappearances was due to vampires. They volunteered to go up to Kalamazoo and help out there. Now, they're together in the truck, they're here and Ty's determined to be the one to eliminate Blake."

"Sounds like at least one good thing came out of all that mess." June said.

"That's exactly what Ty would tell you. I'd say two though, since I got Lisa back unharmed and still human."

Warren looked across the seat at Jean. She sat quietly looking out the car window. He knew she must be thinking about her life and how it had changed.

The inside of the car remained quiet as they drove toward the hospital. Warren sat thinking about Lisa and hoping that her reunion with Pat would be successful and that she would once again have her sister back.

But he also continued to worry about Cassy. She had seen the doctor and the other man burn up in the hospital waiting room. But she had not thus far been exposed to Blake's power and he prayed she never would be. She was considered the rookie of their team and she was still an innocent.

And, of course, he worried about Lisa and what seemed to be Blake's vendetta to have her eliminated. Although Krys insisted that vampires didn't have emotions, Warren could not bring himself to believe that part of the myth. If Blake didn't feel things, then why did he go back to Kalamazoo for Pat and why try so hard to eliminate Lisa. Was it because Lisa had thwarted his attempt to kill her back at the RV park? Blake was definitely showing emotions, although most of his emotions were triggered by rage. That rage had to be squelched or it would mean the death of all of them.

CHAPTER 50

The patrol car Ty was riding in had reached Sapp Brothers Truck Stop. Ty had volunteered to go inside the restaurant to check it out. He came back out to the patrol car to report that everything inside was business as usual.

They cruised the parking lot, noting that there were quite a few trucks parked out back. While driving down the first aisle, Tom spotted a woman standing on the steps of one of the trucks. When she saw their patrol car, she immediately stepped down and walked toward the back of the trailer. Brad sped up and circled around that row of parked trucks. He stopped in back of the trailer as she walked out in front of the car.

Tom immediately got out of the car.

"Hold up a minute there," he said.

She stopped and raised her hands above her head in a gesture of surrender.

"What?" she asked.

She was maybe in her middle to late thirties, but like most of the lot lizards, she looked much older, much more worn out.

"You're name?" Tom asked.

"I'm Susan."

"And you're business out here on the lot?"

"I work inside. I was just going to my car." She answered.

"By way of that truck?"

"He's a customer."

"I bet he is. Do us both a favor. Get in your car and go home."

"Yes sir." Susan said. She walked around him and headed toward the employee parking lot.

Tom turned around and walked back to the patrol car. As he did, the truck pulled out of the space and headed toward the exit.

"She okay?" Ty asked.

"Yeah. Just a working girl."

"Did you notice anything strange about that truck?" Ty asked.

"Not really." Brad answered as he put the patrol car back in drive and started to slowly cruise down the aisle.

"The windows were tinted way too dark, you couldn't see the driver inside."

"And?" Brad asked.

"And that's exactly how the windows in my truck were tinted when Blake was driving." Ty told them.

"We've got an RV park to check out next." Brad said. "Got to keep on schedule."

They pulled out of the lot but kept their eyes on the truck and trailer in question. He got back on I-70 headed south. Brad followed the truck onto the highway, but got off at the next exit to check out the RV park. They cruised through it but there were no RVs present and no evidence that there was any activity in or around the park.

"It's 15 to 20 minutes south to Watkins. There's the Tomahawk Truck Stop there. It's small but worth checking out." Tom said. "Besides, that's the direction our tinted window truck was heading."

Tom sped up and it only took ten minutes to reach their designated exit. He drove up the exit ramp, turned left at the top, drove over the highway and then down the road to the truck stop.

When they turned into the lot, it was immediately evident that something was wrong. There were two buildings. One housed the fuel pumps, convenience store and showers. The second larger building contained the restaurant and a small gift shop.

"Does it seem a little too quiet to anyone else besides me?" Phong asked.

Brad told Tom to drive around back by the trucks. They circled around the fuel pumps and headed between the two buildings toward the back lot.

There were about a dozen trucks parked out back but no activity around the trucks or across the lot.

"Looks like our friend from Sapp Brothers didn't drive too far." Brad said, pointing out his window at the truck they had observed earlier.

"Do truckers usually visit every truck stop along the way?" Phong asked, looking over at Ty.

"No, not really." Ty answered. Without another word, he picked up his bow from off the floor, grabbed his quiver and quickly loaded an arrow into the bow.

Tom drove back around the side of the building that housed the restaurant. He stopped the car next to the curb and quickly turned off the lights. He and Brad took out their service revolvers and checked the clips.

The four men exited the police vehicle and quickly stepped up onto the sidewalk next to the building. Ty stood to the front of their line and took a step toward the restaurant door. Before he could take another step, he noted movement in the parking lot. He motioned for everyone to be still and pointed away from the door.

Phong stepped off the sidewalk to face three men who were walking toward them.

"Can I help you?" Phong asked.

"I think it's more like can we help you?" The trucker in the lead said.

"And what do you think we need help with?" Ty asked as he stepped away from the building to face the three strangers.

"The vampires, of course."

Phong stood staring at the three truckers.

Ty walked up beside Phong. "Are they okay?"

"More than okay." Phong answered.

"Okay, names and weapons." Ty said.

"I'm Sam, I've got a Colt 45."

"I'm Jeff, a 22 pistol."

"Bud, a 9 mm Glock."

"Unload the bullets into your hands."

Without a word, all three truckers emptied their guns and stood with their hands outstretched.

Ty took a small bottle out of his shirt pocket and sprinkled the clear liquid on each of the truckers' hands.

"Holy water." Sam said.

They reloaded their weapons, then walked up onto the sidewalk.

"That makes seven." Tom said.

"Our lucky number." Brad added.

Everyone stood behind Ty who took a step forward to try and look through the side door into the restaurant.

Suddenly, without warning, the door flew open and a woman crawled over the threshold onto the sidewalk. She was covered in blood. She continued to crawl across the sidewalk, over the curb and onto the pavement.

She was saying something over and over again, almost in a whisper. She rolled over onto her back and suddenly saw the men standing by the wall of the building.

"Help me." She said pleadingly.

Phong made a move toward the woman, but Brad cut in front of him and said, "I've got this." He knelt down on the pavement beside the woman.

"Are you hurt?" Brad asked. "Have you been bitten?"

"No." she whispered. "No." She said a little louder.

Jeff had moved off the sidewalk and knelt on the opposite side of the woman.

"I know her. She's one of the night waitresses here. Is she okay?"

Phong had walked up behind Jeff. He put his hand on Jeff's shoulder and told him that she was okay, not infected, just scared.

"I'll take her back to my truck." Jeff said. "I've got Handi-Wipes and some extra clothes. I'll get her cleaned up as good as I can and she can wear a pair of my jeans and shirt for now. Is that okay?"

"That's fine." Ty told him. "We'll be okay here. You just take care of her."

Ty watched as Jeff gently helped the woman get up off the pavement. He then picked her up in his arms. She put her arms around his neck and held him tightly, her head buried against his jacket.

Looking at the two of them, Ty could tell there was more than just a waitress-customer relationship there. He watched as Jeff disappeared around the back of the building into the parking lot.

Ty and Phong stepped back up onto the curb to the side of the building.

"Are we ready?" Phong asked.

Everyone answered with a yeah, yes, guess so and ready as we can be.

Ty took a step up to the door. He tried to look through the glass but it was too dark inside to see anything clearly. He did see some movement but couldn't make out exactly what it was.

Ty slowly opened the door, then quickly stepped inside, Phong following closely behind. Brad and Tom, then Sam and Bud followed.

The inside of the restaurant looked like it had been recently painted red, the paint still wet. The lights were all shut off but they could detect some movement further inside the restaurant. There was just enough light filtering through the front picture windows from the parking lot out front.

The six men spread out, a foot apart, in a straight line. It was hard to comprehend what they were seeing. As their eyes got used to the darkness, they realized that the scene looked surreal, like a painting of what hell must look like.

Phong was the first to move. He crept soundlessly toward a booth by the front window. Without a sound, he grabbed a man off the seat and quickly made a twisting movement. The only sound was the man's neck when the bones in it cracked. Phong slowly lowered him onto the floor.

He then reached into the booth and grabbed hold of the hand of a waitress. He helped her stand up, then whispered something in her ear. When she shook her head yes, he turned and motioned to Tom to take her outside. Tom looked puzzled but, when Phong put his hand up in an okay sign, Tom took the lady and walked quietly out the door.

That left Phong, Ty, Bud and Sam in the restaurant. Before Ty could think clearly about what was happening, a tall man rushed at him, snarling, salivating. Ty immediately fired an arrow and before the man took another step, he burst into flames, then slowly sank to the floor.

Unfortunately, this caught the attention of several other occupants in the restaurant, who stopped what they were doing, turned and faced the men at the door.

Phong was able to count the people standing in the middle of the room facing them. He whispered, "six men and two women" loud enough for the other men to hear him. The men and women started walking slowly toward them.

Phong realized he wouldn't have time to try to talk any of them down, that they were about to attack. He felt relieved to have Ty with him and knew that Brad, Bud and Sam would do their best, whatever that would be knowing that they had never battled vampires before. This wasn't exactly a typical situation, not something they would be adept at.

Without a word, Bud suddenly took a step back, turned slightly toward the door. He flicked the light switch on the wall between the door and the window. The ceiling lights came on and illuminated the entire restaurant.

The light seemed to startle the advancing horde, stopping them in their tracks momentarily. They looked confused, but not for long. Within seconds, they started walking forward again.

Suddenly, Bud spoke up just loud enough for the rest of them to hear. "The third one from the left is mine."

The man who seemed to be leading the pack was huge. He was in a uniform with the Tomahawk patch on it. Ty didn't try to make out his name or his badge number, but let loose with an arrow. The arrow hit the man in the shoulder and the result was instantaneous.

When he burst into flames, the others moved quickly away from him. They spread out across the middle of the restaurant. Now there were five, or at least five they could see.

Phong took a step forward, then actually leapt over the two people in the middle. Without a word, he ran past the counter, turned left and disappeared into another section of the restaurant.

Ty had already reloaded his bow and stood, aiming at the closest man to him.

"Will they fire up like that when we shoot them too?" Bud asked in a whisper.

"You can bet on it." Ty told him.

In unison, Ty fired his arrow at the same time the other three men started shooting their weapons. The restaurant suddenly lit up as if a fireball had exploded in it. The men stood staring at the inferno. The flames died out quickly, leaving only ashes and bones.

"Bud, you and Sam check out the souvenir shop, me and Brad will check out the kitchen."

"What about your friend Phong?" Bud asked.

"Don't worry about Phong. They can't hurt him." Ty answered.

"Why not?" Sam asked.

"Tell you all about it later." Ty motioned to Bud and they headed behind the counter toward the kitchen. Sam and Brad stepped over the bones on the floor and slowly walked toward the gift shop.

Ty walked through the double doors into the kitchen area, Brad close behind. They noted that the stove was still lit up and a big pot was steaming on top of it. Ty didn't stop to see what was in the pot but turned the knob to off as he walked past the stove.

They circled around the worktable toward the back of the kitchen. They separated, Ty going to his left toward the freezer, Bud to the right toward the walk-in cooler.

When Bud opened the cooler doors, he jumped back and yelled for Ty, who stepped up to the open door. Bud was posed with his gun raised and aimed at the inside of the cooler.

Ty looked inside and was astonished to see a family crouched on the floor near the back wall. The woman sat on the floor, holding a boy and a girl in her lap. The man stood up and scooted in front of them protectively, a steak knife in one hand and a butcher knife in the other. He stood motionless, both knives raised in a defensive pose.

"It's okay," Ty said softly, "we're here to help you."

"How do I know that?" the man asked.

Ty lowered his bow so that it was pointed at the floor. He put his hand on Bud's arm and Bud slowly lowered his gun. The man inside the cooler didn't move.

"You need to let us lead you out of here to safety. Do you have a vehicle outside?" Ty asked.

"Our motorhome is parked out front by the street." The woman volunteered from behind the man. "We're on vacation." She added.

"You all need to get out of here, now." Bud told them. "You've got to let us help you."

"Please, honey." The woman pleaded as she got up off the floor, still holding onto the two children.

The man finally put the butcher knife on the shelf next to him. He lowered his other hand to his side but held onto the steak knife, still not completely trusting the two strangers.

The woman picked up the girl, then tapped the man on his shoulder. He turned around and picked up the boy, holding him tightly.

Bud turned his back to the family and took a step forward. Ty walked quickly toward the double doors. The family followed them silently through the kitchen.

When they reached the doors, Bud turned around and told the man and woman to shield the childrens' eyes. They did as they were told. Ty told Bud to go ahead and turned back into the kitchen.

Bud led them through the doors, past the end of the counter and out the side door. He heard the woman gasp and the man say, "Oh, my God," but they didn't stop, they kept following Bud.

When they were out the door and off the sidewalk, away from the building, Bud led them around to the front.

"It's the Winnebago out by the street." The man told him.

They all walked briskly across the parking lot, Bud continually looking around for any movement. When they reached the motorhome, Bud stopped and asked for the keys. He slowly entered the RV, quickly checked it out, came back down the steps and told the family it was safe.

He handed the man his keys back, then patted him on the back and told him to have a safe trip. To his surprise, the man hugged him and whispered "thank you". He then quickly climbed up into the RV.

As Bud turned back toward the restaurant, he had only taken two steps when he heard the door lock click. Before he reached the front of the building, the motorhome was already pulling out of the parking lot and moving slowly onto the road leading to the highway.

Ty met Bud on the sidewalk.

"The kitchen's clear." he said.

They stood for a minute more when Sam and Brad came out the door, declaring the gift shop was also clear. The four of them stood silently, waiting.

The door opened slowly and Phong walked out. He had blood spattered on the front of his shirt and pant legs.

"You okay?" Ty asked.

"Yeah." Phong answered. "There were three more in that off-shoot part of the restaurant."

"And?" Bud coaxed.

"And now there aren't." Phong said.

"Shouldn't we check the fuel store and showers?" Brad asked.

"All four of us should go," Ty said, looking at the two truckers and Brad.

They walked slowly across the lot to the fuel station, quietly opened the front door and stepped inside. The lights were all on and they were able to look down each aisle to the back of the building. Ty walked down the center aisle, while Bud and Sam veered off to the left and Brad went to the right. They walked through the store and met at the desk in the back.

Sam motioned to Bud, pointed to the door leading to the showers. They walked through the door, disappearing from view. Ty and Brad remained by the desk, anxiously waiting.

After a minute or two, Sam and Bud came back through the door, Sam giving Ty the thumbs up.

The four men walked back through the store and out the door. When they returned to the sidewalk by the restaurant, Sam told Phong "All clear".

While they stood deciding who would go back into Denver and who would stay and wait for an ambulance for the two waitresses and the clean-up crew, Ty noticed that Bud had sat down on the curb, his head bowed down into his hands.

"Bud," Ty said after walking over to him, kneeling beside him and putting his hand on his shoulder, "why were you so specific about the third one from the left?"

"He was my brother. We were a team even though we owned two trucks. He had loaded up in Denver yesterday and we were going to meet here tonight. I was going through Denver to Cheyenne. I saw his truck when I got here and figured he was inside. He was younger than me by eleven years, I always felt more like a dad than his older brother. I just had to take care of him now too."

Ty silently kneeled next to Bud a while longer, trying to convey his concern by continuing to keep his hand on Bud's shoulder reassuringly.

Brad had gone back to the patrol car but now stood on the sidewalk, watching Ty and Bud.

"I've got the clean-up crew on the way, as well as an ambulance. Sam can drive back to the hospital to hook up with the rest of the teams. I'll hang out here for a while. Just to make sure there aren't any more hanging out in the lot or anywhere nearby."

"How will you get back to Denver?" Ty asked.

"I'll drive him back in." Bud said, getting up off the curb. "I got to go through Denver anyhow. I can drop him off wherever."

"Okay, then." Ty said. "Let's get back to town.

CHAPTER 51

Krys had been sitting in the police car outside the hospital for a good two and a half hours now. The patrol cars assigned to the hospital had all been in position all night, literally watching all the main entrances, observing the people coming and going. Everything seemed normal, although it was still early, only around 10 p.m.

Around 10:30, another patrol car joined them and Krys was happy to see Ty and two of his partners back in town. She noted that one of the officers was missing, but she couldn't get out of her car to go find out what had been happening. She hoped and prayed it hadn't been too horrible and that the missing officer had not met a bad end.

As she continued to stare at the patrol car, Ty turned toward her vehicle and gave her the thumbs up sign. Krys smiled at Ty, relaxed somewhat and sat back in her seat to continue her watch on the hospital doors and the surrounding areas.

After the patrol car had been parked less than five minutes, Ty got out and, along with Phong, walked around to the front of the vehicle. Suddenly, Ty walked away from the cars. Krys felt somewhat relieved when she noticed that one of the other men in the car accompanied him. She watched as they disappeared around the corner of the building.

Ty was wearing a long trench coat and she knew it was hiding his bow. She felt anxious about him leaving the safety of the car, but she believed in him and didn't question his actions. Now, watching him walk away, she suddenly realized how much she had come to love him.

"Your man will be okay. Phong is one of our best hunters." May whispered to Krys.

"I thought all you did was convert them." Krys said, turning in her seat to face May.

"If they are determined to live their present life, we eliminate them." May told her matter-of-factly.

"Is Ty the one who came up with the idea for the wooden arrows?" Sarah asked from the front seat, not turning around but continuing to watch out her window at the people on the street and sidewalk around the hospital.

"No. That would be Jacob. He's from Hebert. His sister Cassy lives up here. Jacob and his Uncle Andy came up with Warren to help out. Andy is a neat, older gentleman. He's been anointing the arrows with holy water, just to give them an extra edge."

"Like all of our bullets?" May said.

"Your bullets?" Krys asked.

"Larry made sure all of our bullets would act like the sun, as he put it. Every bullet has been blessed and sprinkled with holy water." Sarah told Krys.

"It's a bad situation," Krys began, "but it's nice to know that this time we are prepared to face what's ahead. In Kalamazoo, it was by guess and by gosh. None of us really knew what we were doing. We got the job done, but it was a hard road up there and it took entirely too long."

"Did you see a lot of action in Kalamazoo?" May asked.

"Too much action. We searched one house and found the basement floor covered in vampires, some in tents, some in cardboard boxes. There were quite a few couples and even one baby, about two months old."

"A baby? That's incredible." May commented.

"Lisa took the baby outside with her, not wanting it to be involved in what we were about to do in that basement. Later, when Warren joined Lisa, she realized the baby had been infected too."

Krys paused for a few seconds before proceeding with her story.

"We never knew if the baby was infected through birth or through one of the parents after it was born. Warren took the baby away from Lisa, put a drop of holy water on it and the baby's skin started burning. One of the veteran cops took the baby from Warren and said he'd take care of it."

"Did he?" Hank asked, having turned around in his seat to listen to Krys.

"He did. He took a splinter of wood the size of a toothpick and took care of the infant. Later that same day, when we had all returned to Lisa's house, she found the baby on her bed with a huge stake through it's body. That stake was as big if not bigger than the baby."

"Blake?" May asked.

"It was still daylight so we figured it was one of his familiars who got into Lisa's house and put the baby on her bed. It nearly broke Lisa when she found that baby. She blamed Warren but soon realized it was Blake who was responsible for the child being there and for the large stake, not Warren or the cop who had originally taken the child."

"Blake sounds like the devil incarnate." Sarah commented.

"He's worse than that. He can control you. Never look into his eyes. I made that mistake when he was floating outside the semi window talking to Ty. He looked at me and in seconds I found myself outside the truck standing on the top step. We were parked in Lisa's yard and every night Blake, Pat and more and more vampires would show up on her front yard wanting her to either come outside or let them in. Even though Blake promised Ty not to hurt him or his, he made it very clear how powerful he really was that night. It's something I'll never be able to get out of my mind."

"Did you get attacked out there?" May asked.

"No. Ty said he kept calling my name but I never heard him. I could have very easily been attacked in the position Blake put me in. I've never felt so helpless in all my life. I never want to feel like that again.

"Guess we better get back to watching the grounds." Hank said. "Krys, you think Blake can stop our bullets?"

"I really don't know. He caught an arrow the other night before it could harm him. He's awful fast. He doesn't seem to fear our weapons, he laughs at us for trying to harm him."

"He may be fast," May said, "but he can't stop all of our bullets."

"I hope you're right." Krys said. "I hope you're right."

CHAPTER 52

Jacob sat in the back seat of the patrol car with Molly. He kept sneaking glances over at her on the drive out of Denver.

Darren had informed them that they were going back east toward Aurora and then northeast into Commerce City. They'd be checking truck stops and RV parks. Andy and his team would be doing the same, only they'd be going north and then west. They'd all meet back downtown at the hospital.

Molly looked over at Jacob, startling him when she caught him glancing her way.

"You can ask me, you know." Molly said.

"Ask you what?" Jacob inquired.

"Ask how I became a vampire, of course."

"Okay. How did you become a vampire, of course?" Jacob asked.

"By getting bit by another vampire, silly." Molly laughed.

"Guess I deserved that."

"I worked nights at the hospital. The parking lot never has been well lit. I had unlocked the door to my car, threw my purse and laptop in and, before I could get in, I was attacked from behind. It happened so quick. But I saw him walk away afterward and I'll recognize him when I see him again. I've got a bullet special made for that son of a bitch."

"I'm sorry. I've just never sat and talked to a, a…" Jacob stuttered.

"You can say vampire, it's okay. Although I prefer to be called vamp instead."

Jacob didn't say anything, just sat looking at Molly.

"Now what?" She asked, perplexed and slightly annoyed.

"How can you be so, I don't know, flippant about all of this?"

"What am I supposed to do, lay down and die? I'm 24 years old and I have the rest of my nights ahead of me. Get it? Nights."

"I get it, I think." Jacob said.

"Look, I'm no cry baby. I'm what I would call a bad ass. I've got a rifle and my 22. I can try to convert them like Rick does. But I have to admit I do enjoy elimination just a little more than conversion."

"You are a bad ass." Jacob told her.

"So, can you handle working with a bad ass vamp or not?" She asked.

"If he can't I'll give it my best shot." Darren called out from the front seat.

"Don't worry, Molly." John interjected. "I know for a fact that Darren's no threat. Just ask his wife."

The atmosphere that had been tenuous at best was now much more relaxed and comfortable. Jacob was astonished at how easy the transition had been.

They rode on in silence, each one alert to their surroundings outside the vehicle. They were all alert and ready if and when they approached or were approached by anyone suspicious.

CHAPTER 53

Ty and Phong walked back to the entrance to the ER. They stood to the side of the door watching as patients and visitors came and went.

Two hours into their surveillance, the rest of the teams joined them, including Andy.

Back in the car, Krys continued to watch the people outside, always keeping a steady eye on Ty. After another 30 minutes, Ty, Phong and Andy, along with Mickey, walked away from the ER doors and started walking around the corner of the building once again. They were soon out of sight.

All of a sudden, without warning, a window on the second floor just to the right of the emergency room doors, blew out with the impact of a body, a large man of at least 300 pounds or more, coming through it.

He hit the ground, landing hard on his back, shards of glass raining down all around and over him. He lay still for only a few seconds, then slowly stood up, looking around curiously.

Before Krys or anyone else in the car could move from their seats, the man turned and ran south, in the same direction Ty and the others had previously walked.

The man stopped suddenly at the corner of the building, stood still as if frozen. He turned around as if to head back to the ER, took one step, then two, then burst into flames in mid stride.

As Krys watched, the flames quickly died down. Ty appeared at the corner of the building, bow in hand. He stood, staring at the ground. The man's bones lay at his feet, now just smoldering. Andy and Phong soon joined Ty.

Jacob appeared as if out of nowhere to join Ty near the ashes. They talked for a few seconds, then turned and once again disappeared around the corner of the building, Andy and Phong close behind them.

Krys had stepped out of the car and stood staring at the second story window, the curtains waving in and out, blown by a much stronger, much colder wind than had been present earlier in the evening.

She took a step backwards, bumping into May who had silently come up behind her. Still looking at the window, she suddenly gasped when Blake appeared in the opening, staring down at her. She shivered involuntarily.

Before she could alert anyone, Blake stepped back from the window and disappeared back inside the hospital room.

"What's wrong?" May asked.

"Blake." Krys said as she turned and ran toward the hospital, heading in the same direction where she had last seen Ty, Jacob, Andy and Phong. She realized that May was running beside her. She continued to run ahead, anxious to find Ty and let him know she had seen Blake.

CHAPTER 54

Inside the hospital, Blake appeared to be floating across the floor, followed by a nurse and two orderlies. As Blake proceeded further down the hall, one by one, the orderly, the nurse and then the second orderly side-stepped into different rooms.

Outside, Krys had caught up with Ty about half a block away. She was out of breath and could only speak one or two words at a time.

"Blake. Inside." She blurted out, still trying to catch her breath. "Second floor."

The three men immediately turned and headed back to the ER entrance with Mickey in the lead, instinctively knowing in which direction to go.

As Ty ran past Krys and May, he yelled "Stay here."

"Not in this lifetime." Krys yelled back and she and May started running behind the men.

They rounded the corner of the building to see Sarah, Rob, Hank, Paul and Eric all standing next to the ER doors, fully armed. They were diverting the people away from the area, asking them to leave and directing them to other hospitals.

Paul was on his cell phone. He hung up and told them that Larry would soon be at the hospital with other policemen. He wanted to evacuate the hospital quickly to avoid having any more patients infected by Blake or his followers. They were expecting ambulances and buses to arrive soon to help transport as many of the patients as possible. The other hospitals in the area had already been notified and were standing by.

Without another word, they all entered the hospital, walking in single file past numerous people sitting patiently waiting to see a doctor. Although they raised the curiosity of the check-in nurse and the security guard, no one tried to stop their procession.

"Second floor?" Ty turned to ask Krys, instinctively knowing she would be standing behind him.

"Yeah, second. That's where that man came crashing through the window. Blake was standing inside that room looking down at us."

Ty stopped at the elevators. He quickly pushed the up button. Everyone was startled when the arrow lit up and the bell rang announcing that elevator number three was already on their floor.

Everyone took a step back and stood anxiously waiting for the doors to open, ready with their bows if needed. When the doors slowly opened, the elevator was empty. Ty, Andy, Jacob, Krys, May and Paul all piled into the elevator.

"The rest of you follow in the next one. We'll wait upstairs for you to join us." Paul told them.

Ty pushed the button for the second floor. Before the door was completely closed, they all heard the bell indicating that another elevator had arrived. Their elevator began its slow ascent, everyone checking their weapons, making sure they were all ready.

The elevator stopped and the door opened slowly. As Andy stepped out, Mickey by his side, the quietness was blatantly evident. The nurse's station was empty, as was the hallway in both directions.

Within seconds, the second elevator arrived. When the door opened, Paul stepped out, then turned and told the occupants to go up to the third floor, divide into two groups and walk the halls, searching the entire floor and checking out every room, including broom closets and bathrooms. Every inch of that floor was to be investigated.

Ty motioned to Krys, Sarah, May and Hank to follow him to the right hallway. As they headed down the hall, Andy, Jacob, Rob, Paul and Eric started walking toward the opposite hallway, Mickey in the lead.

Andy's team walked slowly down the hallway. When they approached the end, they turned to their right. Mickey stood still, looking down the hall, alert to any sound.

Jacob caught up to Andy and together they followed Mickey down the hall. They were headed toward the room where the window had been blown out. They all walked side by side behind Mickey, no one speaking, trying not to make any sound at all.

CHAPTER 55

Ty, Krys, May, Sarah and Hank followed the hallway which eventually turned to their left. Ty's plan was to meet back up with Andy and his team near the room where Krys had seen Blake.

As they walked slowly onward, Ty thought he heard a woman scream, but it was muffled as if farther down the hall, maybe behind a closed door. He was beginning to wish he had Mickey with him right now.

Suddenly, no more than 30 feet in front of them, a man stepped out of a patient's room. He stopped and stared in disbelief at Ty's group, blood dripping down his chin onto his white lab coat.

Ty's reflexes kicked in and, without a second thought, he fired his bow. The arrow flew true and hit the man dead center in the chest. He immediately burst into flames, falling face first onto the floor, not having made a sound.

As they drew closer to the room the man had just exited, a woman in a hospital gown burst through the door, unsteady on her feet, holding onto the door frame. As soon as she spotted Ty's group, the look of pure terror on her face relaxed.

"Please, help me." She whispered in a hoarse, almost inaudible voice. Her knees buckled and she collapsed to the floor, her arms held out pleadingly.

"I can stay with her." Krys volunteered.

"No." May said from behind Krys. "I'll take her down and have her checked out. If she's been bitten, I'll know what to do. You all take care of your business, I'll take care of her."

May knelt down on the floor next to the lady. The patient was hyperventilating and making jerking movements as if having a seizure. It was evident by the blood still trickling down her neck onto her hospital gown that she had been bitten. She was very agitated, arms flailing as she moaned and tried to grab hold of May, who continued to kneel quietly beside her but avoiding any direct contact.

Suddenly, as if out of nowhere, Kaylee appeared beside May. She walked over to the lady and sat down in front of her, close enough to help calm her down by diverting her attention. The lady slowly held out her hand to Kaylee, no longer paying attention to the people around her. Kaylee put her head in the lady's hand in a gesture of supplication. The lady quieted down completely, picked Kaylee up and held her close to her chest. May helped the lady to her feet, noting that the smell of blood surprisingly didn't seem to affect the dog.

"Kaylee, go with May." Rick's voice spoke up from behind the group. Everyone turned around, surprised but also relieved to have him here with them.

May led the lady down the hall toward the elevators. The woman was now completely calmed down and talking soothingly to the dog.

The rest of the group advanced forward, Rick in the lead walking beside Ty. They could hear a commotion ahead of them, even though the hallway remained empty.

They proceeded slowly, cautiously.

CHAPTER 56

Meanwhile, Andy's group was drawing closer to the room where the window had been shattered. They could hear the wind blowing, howling in the darkness.

Suddenly, as if from nowhere, a woman in a nurse's uniform and a large man in scrubs appeared two doors down the hall.

Mickey, who had been only a couple of feet ahead of the group, stopped and stood perfectly still, growling low.

Andy and Jacob stood behind Mickey, watching the couple. Sarah, Rob and Paul walked up beside Andy and Jacob, making a line from one wall to the other, preventing anyone from walking past them.

The nurse spotted them first. She snarled at them, then shouted, "Leave here."

The man had also turned when he heard the nurse shouting out.

As if tuned to each other, they simultaneously ran toward the group, the man snarling like a rabid dog, the woman screeching at the top of her lungs. Their intent was evident in their faces and their actions. There would be no time for talking.

Andy and Jacob both raised their bows, aiming at each of the oncoming people. Sarah and Paul took a step closer to Andy and Jacob, forming a solid barrier line, determined not to let either one of these two through to do more harm. Rob stood slightly behind Sarah and Paul, gun raised and aimed.

As if on cue, Jacob and Andy fired their bows at the same time Sarah, Rob and Paul fired their guns. Not sure what hit the two vampires first, the arrows or the bullets, the team continued to stand its ground, no one flinching, silently watching.

Within seconds, the nurse and the man burst into flames. Before they hit the floor, the fire alarm sounded and the sprinklers automatically started raining down water on the group, soaking them almost immediately.

Although the two bodies on the floor were similarly soaked, they continued to burn until only their bones remained.

Andy turned to Paul. "See if you can get those sprinklers turned off."

"No problem. I've worked in this hospital before, know where everything is located. May take me a minute or two, but I'll get them turned off."

As Paul turned back down the hallway in the direction they had just come from, Andy, Jacob, Sarah and Rob turned back around, ready to proceed on their designated route.

They walked two by two close to the walls on either side, trying not to get any more wet than they already were. The sprinklers were spaced about six feet apart but were all located in the ceiling down the middle of the hallway. By walking close to the walls, they were able to proceed without getting the brunt of the water raining down on them.

Mickey, on the other hand, walked down the middle of the hall, reveling in the raining water. Every couple of feet she would shake herself, sharing some of the water with the rest of the team.

"Thanks a lot." Andy said. "You're a big help there, Mickey."

They proceeded down the hallway cautiously.

CHAPTER 57

Ty's group was closing in on the room with the broken window. There were two more doors between them and the room in question. They, like Andy's group, had gotten soaking wet from the sprinklers, but they advanced nonetheless.

Suddenly, the door on their left ten feet ahead was pulled open. An orderly exited carrying a child in his arms. The child was maybe 5 or 6 years old. She was very small, weighing only about 40 to 50 pounds. Both the orderly and the child were bloodied. The child was hysterical, struggling to get free of the man's grip. She was screaming and scratching at the man, wiggling around trying her best to get away.

The orderly turned and faced Ty's group, holding the child out in front of him.

"Go ahead, shoot me, fools." He screamed.

Ty aimed carefully but was unable to get a clean shot because of the child. In her struggling she was unintentionally shielding the orderly from their arrows and bullets.

All of a sudden, they heard the sound of breaking glass from inside the room the orderly had just exited. Although the noise was deafening, neither the orderly nor anyone in Ty's group turned toward the door.

Krys noted a shadow against the open doorframe. Before she or anyone else could react, Mike appeared from out of nowhere. In a split second, he karate chopped the orderly on the back of his neck, grabbed the child from the orderly and disappeared back through the door into the room.

The orderly staggered back a step or two, shook his head and leaned toward the opposite wall as if he were about to fall and needed the support. He looked down at his hands which were still spread out in front of him.

A look of disbelief appeared on his face when he realized he was no longer holding the child.

Ty acted spontaneously, brought his bow up, aimed and fired. The arrow hit the orderly in the abdomen. He immediately burst into flames and fell to the floor.

Mike stepped back through the doorway, still holding the little girl in his arms. She had calmed down and lay nestled comfortably, sucking on her thumb.

"She's okay." Mike told them. "We got her in time."

Krys stepped up and took the girl from Mike.

"I'll take her out of here." She said as she turned back down the hall and started walking silently toward the elevators, cuddling the child and cooing to her as they left.

Mike motioned to the rest to follow him and started back down the hallway. As they walked, he checked each room and closed the doors after noting that the rooms were totally empty.

They walked another ten feet down the hallway when Ty suddenly stopped. Andy and his group were standing two feet ahead of them.

"Got a hunch. Follow me." Mike said as he turned back down the hall and rushed through the group, heading back toward the elevators.

Everyone followed him without question, never faltering. The room with the broken window became an afterthought. They instinctively knew that following Mike would bring more results than continuing their search in that last room.

When they reached the elevators, instead of pushing the down button, Mike veered to his right. Twenty feet down the hallway, a sign hanging from the ceiling announced the stairwell. Mike hit the door running and sprang down the stairs, seemingly not touching a step.

The rest of the group followed, trying to keep up but failing miserably. When they reached the first-floor landing, Mike was standing outside the stairwell holding the door open for the rest of the group.

CHAPTER 58

After handing the girl to a nurse in the ER, Krys left the hospital, walking across the sidewalk toward the parked police cars.

Suddenly, out of the corner of her eye, she noted a movement. As she turned back toward the hospital, she was startled to see another figure fly out of that same broken second story window. The man dove headfirst through the window but then somersaulted and hit the ground feet first. When he landed, he bent his knees to cushion his fall. His head was bent down but Krys knew immediately that it was Blake.

She stopped dead in her tracks. He straightened up, raised his head and smiled maliciously.

"Good evening, Krys." Blake said. "Nice to see you again."

"Sorry I can't say the same to you." Krys answered sarcastically.

"So, where is your other half?" Blake asked.

"No idea. But then I don't think I need him right now. Or do I?"

"It doesn't matter. Like the rest of you, he's helpless against me."

"How do you figure?" Krys asked, wanting to keep the conversation going, giving everyone in their hunting party time to arrive.

"Well, let's see. I've got you here to keep my attention averted on you while Ty and the rest of the humans have time to get back down here to help you out."

"You think I need help?" Krys asked.

Blake stood completely still, watching Krys but not answering her. He was completely aware of his surroundings and could sense the arrival of the others.

Krys saw a movement out of the corner of her eye and suddenly Rick and Pat were standing beside her. She hadn't heard them approach. It was as if they appeared out of nowhere.

"Your numbers have increased, Krys. Hello, Pat. I've missed you."

"I haven't missed you, Blake." Pat spoke softly. She stood close to Rick, their arms touching. Pat exuded confidence as she stared back at Blake.

"Over here." A voice shouted from somewhere behind Krys. Before she could move or turn around, Ty walked up beside her. He was followed by Warren and Larry, along with Mickey who stood poised in an attack position. Jacob and Andy slowly walked up to join the group, along with four of the officers who had accompanied them to the hospital.

Without a sound, Lisa walked through the group to stand beside Warren.

"Your numbers keep growing. Nice to see you again, Lisa. Sorry our little snow drift didn't work out." Blake said, mockingly.

"Nothing is going to work out for you now." Lisa shot back at Blake, the hatred evident in her tone of voice.

"Whatever you say, my dear." Blake said.

The number of officers steadily increased and everyone started spreading out in an effort to completely surround Blake, not giving him an out in any direction.

"Hello, Larry. It's a shame you had to bring all these fine officers out in the cold. Your police force is helpless against me. You do realize that, I hope."

Larry had walked up behind Ty so quietly that Ty never realized he was there.

"How does he know my name?" Larry asked Ty in a whisper.

"I know all of you. I know all your weaknesses. I know everything."

"Then you must know that there's strength in numbers." Warren said. He stood with his hand poised just above the grip of his handgun.

"Looks like a standoff to me." Blake commented, still smiling.

"More like the Little Big Horn," Andy said. He knelt down next to Mickey, gently holding her at bay.

"So what's your next move, Ty?" Blake asked.

"To eliminate you once and for all." Ty answered.

"And how do you intend to do that?"

"Look around you. I believe we have it covered."

"You think you do. Even if you were to succeed, which you won't, I'll be back."

"No, you won't." Rick spoke up. "We'll make sure of that."

"You'll never be free of me." Blake stated, confidence oozing from him both in his voice and in his posture.

Krys had been watching and listening. She wondered how Blake could keep standing there, not showing any fear or anxiety on his face. He must truly believe he was immortal, he could escape unharmed even though the cards were definitely stacked against him.

"We end this now." Ty spoke to all of those standing with him.

As Ty raised his bow, the rest of the group followed suit and raised their various weapons. The only sound heard was that of the hammers clicking on the guns. The wind, which had been gusting violently all day, was now silent.

"Give it your best shot." Blake said, smiling evilly. He stood still, looking straight at Ty, then over at Krys.

Blake's gaze wondered from left to right, seeing Pat and Rick standing close together, no weapons raised by either of them. He saw Andy and his faithful dog, a nuisance as far as Blake was concerned.

He saw that he was surrounded by these so-called hunters. More men and women walked up to join the circle, some in uniform, some in plain clothes. He looked from one to the other, as if sizing them up, showing no fear, no emotion of any kind.

His gaze froze on one of the S.W.A.T. men who stood to his right. The man was tall and thin, close to Blake's size.

Jacob walked out of the shadows with Cassy to stand on the opposite side of Mickey. Like the rest of the group, he stood staring at Blake, not comprehending how Blake could be so at ease under the circumstances. He had to know he was out-numbered and out-gunned. Why was he being so nonchalant? Cassy stood quietly staring at Blake.

As they all stood mesmerized by Blake's lack of fear, he started rising off of the ground. They were all waiting for him to try to take flight. Instead, he began to spin in a circle, his speed increasing steadily. Soon he was nothing but a dark blur. The loose dirt and grass on the ground began to stir and rose to surround Blake's spinning figure, making him almost invisible in the swirling debris.

"Watch him." Someone from the back of the group shouted.

"Watch what?" Andy yelled, some of the dirt spreading out and blowing into his eyes.

"Fire" Larry shouted.

Suddenly, the air was filled with the sounds of guns firing and the click of the bows as the arrows were shot in Blake's direction. Everyone aimed at the center of the whirlwind, the rising debris obliterating Blake. They were firing blind but aimed at the general area where they had last seen Blake standing.

From within the vortex, bright flames suddenly shot straight up into the night sky. These flames somehow different than those seen when any other vampire burned.

These flames burned much brighter and the men and women alike could feel the heat from the flames. They burned bright yellow, then slowly turned into a dull blue.

The spinning motion seemed to increase for a second or two, then rose as a tornado would when dissipating back into the clouds.

The silence was eerie. They were all staring at a pile of bones, still steaming from the heat of the flames.

Jacob, Ty and Andy all stepped closer to the bones on the ground. Ty bent down and touched the skeleton, the bones all still attached to each other. He touched them almost reverently, not fully comprehending that they had eliminated Blake. It had been so much easier than they had expected it would be. And so much quieter.

"Now what?" Andy asked.

"Now I cut the head from the body. We cremate the bones but keep the head separate. The bones get buried in one grave but the head will be buried separately, a long ways away from the bones. As long as he isn't whole, he can't be brought back."

Pat and Rick stepped up beside the three men.

"It's really all over?" Pat asked.

"This part of it is." Ty answered.

"We still have his followers to round up and either dispose of or convert." Rick added. "Whichever way they choose to go."

"I believe you'll convert more than you'll dispose of at this point. With Blake gone, they have no leader. They'll be wondering around trying to figure out what to do next."

Krys walked up next to Ty, along with Lisa and Warren. The four of them stood looking at the bones on the ground.

"It doesn't seem real. It was just too easy." Warren stated, more to himself than to those around him.

Lisa stepped closer to Warren, put her arm around his waist.

"Look over there." She said, nodding her head behind them.

About 20 feet away stood Rick and Pat. Rick had encircled Pat with his arms and she stood with her head on his shoulder. They both looked content and Pat finally looked totally at peace.

"Me and the teams will finish our search in the hospital and the grounds around here." Larry announced as he motioned for the S.W.A.T. teams and the policemen and women to head back inside.

"I trust you all will proceed as planned?"

"We got this." Jacob said.

"I still can't believe how easy it was." Lisa stated.

"His ego didn't let him believe we could actually destroy him." Ty added. "He truly felt he was invincible."

"He wasn't, was he?" Pat asked.

"No, he wasn't." Rick chimed in. "We'll make sure he doesn't ever come back here or anywhere else." Rick continued to stare at the bones on the ground, a puzzled look on his face.

Andy had left the group and headed back toward the police cars parked by the emergency room. He soon came back carrying two black garbage bags.

Andy knelt beside the bones, Jacob joined him. They started picking them up one by one and placing them in the first bag.

Larry suddenly appeared back outside of the hospital and slowly walked over to the group.

"My men will cover the rest of the hospital. I'll make sure the arrangements for cremation are carried out."

"Just be sure the ashes from the head are kept separate from the rest of the bones. They have to be buried in a separate grave too." Ty told him.

"No problem." Larry stated.

"So, if we're done here, why don't we head back to my place." Cassy said. "I've got a bottle of Hennessey just waiting to be opened."

"We'll meet you all out there." Krys said, standing next to Ty and holding onto his arm tightly. "Soon as we make sure the arrangements for the disposal are made and being carried out."

"I've got to get back inside just to make sure everything is taken care of." Mike told Cassy. "I'll meet you at your place later, if it's okay."

"It's more than okay." Cassy told him. "We'll hold off on our celebration until you get there."

"Mind if we go with you?" Jacob asked Mike, Andy standing by his side with Mickey standing alert between them.

"Not at all." Mike answered. "Glad to have the company.

"Great. We'll see you in a while, sis." Jacob said as he turned toward the hospital entrance.

Cassy walked quickly over to Jacob and gave him a kiss on the cheek. Then she stood on her tip-toes and gave Andy a kiss also.

"Be careful in there." She said as she turned to go back to her Jeep.

"And..." Mike asked.

"And what?" Cassy asked, smiling coyly.

"And what about me? I'm in grave danger here too, you know."

"If it will make you feel better, then I guess." Cassy said.

Before she could say another word, Mike stepped up, took her in his arms and kissed her deeply. When he let go, he smiled down at her, turned and swiftly walked back toward the hospital entrance.

Cassy stood, stunned, watching as Mike walked away. She jumped when Krys laid her hand on her shoulder.

"That was pretty spectacular." Krys commented.

"What?" Cassy stammered. "Oh, yeah. Unexpected but pretty nice."

"I don't think nice is how I'd describe that kiss." Krys said.

Cassy turned to Krys, a smile forming slowly on her lips but with a puzzled look still on her face that wasn't fading too quickly.

"You're right. It was much more than nice." Cassy said.

"So, if the shock has worn off, can we head out to your place now?" Krys asked as she turned back toward the parking lot.

CHAPTER 59

Mike led the way back into the hospital. The three of them, along with Mickey, walked across the entry way to the elevators. They stood silently, waiting for one of the doors to finally open.

"So, Mike," Jacob began, "you do know that Cassy's my sister."

"And my niece." Andy added.

"I'm aware. Is there a problem?"

"Not from me." Jacob answered.

"Me either. I learned a long time ago never to argue with the law. And especially don't argue with a woman." Andy said, smiling.

"That's a good deal then." Mike said. "I just hope Cassy feels the same way."

"If she didn't," Jacob said, "we'd still be outside, picking you up off the ground. She may look like a lady, but don't ever get her riled up. She can be brutal."

The elevator arrived. Each man took a step back as the door opened slowly. It was empty, much to their relief.

They entered the elevator and Mike pushed the button for the second floor. They rode up silently, quickly reaching their destination. Each stood alert as the door slowly opened.

The hallway was dark but vacant. They stepped outside the elevator, each one listening for any unusual sounds. But it was completely silent.

Mike took a few steps, Jacob and Andy following close behind.

Suddenly, Mickey stepped in front of Mike. She started emitting a deep growl as she blocked him from going any further.

"Hold." Andy commanded in a whisper from behind Mike. Mickey continued to stand in position. To Mike's amazement her growl grew even deeper. She remained locked in place but continued to look down the hall, never stopping that deep, threatening growl.

Andy and Jacob stepped forward, one on each side of Mike, forming a barrier between them and the elevator.

Before a word could be said, a woman dressed in scrubs flew through the door of a room about ten feet down the hall. She landed hard across the floor, her head banging loudly against the wall.

She lay still for a few seconds, then moaned as she tried to get up off the floor. She got to her knees, then looked down the hall seeing them for the first time. The front of her shirt was red with blood, but her face and neck looked clean.

Unexpectedly, a tall man, also dressed in scrubs, walked through the door of the same room. He stood still, looking down at the woman who was still kneeling on the floor. He had not yet noticed the three men and the dog standing further down the hallway.

Jacob slowly raised his bow, aiming at the level of the man's chest. The motion caught the man's attention and he quickly turned to face the three of them. Unlike the woman, his face was covered in blood, some of which had dripped down his neck onto his shirt. He opened his mouth displaying long fangs, then slowly let out a loud screech. He snarled viciously and the blood dripped out of his mouth, over his lips and down his chin.

Before the man could make a move, Jacob pulled the trigger on his crossbow. The arrow flew, hitting the man dead center in the chest. He immediately burst into flames, slowly sinking to the floor.

The woman screamed and started crawling away from the burning figure. She crawled toward the three men. Andy stepped forward, put out his hand to help her to her feet.

"Wait." Mike yelled.

"It's okay." Andy said. He reached down. The lady took his proffered hand, then slowly got to her feet. She was visibly shaken and a little unsteady. Andy put his arm around her waist and held her tight.

"She's okay?" Mike asked.

"She'll be just fine." Andy told him.

"How did you know?"

"I didn't." Andy answered. "Mickey did."

"I should have guessed."

"Go ahead and take her downstairs." Mike told Andy. "Me and Jacob can check the rest of the floor."

"Okay, but keep Mickey here with you."

"You bet."

Andy walked back down the hall, supporting the woman along the way. He pushed the down button on the elevator and the door opened immediately. He took the woman's hand and led her through the door. The door closed slowly and they were gone from sight.

Mike and Jacob started walking back down the hall, Mickey leading the way. They covered the entire second floor without any further incidents. About 20 minutes later, they found themselves standing once again in front of the elevator doors.

When the doors opened, they jumped back in surprise, both letting out a sigh of relief when they realized it was Andy standing inside.

"Everything okay?" Andy inquired.

"It's all clear. How's the woman doing?" Jacob asked.

"She'll be fine. She wasn't bitten. Evidently the blood came from one of the orderly's previous victims. She's shaky and will have a few bruises but she'll be alright."

"Some good news for a change." Mike commented.

"We could use a lot more of that." Andy added thoughtfully.

The three men stepped into the elevator, Mickey following obediently. The door slowly closed and the elevator silently descended back to the first floor.

CHAPTER 60

Cassy, Krys and Ty arrived back at Cassy's house before the rest of the crew. Cassy and Krys went immediately into the kitchen to make sandwiches and a pot of coffee. Ty headed to the bathroom for a hot shower.

About two hours later, Andy came through the door followed by Rick, Pat and Lisa. Five minutes later, Larry and Warren showed up.

Cassy kept sneaking a peak at the front door.

"He'll be here soon." Andy told her. "He had a few things to clean up at the hospital first."

"He who?" Cassy asked, trying hard to sound innocently unaware.

"You're kidding, right?" Andy asked, giving her a knowing wink and then a big hug.

As they were sitting down at the table, the sounds of Mike's motorcycle grew increasingly louder as he neared the house. It idled for a few seconds, then became silent.

Cassy had been watching her brother and was wondering why he was so quiet. "Are you okay?" she asked him.

"Yeah. We found another one but disposed of him quickly. Other than that, everything's fine." Jacob answered.

"And?" Cassy asked, looking directly at Jacob.

"And what, sis?" he questioned her.

Before Cassy could answer him, Mike walked through the front door. Cassy got up and almost ran across the living room, grabbed his hand and led him back into the dining room to the chair next to hers.

They all sat silently, eating sandwiches and enjoying the hot coffee.

When they were through, the girls quickly cleared the dishes and put the leftovers away. They all migrated into the living room, Cassy following close behind with a bottle of Hennessey and some plastic glasses.

"Aren't you afraid the Hennessey will eat through the bottom of the glasses?" Larry teased as she handed him a glass and poured a double shot into it.

"Not if you drink it fast enough." She smiled back at him.

When everyone had their glass in hand, Larry stood up.

"I'd like to make a toast if no one objects."

Everyone muttered okay or go ahead.

"To all the hunters and to our success tonight." He raised his glass high and then downed the shot in one gulp. He caught his breath quickly, then let it out slowly.

"Wow!" he exclaimed. "A man could get used to this stuff real quick."

"A friend of my mom's always told her to drink top shelf and never mix it." Cassy said.

"That friend's name wouldn't by any chance be Billy?" Krys asked.

"Well, yeah." Cassy said, surprised by Krys's question. "How do you know about Billy?"

"I've known Billy for years. Used to party with him on Colfax now and then. As a matter of fact, we ran into him a couple of weeks ago at a truck stop. Didn't think he'd still be driving, but then doubt he'll ever quit."

"My God," Cassy exclaimed. "It really is a small world. But then Billy always did get around."

As they sat talking, Larry's phone suddenly rang. He answered, then excused himself and stepped out the door onto the patio.

"Wonder what that's all about." Andy asked.

"Police business, I'm sure." Mike said, keeping his eyes peeled to the front door.

After five minutes or so, Larry stepped back inside, a worried look on his face.

"What's up, Chief?" John asked.

"Seems one of our S.W.A.T. team is missing, Greg Willingham."

"He was in our circle when we confronted Blake. He was standing near Andy." Jacob said.

"Did he maybe go back into the hospital afterwards?" Krys asked.

"Did anyone see him after we got Blake?" Larry asked, looking around the room at each one of them, hoping for a positive answer.

No one said a word, each trying to remember if they had seen Greg after the incident with Blake or not.

"So now what?" Mike asked. "Put out an APB?"

"Not yet. We're going to do a DNA on the bones, just to be 100% sure."

"You don't think it was Greg and not Blake, do you?" Warren asked, anxiously.

"I don't know what to think. We just want to be positive before we have the bones cremated." Larry answered.

"If it is Greg and not Blake, then what?" Cassy asked.

"Then we start the hunt all over again." Mike told her.

The room went completely silent, each one contemplating what Larry had just said and what it would mean to each of them. Ty especially wondered what would happen if it wasn't Blake. He knew his hunt would continue, but would Krys want to go any further with it?

Ty took Krys's hand in his. "It has to have been Blake."

"And if it wasn't?" she asked him.

"Then we keep hunting until it is."

"Are you sure you're up to it?" she asked, holding his hand even tighter.

"I can't stop until it's over." Ty told her as he leaned over and gently kissed her on the cheek.

"I'm with you until the end, no matter how long it takes." She told him, hoping it would somehow reassure him.

Soon after, Larry left to go back to the station. Ty and Krys headed out to their truck. Warren and Lisa said goodnight to Rick and Pat as they left to return to Rick's house, then they retired to Cassy's extra bedroom.

Jacob and Andy soon went to bed also, but not before letting Mickey, Sam and Bright Eyes out one last time.

The animals went out but didn't stay outside more than five minutes. They usually would romp around the yard and wear each other out this time of the evening. But not tonight.

Cassy and Mike lingered in the living room once everyone had left. As they sat silently on the couch, Mike gently took Cassy's hand in his.

"So, did you ever in your wildest dreams think you'd be sitting here on your couch holding hands with a vampire?" He asked.

"I don't think of you that way." Cassy told him.

"How do you think of me?"

"As a very nice cop who works nights." She answered in all earnestness.

"And…" Mike prompted.

"And as someone who won't be going camping in the woods any time soon, at least not in the daylight."

Mike laughed loudly and soon Cassy joined in. It was so easy to be open and honest with him and she felt herself relaxing completely.

"Tell me something though." Cassy said.

"And what's that?"

"When we kiss, your fangs won't get in the way, will they?"

"I'm not sure. Maybe we should try and see what happens."

They slowly leaned into each other. The kiss was gentle, but soon grew in passion.

When they finally pulled apart, Mike looked deep into Cassy's eyes.

"I was thinking my life as a human was over, but now…"

"Now?" Cassy coaxed.

"Now I'm thinking it might just be beginning."

CHAPTER 61

As soon as Larry sat down at his desk, he called the crematorium. He ordered them not to cremate until he could get a lab technician down there to do some studies. He would let them know when to proceed.

He was somewhat startled when his phone rang. It was the middle of the night and not his usual time to be in the office. He answered on the second ring.

"Hello, Larry Moore here." He answered somewhat hesitantly.

There was a silence on the other end for a few seconds, then a gravelly deep voice said, "You didn't really think it would be that easy, did you?"

Before Larry could even think of an answer, the line went dead. He sat for a minute longer in stunned silence listening to the dial tone.

Who should he call first? He didn't want to call Warren or Ty or Andy, knowing they all needed their sleep. Morning would be soon enough for the bad news. There was no doubt in Larry's mind as to who had been on the other end of that call or what it would mean to the folks out at Cassy's or across the entire United States for that matter.

Larry slowly got up from behind his desk and walked to the couch, there was no way he was going home tonight.

He sat on one end of the couch, took off his shoes, then lay back. His tall frame covered the entire couch, his legs hanging over onto the floor.

He lay there, eyes wide open, listening to all the sounds around him. His mind was in a scramble wondering if Blake would stay in Denver and wreak more havoc or would he find some new town or city to start all over in.

Larry knew one thing for sure and that was that it would be a long and excruciatingly rough time waiting to hear of another outbreak of missing people, then missing bodies. But he knew from experience now that the only way to track Blake would be to wait and stay vigilant.

As much as he despised the idea, he prayed that the next bad news would be from another part of the country and not here in Denver. As short-lived as the horror had been, he didn't want to believe they would have to go through it a second time.

From what he knew of Blake's history, he truly believed that another city would be involved. Blake seemed to thrive on the anonymity a new city gave him, plus the unhindered time he would have to start all over again.

Larry thought of all the people who had been involved in the hunt here in Denver. Warren and Lisa were finally together and would be going back to Hebert to start a new and much deserved life.

Pat had found Rick and would be staying here in Denver. He was happy for Rick because he had been alone for so long. He had put his whole heart and soul into his job and never took the time to enjoy himself. Larry was sure that Pat would change all of that rather quickly.

Andy and Jacob would both be going back to Hebert. Andy had his ranch and Jacob had a thriving business to tend to. They were both good men. Andy had a heart larger than any he had ever known. He was the kind of man that, when you walked through his front door, you were family. No questions asked.

Jacob was a total computer nerd who readily admitted to that fact. However, he had a very imaginative mind and had worked miracles for them with his wooden arrows. Wherever Blake showed up, Larry would be sure that the police department had an abundant supply of those weapons as well as holy water for their bullets.

Of all the people involved, he dreaded most telling Ty that Blake was still alive. Ty had made it his life's work to eliminate the vermin, feeling guilty for helping him drive cross country to spread his disease all over the U.S. He seemed so much more at ease after they believed Blake had been disposed of. How would he take the bad news that they had failed again?

But no matter what Ty decided, Larry knew that Krys would be right by his side. He almost envied Ty his relationship with Krys, for them not having been together that long, they were both totally committed to each other. It was a rare thing to behold.

Larry's eyes were getting heavy and as much as he feared going to sleep, he knew he had to rest before the gruesome news would be taken back to Cassy's in the morning.

CHAPTER 62

When Ty and Krys came through Cassy's front door the next morning, they were greeted with the smells of fresh coffee brewing and bacon sizzling in the kitchen. Ty had already called in for a load and they would be leaving out this afternoon, headed for the east coast. He was anxious to get back on the road, get back to normal once again. That is if life would ever be normal again.

Andy, Warren and Jacob were already at the table nursing their coffee. Cassy and Lisa were busy in the kitchen. Krys joined the girls and Ty sat down at the table.

"Larry called," Warren told Ty. "He'll be here in a few minutes. Says he has some news for us."

"Hope it's good news." Jacob piped up.

"He sure didn't sound too good." Warren added. "But he may just be tired."

Krys brought Ty a cup of coffee, then returned to the kitchen.

As the girls kept busy and the guys sat quietly at the table, there was a knock on the door and then Larry walked in and went directly to the table.

"Well?" Warren asked anxiously.

"Awful deep subject." Andy commented.

"I know, for such a shallow mind." Warren finished the statement, trying hard to be funny but not really succeeding.

Larry said, as he sat down at the table. Krys brought him a cup of coffee, then lingered behind Ty expectantly.

"I got a phone call last night when I returned to my office." Larry began.

"It was verification that the bones belonged to Blake, right?" Warren interrupted.

"No. It was Blake." Larry continued.

"Say what?" Jacob asked.

"How is that possible?" Andy queried.

"I don't know. The line was silent at first. Then he said, 'You didn't think it would be that easy, did you?"

"You sure it was Blake?" Ty asked.

"I'm positive. No one else has that voice. We're checking on the bones but I'd bet my pension that they belong to our missing officer."

"Did you know him?" Warren asked.

"Yes. I did. Greg worked for me before he joined the S.W.A.T. Team. He has a wife and a pair of 3-year-old twin girls."

"Oh, my God." Krys said, drawing in a breath, holding her hand over her mouth.

"I don't envy his captain that home visit." Warren said.

"His captain won't be the one going to the house, I will." Larry said. "I've known Greg since he was a pup, brought him onto the force straight out of the academy. I was Godfather to his girls when they were baptized. His wife, Carrie, is like a daughter to me."

"So, now what?" Ty asked.

"Now we sit and wait." Larry answered.

"Yeah, sit and wait for another town to report missing bodies. Then start all over again." Ty added.

"Mike will be our liaison on the road." Larry began. "If you and Krys can keep in touch, that will help."

"Don't forget about me." Cassy added. She had walked from the kitchen and had been standing behind Larry, quietly listening. "Between my CB and my big mouth, I should be able to get a lot of information from the truckers out there too."

"We leave this afternoon for the east coast." Krys volunteered.

"And I'm leaving out in two more days heading west." Cassy added.

"Me and Warren, we're going home to Hebert." Lisa told them.

"We'll be leaving tomorrow. Lisa wants to see Pat tonight and visit a while before we leave. And I can let Rick know what's going on tonight when we see him." Warren said.

"I'll be going back to Kalamazoo to close out my house and Pat's and put them up for sale. I'll get in touch with Kee and let him know what's happening and to be on the lookout too." Lisa said.

"So, that'll cover both coasts and the North." Larry noted. "Then it's just a waiting game. Let's just hope we won't have to wait too long and we can get an early start the next time. Nip it in the bud, so to speak."

"I keep seeing Blake spinning and just didn't see anything else unusual out there. How did we not see it happening?" Warren asked out loud to no one in particular.

Lisa stood behind Warren, her hands on his shoulders.

"Does it really surprise anyone that he's still out there?" Lisa asked.

"Not really," Ty interjected. "I just had really hoped that it was all over. Prayed it would be all over."

"Well, wherever he shows up next, we'll be there." Krys said determinedly.

"Yeah. And then I swear we'll finish this once and for all." Ty added.

"I've got to get back to the office." Larry said as he rose from his chair. He turned to look at Cassy.

"If you see Mike before I do, tell him what happened and ask him to call me. I'll be in my office all day and most of the night."

"What makes you think I'll see him before you do?" Cassy asked, trying hard to lighten the depressing atmosphere in the room.

"Come on, sis," Jacob said with a sly smile, "really?"

"Okay, little girl." Larry continued. "When you see Mike, tell him what happened and ask him to call me. Better?"

Larry kissed Cassy on the top of her head and laughed out loud when her cheeks turned a dark pink as she turned and quickly walked back into the kitchen.

CHAPTER 63

Cassy, Krys and Lisa served breakfast to a very quiet table full of men. They all ate, but did so slowly, each one deep in thought. When breakfast was over and the table was cleared, they all moved into the living room. The mood was not as uplifting as it had been when they had returned from the hospital the night before.

After a while, each one got up to prepare for their departure. Ty and Krys got the truck ready to leave with extra bags of groceries from Cassy for their trip. She had packed a lot of homemade pastries and sweets, which would keep quite nicely in the refrigerator Ty had in the sleeper.

Ty and Krys were the first to leave. They said their goodbyes to everyone and promised to keep in touch with them all. Of course, Krys was in tears when they said their goodbyes, but no one mentioned it to her. They left the house hand in hand and soon those left inside heard the truck start up, idle for a short period of time and then pull out.

Warren gave Andy the keys to his pickup so that he and Jacob could also get on the road. He would be using Cassy's Jeep while here in Denver for another day and then he and Lisa would fly back to Illinois. His Deputy, Earl, would pick them up at the airport.

Shortly after 1 o'clock, Andy and Jacob said their goodbyes. Mickey got hugs from Cassy and Lisa before she jumped up into the bed of the pickup and settled in for the ride home.

"Bet she's in the back seat before they get ten miles down the road." Cassy told Lisa.

"I don't take sucker bets." Lisa retorted, smiling broadly.

Warren and Lisa hung around Cassy's for most of the afternoon, waiting for the evening so they could go see Rick and Pat. Warren was anxious to get back home to his quiet life, a life he knew was about to become much more fulfilling with Lisa there with him.

Lisa planned to stay in Hebert a couple of weeks before going back to Kalamazoo to put the houses up for sale and pack her things up for her move back. Pat was would have all the papers in order for Lisa to handle her business and her house. She had decided to stay in Denver with Rick, not unexpectedly.

Cassy had a few things to do before her date with Mike. She told Jacob before he left that she felt like a teenager waiting on her first date. Mike had planned a nice dinner and then a drive afterwards. He had said he'd bring the food with him and that she wasn't to fuss.

Larry stopped by before Warren and Lisa left for Rick's place. The remains had proven to belong to his officer, although Larry admitted it didn't surprise him when he got the news. He had just left the widow's house. She was understandably devastated but he hadn't told her the entire story of how her husband had died and never would. All he told her was that it was in the line of duty and he was a hero and would be honored as such. He had also told her that the department would help her in any way it could.

The phone call to his office had been traced to a pay phone on Colfax. There were so many prints on the phone and the booth it would have been impossible to even try to dust for Blake's specific prints.

"Besides, does a vampire even leave prints. And if he's as old as he says he is, they won't be on file anywhere except maybe in a crypt in Transylvania." Larry added.

Larry told Warren he would keep in touch if he had any news. Mike would be going undercover, riding his Harley to any town or city with suspicious disappearances.

Cassy assured them that she would put out the word to the truckers and knew Ty and Krys would be doing the same. They'd have every trucker in the United States looking and listening for any news.

Warren and Lisa left to go to Rick's. Larry stayed at Cassy's long enough for a cup of coffee and then left to go back to his office.

CHAPTER 64

Warren and Lisa arrived at Rick's just after sunset. To their surprise, Rick and Pat had the BBQ fired up and were setting the table with some very interesting appetizers.

"Supper will be ready in about half an hour." Pat told them, smiling broadly. "Care for a drink?"

"I'm driving." Warren answered. He stood with a look of surprise on his face. It all seemed so natural, like visiting any other friends he had. No hint that this home was any different than any other.

"No, you're not." Rick announced as he came in through the patio door.

"I'm not?" Warren asked.

"We have five bedrooms in this rambling old house and I know Pat and Lisa will want some private time before you two leave out. So, you are our guests this evening."

"But I have Cassy's Jeep." Warren protested.

"I've already called Cassy. She's going out with Mike tonight, so won't need it until tomorrow. She said to bring it back around 10 and she'll drive you to the airport. She doesn't have to leave out until later in the day."

"Okay." Warren said. "In that case, I'd love a drink."

"And you don't have to worry," Rick said, looking directly at Warren. "We've both had our fix. You'll be perfectly safe here tonight."

"I suppose being a vampire also makes you a mind reader." Warren said, laughing.

Both Rick and Warren relaxed somewhat after that. The women went back to the kitchen, talking a mile a minute with easy laughter heard on a regular basis.

Rick mixed Warren a drink and the two of them walked out onto the patio. Rick checked the BBQ, then joined Warren at the table.

"It all seems so natural." Warren commented.

"It's as natural as we want to make it. The only difference for now is that we do our entertaining after sunset."

"What about Pat?" Warren asked. "Is she okay with all of this?"

"I'm fine, Warren." Pat announced from the doorway.

She and Lisa joined the men. Pat sat next to Rick, having given him a quick kiss on the cheek after she sat down.

"You do seem okay." Warren told her.

"I'm good. You don't have to worry about me, either of you. I've always been driven to succeed. I never really stopped to smell the roses, so to speak, until now."

As Pat talked, she took Rick's hand in hers. The smile between them spoke volumes.

"How do those roses smell now?" Warren asked her.

"They smell free." Pat answered. "I've never been so relaxed or so content in my life. It's amazing to me that after all the horror, something so wonderful could happen. And I know it's only been a couple of days, but then it's just so natural. We're really two of a kind, in more ways than one." Pat looked at Rick and they both started laughing.

"You really don't have to worry, Warren." Rick added. "Pat will always be loved and cared for and, considering our circumstances, that will be for a very long time." Rick squeezed Pat's hand and then kissed it gently.

The rest of the evening was very relaxed. Warren went to bed around midnight. Rick went into his office and his computer. Lisa and Pat stayed up and talked until past 3 a.m.

The next morning, Warren woke to a delicious smell that he didn't recognize. When he came down the stairs, Rick was at the kitchen table with a cup of coffee. The women were busy in the kitchen cooking breakfast.

"Good morning," Rick greeted him cheerfully. "Thought you'd like to eat before you hit the road."

"But it's daylight and…" Warren began.

"My windows have a special coating on them. As long as we don't go outside or open them during daylight hours, we're fine."

"I learn something new every day." Warren said. "But it seems to finally be something good for a change."

"Most of it, anyway." Rick added.

"Yeah, Blake." Warren said. "Does his being alive affect you and Pat in any way?"

"Not really." Rick answered. "Blake isn't in Denver anymore. If he were, I'd feel him. I don't know where he's gone, I just know he isn't here. And he's too smart to come back. But what about you?"

"Me? I'm going home to live the life I've always wanted. Back to my small quiet town and my small quiet house in the woods. Back to deer romping in the yard and sometimes on the porch, to birds singing in the trees outside my bedroom window every morning."

"What happens when Blake reappears, and you know he will?"

"Unless he reappears back in Hebert, I'm not going to be involved." Warren stated emphatically.

"That's good to hear, for more reasons than you know." Rick said.

"I'll second that." Lisa added as she brought Warren a large cup of coffee, kissed him lightly on the cheek and then returned to the kitchen.

CHAPTER 65

Larry sat in his office, engrossed with his monitor. So far, no police department had any unusual number of missing people. He realized it had only been a week, but he was unexpectedly anxious to know where Blake had disappeared to.

The funeral for Greg had been yesterday and it was a great tribute to a great cop. The procession had wound down Wadsworth to Olinger Cemetery. All the side streets had been blocked off by fire trucks and EMS vehicles. The curbs were lined with citizens. They held up posters that stated they were praying for the family. The procession was at least two miles long and it seemed that every policeman and woman in Colorado were present, as well as city officials.

Larry had stayed in close contact with Mike, who was also anxious for news of Blake. Mike had a motorhome that Rick had supplied and had altered to fit Mike's needs. The windows were tinted so he could drive during daylight hours.

The back wall folded down to make a ramp for Mike's Harley which would be nestled snuggly inside the motorhome until Mike was ready to use it. That back room had walls covered with spare parts and all the tools needed to keep his bike in tip-top shape.

Larry had been in touch with Warren and it was good to hear that Hebert was slowly coming back to life. They had new people moving in and new businesses opening up. Lisa was planning on opening up a craft/thrift store as soon as her house was sold in Kalamazoo. She said it was something she had always wanted to do and now was the perfect time and place to do it. Her best friend, along with her husband and son, were in the process of moving to Hebert so that they could partner together in the business.

Warren also told Larry to plan on a few vacation days in about eight weeks. He would have a wedding to attend.

Larry looked back at the computer screen. There was one missing person report that caught his eye, maybe because it had been reported twenty-four hours after the body had originally been found. It wasn't a positive sign that Blake was involved because of the city. There was a lot of voodoo still present in New Orleans and who was to say that the body hadn't been stolen from the morgue for reasons unknown to the uneducated populace.

Larry made a mental note to keep his eyes out for any more incidents in New Orleans or anywhere else. He felt confident that Blake wouldn't try to return to Denver, it hadn't turned out to be too fruitful for him there. He had converted a lot of people but then Rick had taken that away from him, either by convincing them his way was better or eliminating them.

Now, it was just a waiting game. And Larry hated waiting games with a passion. He wanted Blake found again and this time eliminated permanently. He wasn't sure if he would venture away from Denver to help out once Blake was located, he was torn between keeping Denver safe and avenging Greg's death, along with the many other citizens whom Blake had infected. He would just have to wait and see what happened. But whatever he decided, he was confident it would be the right move for him.

THE END?

Not yet…

EPILOGUE

Once again Blake found himself in a semi. And once again, his partner was totally unaware of who he really was.

She had advertised for a partner who was willing to drive nights. She was in her late 20s, not married, no attachments. She said she had never, in her six years of driving, liked to drive after dark. She loved driving and wanted to see the country, the good and the bad of it. She had already seen rainbows in the desert in Arizona and the flooded crops in Missouri.

Blake had met her at Sapp Brothers Truck Stop in Denver and, of course, started driving the next night. He had the sleeper transformed to suit his needs before they ever left Denver, all of it being done while she slept peacefully in the new top bunk.

He kept the CB on, which was unusual for him, and listened to the truckers talking about Greg's funeral. Besides all the police vehicles and politicians in the funeral procession, there were quite a few semis bobtailing. They felt respect for the cop who had given his life to protect the citizens of Denver, including the truckers. To them, it was a tribute to not only Greg but the entire police force.

Blake had to laugh at the talk on the CB. These truckers felt they were invincible and that they would be helpful in regards to locating him once again. It never ceased to amaze Blake how easily these humans could be manipulated. They made his mission in life so much easier.

Blake and his new partner, Kelsea, left Denver the next night with her sound asleep and Blake driving south, headed for a c city of myths and legends and superstitions – the perfect place for Blake to relocate to.